THE LAST
Winter Rose

A NOVEL OF RICHARD III

CAITLIN SUMNER

Copyright © 2024
The moral right of Caitlin Sumner to be recognised as the
author of this work has been asserted.
All rights reserved.

No part of this manuscript may be reproduced, stored in a
retrieval system, or transmitted, in any form or by any means,
without the prior permission in writing of the author, nor be
otherwise circulated in any form of binding or cover other than
that in which it may be shared in a limited capacity with relevant
parties.

No part of this manuscript was created using generative AI.

The author expressly prohibits any use of any part of this
manuscript for the purposes of training any AI technology,
including and without limitation any technologies capable of
generating works in any style or genre of the written word.

Typeface Sabon 11pt

Published Independently by Prometheus Press via Amazon
Publishing
ISBN: 9798328914512

Cover designed by and copyright © Caitlin Sumner

This book is for my mother, who raised me on Richard III and the belief that he was a good, kind man, and one of the best kings that England ever had.

Part I - Young Prince

October 2, 1468

The sun rose cold on the day of his sixteenth birthday. Frost tipped the leaves and turned the garden as white as the rose embroidered on every piece of his livery, carved and painted in stone above the gateway, carved in wood on the doors to the great hall. Birds came awake slowly, shaking their feathered heads in confusion as they fluttered down to the garden from their trees, examining the fresh snow with curiosity. Winter had come early to Yorkshire, and for the first time in his life, Richard was glad he would be going south soon, to the warmer climes of London and its gentler winter.

This land was his home, but winter? Winter ached, a little more each year. His bones would begin to feel as if they were made of lead, bruises from training took longer to heal, his steps grew slower, and his spine...

The curve was not obvious, not yet. He'd been told it would worsen as he grew older, but the pain was like an old friend already. Dull, mostly, but sometimes sharp and hot like a sword just drawn from the forge fire. And the deep chill of a Yorkshire morning, the welcome, but draughty halls of Middleham...this year he would not have to feel their discomfort.

He'd received the summons only a week ago, to join his brothers, Edward, the king, and George, the Duke of Clarence, in London for the winter. He suspected his mother may have urged Edward to bring him to the city, but Edward, though ten years Richard's senior, the eldest of Duchess Cecily's children, had always taken the time for his younger brothers and sisters. He had especially made the time when Richard had been nothing more than a child, when he had seen such horrible things after their father was killed. Edward had been only eighteen himself at the time, when he had taken all their father's responsibilities on his shoulders, and then he had taken up the crown of England as well. Richard still couldn't fathom how Edward had found such strength and resolve and he admired his brother greatly for it.

"You should come inside," a soft voice drifted toward him and Richard turned, distracted from his thoughts, wincing as he remembered it hurt to twist like that now. Four years and he still forgot that he'd never again have the mobility he had as a child and that it would only worsen with age.

"I'm all right," he said and Anne huffed, stepping out onto the walkway with an extra blanket in her arms, her heavy cloak wrapped around her.

"You shouldn't be in the cold, Richard," she admonished and he smiled, stooping to allow her to drape the heavy wool over his shoulders. At twelve years old she was still small in stature and might never get much taller, barely coming up to the top of his shoulder.

The Last Winter Rose

But she had the kindest heart of anyone he had ever met and she was his entire world. She burned like the hottest fire, though he knew few around them could see it. They preferred to see her as a weak girl child, not someone who could move mountains if she chose.

"Is this to be my life? Always looked after and fussed over like a child?" he asked.

He was teasing and they both knew it. His words brought a rueful smile to Anne's lips as she stood beside him, eyes on the sunrise and the frosty dales. She was going to miss him when he went away.

"I just worry," she said softly and Richard smiled again, reaching for her hand and covering it with his own. They were the best of friends, though they were both getting too old for the friendship children had with each other. Anne was nearly old enough to marry, he was leaving for London in three days. He didn't know when he'd see her again, and there was every chance he might never.

"You needn't worry about me," he assured her gently, trying not to think of a day without her smile. "I can look after myself."

"You nearly killed yourself again last week," she said, her voice flat. "You always trip over things because you don't look where you're going. You come out on the coldest mornings in only a shirt, and if I didn't remind you to have your hair kept neat, you'd look like a Viking invader of old."

Richard snorted, grip tightening on her hand. She wasn't wrong, he was a bit clumsy, and he was usually too busy to remember about his hair. That was the fascinating thing about hair, it just kept growing, unless you were like Henry Percy, whose hair had started to creep backward from his forehead when he wasn't much older than Richard was now. At nineteen, it was already clear he'd be bald as an empty platter before he was thirty.

"Who's going to look after you when I'm not there?" Anne said softly and Richard's heart jumped in his chest as he came to a startling realisation.

He was looking at her, not directly, but out of the corner of his eye, watching her face as she watched the sunrise, her breath a billowing cloud and frost already settling on her hair, the morning was so damp. It wasn't quite snowing now, but it would again before the day was out. And when he looked at her, saw the faraway look in her soft blue eyes, he realised he was in love with her.

The thought barely had the time to form before it was swept away by the sound of footsteps and he reluctantly drew his hand away from hers.

"There you both are," Lord Warwick grumbled as he stomped his feet and stopped behind them, glancing out over the wall before turning around. "Come inside, cook has breakfast waiting and Richard, you need to start packing your things."

"Yes sir," Richard said, sighing as Lord Warwick disappeared back inside, his long cloak swirling around his ankles.

Anne reached for his hand again and he smiled at her as she nudged his shoulder gently.

"No need to look so sour," she said lightly. "Just remember to watch your feet."

Richard chuckled, glancing around before he pulled her close and hugged her tightly one last time, stepping back and holding his arm out to her with an exaggerated bow that left her giggling as they went into the warm hall for their morning meal.

The breakfast was plain as it always was on a Sunday morning, the only time during the week when they all sat around the table in the great hall to take their meal. Afterward, they would attend a short Sunday service in the town church, and then Richard would have to pack his few things to be ready to leave.

Isabel, Anne's elder sister, was already at the table, as was her mother, also named Anne, the countess of Warwick. She was the reason that Richard Neville now held such great swathes of land throughout England and was titled the Earl of Warwick. Some also styled him the Kingmaker for his part in assuring Edward's ascension to the throne when the old king Henry had been deposed, but those were the whispers of everyday folk in markets and alley taverns, not for the hall table. King Henry was mad and feeble, and eight years ago the people had risen up, led by Warwick and Richard's father, the Duke of York. He would have been king, had he not been killed first, leaving Edward to take the throne in his place.

Anne settled in her seat next to Isabel, reaching for a roll from the middle of the table, not looking at Richard. Across the table were three other boys who were fostered at Middleham, all sons of minor nobles. Richard took his seat next to Francis Lovell, the only one of the three he cared to share conversation with. The other two were younger, eleven and twelve, and still bore all the poor characteristics of childhood. Francis, about to turn fifteen, had a good head on his shoulders and was a smart conversationalist. He and Richard spent much of their time together training and riding and learning to hunt.

"She's mad this morning," Francis whispered as Richard sat down and he glanced at the countess, wincing at the pinched line of her mouth. She didn't say anything as her husband swept into the hall and took his seat and Richard reached for a bowl and helped himself to a scoop of porridge.

"What happened?" he asked quietly and Francis shrugged.

"I heard shouts this morning, but couldn't make out what was said. Likely something to do with Lord Neville travelling to Warwick castle and leaving his lady wife here for the winter."

Richard frowned, but kept his thoughts to himself. What the Earl and his Lady did or said in their private lives was none of his business.

"It's so exciting, isn't it?" Francis continued, voice louder now. "London! I've missed the city."

Richard snorted, pulling a bread roll apart and spooning some honey into the middle before he smashed it together again and took a bite. He hated London, it was loud and crowded and filthy, and he had no desire to ride south except to escape the horrible cold that would come sweeping in from the north in the next weeks.

"I wish I was going with you," Anne said quietly, so her parents couldn't hear. Isabel scowled next to her.

"Why would you want to go?" she demanded. "You're just a child."

Anne's face fell and Richard carefully extended his foot under the table, poking her shin lightly with his toes. She glanced up at him and smiled, shrugging. Isabel had become withdrawn the last year, convinced she was no longer a child, that she was a woman grown who should already be married and having children. She was not quite fifteen, a year younger than Richard, but something in her had changed. Anne had said it was because Isabel had her woman's blood and she thought that somehow made her special. Richard refused to have an opinion, but Anne hadn't seemed to care, she had just been angry with Isabel and needed to complain about her older sister.

They ate in relative silence for the rest of the meal, which was hurried along when one of the ladies rushed in with an armful of cloaks. Richard stuffed another roll in his pocket as they all rose from the table and pulled on cloaks and hoods, preparing to walk down to the church for services.

They sat in the first pew, first Lord Warwick, then his wife, then Isabel, Anne, and Richard. Francis and the other two sat in the pew behind them with two of the stable boys who had been scrubbed and brushed and combed by their mothers, who sat further back with the other household servants. Anne shivered and Richard glanced at her, seeing her hands bare and twisted in her lap.

"Where are your gloves?" he asked quietly, as the priest entered and there was a rustle as everyone stood.

"Eleanor forgot them," Anne mumbled and Richard pulled his own gloves off, passing them to her. She smiled, tugging them on before she wrapped herself tighter in her cloak, another shiver passing through her.

"Here," Richard said, tugging his own cloak off and draping it over her shoulders. She scowled at him, but didn't protest. No one else seemed to notice.

"You'll be cold," she said, trying to tug the heavy wool off and push it back toward him.

"I'll be fine," he whispered. "Now hush."

Anne frowned, hunching her shoulders into the double layer of warmth, and sighed as her shivers subsided. Richard's cloak really was warmer than hers. She hid a smile behind the heavy scarf wrapped around her neck and turned just enough that she could reach out and grasp Richard's hand, out of sight of Isabel and her mother, who were looking directly ahead at the altar. Richard didn't look at her, but his fingers tightened on hers and she knew he was hiding a smile. Behind them Francis coughed to cover a laugh.

October, 1468

Two weeks later they entered London. It had been four years since Richard was last in the city and it hadn't changed at all. It was still loud, still dirty, and still packed with too many people. He already missed the open countryside and they'd barely crossed the first gateway.

"This place is horrid," he muttered and Francis chuckled.

Richard glowered slightly at the entourage around them, six guards, two messengers, a cook, and a boy carrying Edward's York banner, announcing Richard's arrival to anyone they passed. As a member of the royal family, brother to the king and legally second in line for the throne if Edward and George were to die, Richard never went anywhere alone. There were always guards, and since he had met Francis three years before, there was always a shadow just behind his left shoulder. He was only thankful that he and Francis got on so well, being so close in age.

Francis, though younger than Richard, had already inherited his title of Baron Lovell of Oxfordshire from his father at the age of nine. He hadn't seen his family home since his mother sent him to foster with Lord

The Last Winter Rose

Warwick at his small castle in Middleham, far to the north in the heart of Yorkshire, the very next year. Francis was already a skilled swordsman, strategist, and a keen observer of the world around him, and after Anne, Richard's best friend.

It had taken a promise from Richard that he would take full responsibility for Francis to convince Lord Warwick to allow him to accompany Richard to London, despite his age. They'd passed Francis' fifteenth birthday on the road, only a few days after Richard's, and he'd proudly taken his place as Richard's official personal bodyguard ever since.

"You'll get used to it," Francis said and Richard frowned, unable to move his horse around the piles of excrement in the street because there was no clear place to step. Francis had spent his youngest years here in London and Richard didn't know how anyone could stand it, much less grow accustomed to it.

"I don't want to get used to it," he said under his breath, but he followed Francis as they wound their way through the outer city and toward the palace at Westminster where Edward spent most of his time when he was in the city.

Richard preferred Windsor, further out in the country and away from the noise and press of London, or Baynard's castle, where his mother lived a quiet life as the mother of the king, her every need attended to. He remembered her joy the last time he had visited, and he knew he would have to see her as soon as possible. He still remembered the chilling screams and horrible fear of their ordeal, the cold nights with little food, and having to leave his mother behind with only George for company as they fled across the sea to cousins who barely acknowledged them until it was certain Edward had won the throne. He remembered when his mother was given the news that his father and brother Edmund had been killed, the way her face broke and she sank to her knees with a sob, clutching them as her two young boys and their sister Margaret wrapped her in their arms, terrified and suddenly so alone.

"We're here," Francis said, pulling Richard out of his thoughts. And indeed, they were already passing into the gates of the palace, the guards at attention. Richard was pleased to see that the castle, at least, was in good order, the guards sober and uniforms clean, and no sign or stench of refuse. The king's banner flew from the parapets and it brought Richard some comfort to see it.

They were greeted by a herald in the yard and grooms took their horses as they dismounted. He bowed, introducing himself, though Richard almost immediately forgot his name, only managing to keep his title in his mind, and they followed him deep into the palace, its halls familiar in a distant kind of way. Richard had spent little time here when he was younger, but there was still a brush of remembering here and there.

Francis stayed with him until he was shown into a room that held only one other person, his elder brother, King Edward IV. The doors closed behind him and Edward looked up from his reading at the sound.

The Last Winter Rose

"Brother!" Edward beamed, stepping forward to embrace Richard, slapping him heartily on the back. Richard held back his grimace and instead returned his brother's wide smile and greeting.

"Your Majesty," he said, bowing as well as he could with Edward's arm around his shoulders.

"It's good to see you," Edward laughed, easily propelling Richard out of the audience room and back into the private area of the palace. "I've had rooms made up for you, I hope they'll be satisfactory. They'll be less draughty than that old wreck at Middleham, I dare say."

"It's the Yorkshire wind," Richard chuckled. "It's insidious." He kept his other comments to himself, because Middleham may be old and simple, but it was well kept and had been a place for him that felt like home. Not even Ludlow, where he'd spent his childhood, had felt like that.

Edward talked the whole way to the guest rooms, barely letting Richard get a word in, but he didn't really mind. It was good to see his brother happy, settled, apparently enjoying life as king. Edward hadn't been prepared for the crown, he hadn't really wanted it when it came to him, but he'd fought hard for it after their father had been killed. He'd taken to ruling well in the last eight years and the country was more or less at peace. He'd proved to be a fair ruler and Richard was proud of him.

He showed Richard to his room and then made his apologies, disappearing to some meeting or other.

13

Richard imagined he'd have a day or two to get familiar with the palace before he, too, would be required to attend the endless stream of government meetings, now that he was going to be, in some capacity, a part of his brother's council. Edward had wasted no time telling Richard his plan, talking of little else on the walk between the audience chamber and where he stood now. He couldn't say he was looking forward to the prospect very much. There was nothing he could do about it, however, so he simply sighed and looked about, familiarising himself with his new chambers.

The rooms he'd been give were large, much larger than he was used to. They were richly decorated, both the outer room and the bedroom warmed by roaring fires. The first room had a table with two chairs, a shelf for books with some already placed on it, a desk under the window well stocked with ink, quills, paper, and parchment. There was a long couch in front of the fireplace as well as a high-backed chair, both upholstered in a deep red brocade, and the floors were carpeted in thick rugs, unlike Middleham where the floors were covered in fresh rushes at the beginning of summer and the end of autumn.

Richard tossed his cloak idly over the end of the couch and let out a breath, forcing himself to relax. He didn't really know what he was doing here, what part Edward wanted him to play. He'd come because his brother asked him to, yet in his enthusiasm about Richard joining his council, Edward hadn't exactly been clear as to why, or what role Richard would hold.

The Last Winter Rose

Although, Richard supposed, as king, Edward might not even feel the need to explain. Whatever the reason, Richard felt sure he wasn't up to the task, not yet, not so young. He sank onto the couch with a sigh, gazing at the fire. It was quiet here, the noise of the city blocked out by the sturdy walls and tightly sealed windows. Tomorrow, tomorrow he would go and see his mother.

It would be so good to see her again, he saw her so rarely. She'd taken up residence in Baynard's castle not long before Edward had come to the throne and she seemed quite content to stay there for the rest of her days. She'd never come north to see Richard, and he'd only visited her once in the four years he'd spent at Middleham. It was that, more than anything, that had brought him to London in the first place.

Dinner was served in the main hall and Richard found himself next to Edward for the evening, the queen nowhere in sight. He had yet to meet her, officially, even though she had been married to Edward for four years, but it seemed tonight would not be the night. Edward excused himself early and Richard, tired from travel, went to bed not long after.

The next day it wasn't hard to slip out of the palace and make his way across the city, Francis and one guard following him at a respectable distance. Richard smirked to himself, sure Francis hadn't realised that Richard could see him following. He slipped into an alley and waited for Francis to draw level before stepping out behind him and tapping his shoulder. Francis rolled his eyes after recovering from his surprise and they carried on together.

The doors to the castle were open even before they crossed the gateway and Duchess Cecily swept into the yard to greet him with open arms.

"My boy," she cried as she held him close and Richard embraced her, sighing as a weight lifted from him. He'd missed her so.

"Mother," he said quietly as she held him, pulling back to kiss each of her cheeks as she looked him over.

"You're looking well," she smiled. "Francis."

"My lady," Francis bowed in greeting and he and the other guard from the palace took seats just inside the door while Cecily pulled Richard along to the east sitting room, her favourite.

It was easy to see why the room was her favourite. It was a beautiful sitting room draped in bright tapestries, books everywhere overflowing their shelves, and soft morning sunlight pouring in through hundreds of diamond shaped glass panels, some of them coloured in brilliant hues of orange and red and blue. He'd nearly forgotten how much his mother liked to read and he absently brushed the spines of a pile of books as he walked past. Most were in French, a few were in Latin and one or two were in English, but since they were only just starting to print books here in England, nearly all of these had come from the continent.

"You should take some back to Westminster with you," she said, noticing his attention. "I can't imagine

The Last Winter Rose

Edward has a proper library yet, and goodness knows what the old kings kept, if they even had books."

Richard chuckled, shaking his head as he took a seat on a red and gold couch that must have been brought hundreds of miles just to adorn his mother's home. It was exactly to her taste and he was happy to see that she was living a good life here in London.

"I suspect I'll be too busy for books," he chuckled, though he told her about the few he'd found in his room. Apparently, Edward had also remembered Richard's love of reading that he shared with their mother.

"How are you, really?" Cecily asked, reaching for his hand. He let her take it and held her fingers tightly.

"I'm well," he said quietly. "Most days, anyway."

His mother was the only other one besides Anne who knew about his back and the pain it caused him. She had been the first one to notice that he'd started to move stiffly and had brought her personal physician to examine him. They were the only people in the world who knew the details of what his condition was and what it would do in the coming years.

A lady in waiting brought a tray of food and they ate as they talked. Richard told her about his life at Middleham, asked about her life the last few years. She had been well, she told him, more tired than she used to be, but in high spirits. He told her about the trip to London, the storm that had delayed them near Nottingham, and he asked her why Edward had brought him here to sit on his council.

"You know I'm not old enough," he said and Cecily smiled her smile that meant she was up to something.

"Your brother wasn't old enough to be king," she said. "Age is a number, not a guarantee of maturity, and you, my son, are by far the most mature of my children. You've had to be."

They shared a sad smile and Richard sighed, gazing out the window at the river for a moment. Somehow it had become true of him as the youngest. Anne, his oldest sister, and three years Edward's senior, was much the same. Though he hadn't seen her in several years, he remembered that she was strong and stubborn. She'd been grown already when he was just a child, so Richard had barely known her, but maybe it had been enough, enough for him to learn how to carry such a heavy maturity on his young shoulders.

"You need a sigil," Cecily said decisively, bringing Richard's attention back to her. "You're old enough for one, you have your own titles. Have you given it any thought?"

Richard nodded, picking at the loose thread on a pillow. "I have," he said quietly. It was good to see his mother smile and when she waved her hand for him to continue, he chuckled. "A boar," he told her. "I brought one down last spring when we were hunting and it was... they are formidable if crossed, but peaceable if left alone."

"Just like my sweet son," Cecily smiled, reaching out and brushing his hair back out of his face and he favoured her with a soft smile.

The Last Winter Rose

"I'm almost grown, mother," he said softly, covering her hand with his own. "I'll be a warrior before long."

"Richard, you have the best and kindest heart of all my children, even dear Edmund, who wouldn't hurt a mouse had he been given the choice. You are the best of them, and I think you have chosen a sigil with great wisdom. Although I would suggest perhaps, make it white," she said, her eyes twinkling mysteriously.

"A white boar?" he asked with a chuckle. "Who has ever heard to such a thing?"

Cecily smiled. Her son was caring and smart, but he was still so young. "Think, Richard," she said. "The symbol of our house is a white rose, now the symbol of a *royal* house. Your white boar will remind people you are of royal blood."

She was right, she usually always was. He nodded, happy with his choice, and they spoke for a while longer before the sun passed midday and Richard had to return to the palace. She walked with him out to the courtyard where Francis and the guard were waiting.

"You must come and see me again," Cecily said, face sad at the prospect of not seeing him for several weeks, but he was closer now, just across the city and he reached out to embrace her.

"I'll come as often as I can," he promised, holding her tightly before he pulled his hood up and left the castle with his two shadows in tow.

November, 1468

Richard winced as the sword whistled past his ear, barely missing his shoulder. He tried to move out of the way of the next swing, but it rang across the practice yard with a sharp clang as the flat of the sword met his heavy armour and he staggered back.

The pain was agonising. He could barely breathe, the weight of the plate armour like wearing sacks of stones around his neck and across his shoulders. His back was screaming, but he couldn't say a word.

No one knew.

Edward didn't know, the trainer in the Tower yards certainly didn't know. Only Richard's mother, her physician, who was sworn to silence, and Anne knew about how his spine was curving unnaturally to the right, about the pain that plagued him day and night since he was twelve.

It wasn't so bad most days, but days like today when he spent hours in the practice yards wearing plate armour heavy enough that his slight frame would struggle to carry the weight to begin with, those days were Richard's personal hell.

The master of the Tower yards was a man named Thomas and he didn't care one bit that Richard was a

The Last Winter Rose

royal prince, brother to the king, second in line for the throne. The only thing that mattered to Thomas was your ability to stay alive when someone put a sword in your hand, the ability to kill your enemy when they were coming at you with fire in their eyes and blood on their blades. Killing, Thomas was fond of reminding Richard, was something he would be a poor hand at.

"Don't they teach their brats to fight in the north?" Thomas sneered, making a jab at Richard's years spent at Middleham. No one south of Warwick particularly cared for Richard Neville, but jibes and jeers didn't faze the young Richard. He'd always thought insults were a waste of breath in a fight. He gripped his sword tightly and raised it in front of him, teeth gritted and jaw clenched. He took his stance and waited for Thomas to attack.

"You'll never kill a man if you wait for him to come to you," Thomas called, and charged.

Richard moved his sword to defend, but next thing he knew he was on his back in the mud, staring up at the dark grey London sky, pain threatening to make his vision go black.

"Now," Thomas said, leaning over him to block what little light there was. "You'll never win a fight like that, young lord."

He reached a hand out and pulled Richard to his feet, keen eyes watching.

"The armour is too heavy," Richard gasped, leaning hard on his sword, aware of Thomas' critical gaze.

21

"Aye," the grizzled older man said after a moment. "It might be at that."

Richard glanced up at him in surprise and Thomas nodded to himself.

"Tomorrow, dress in light mail, not the plate," he said, rubbing at the beard that struggled to grow through the scars on his face. "I suspect we'll find your advantage then."

Richard stared at him as he turned away, already halfway across the yard before he found his voice again.

"What's that?" he called, and Thomas paused, turning with a wolfish grin.

"Speed, lad," he called back. "I'll make you the fastest prince west of Rome, and in Rome all they know how to do is run away." He laughed as he disappeared and Richard found himself grinning as he half limped to where two pages were waiting to help him remove the heavy plate. Once he was out of most of it, he sent one of them inside to draw him a hot bath. He was going to sit in the tub until the water turned to ice and no one was going to stop him.

The next day Richard dressed in sturdy breeches and a cotton shirt and instead of his plate he donned a heavily padded wool and linen gambeson and a long tunic of chain mail. It was almost nothing in comparison to trying to carry the weight of plate armour and he wanted to weep with joy. It was still heavy, it was never not going to be heavy, but he could move. He was agile. And he proved it when he knocked Thomas into the dirt and the old soldier grinned up at him.

"We found your strength, lad," he said, as Richard helped him back to his feet. "Now I'll make you as fast as a viper."

And he did. Richard felt better than he ever had in his life despite the fact that he was exhausted constantly. The movement was good for him, he thought, and soon rising at dawn became a habit, rather than a chore.

He missed Middleham most days, but London was fascinating, once he got past the initial shock of the noise and the smell. It had been easier when his visits had only been a few days or a week at a time, but now he would be in the city for the foreseeable future, and he would learn to live here. Despite being a prince of the realm, he had a surprising amount of freedom and he and Francis, along with two guards, spent long days exploring the maze that was London. The city was a warren of alleys and dark corners and they wanted to find every secret she had to offer. The markets were bursting with goods from faraway lands, smells and tastes and colours that Richard had never even dreamed of. He'd been across the channel, yes, but most of that time they'd been taking refuge with their relatives, so he and George had stayed confined to their rooms and dined on simple fare.

The London winter was cold and wet, and when the first snows fell, Richard thought of Anne. He thought of her often, wondering if she missed him, if she would like a fabric or a trinket, and he often had to resist buying things simply because he thought she might like them. He thought about asking for her hand in marriage, about making her his wife, but he wanted to wait until she was older. Until they were both older.

His position at court remained unclear to him, but after a few weeks he realised that was the point. He wasn't yet a full member of the council, nor was he Edward's advisor. The only thing he seemed to be, officially, was the king's younger brother, and that gave a weight to his words they otherwise wouldn't have had. He was training for a seat on the council, but it remained unclear which one. Edward seemed to be watching him, shuffling him around to different ministers and council members, seeing where best he fit in. That was, at least, when Edward attended council.

Richard sat in on many meetings, and more than half of them were without Edward, who was often otherwise occupied with his wife and their young family, the magic of a beautiful woman and two young daughters, with a third child on the way, not having diminished in the slightest. That, or the king was sleeping off the night before and however much he'd drunk.

So, Richard listened, and he learned. He learned what a kingdom needed to run, he learned about trade, wars in Europe, the cost of maintaining their troops, the cost of protecting London, the cost of, ostensibly, keeping London clean. Francis had laughed for nearly five minutes when Richard passed this thought on. London hadn't been clean since the Romans had sailed home a thousand years before.

He had, by the end of November, met the queen, the redoubtable Elizabeth Woodville, and she had been polite, but distant. The girls were adorable and Richard had loved them from the moment Edward brought him to meet them. Their bright laughter and indomitable spirit made Richard wish for daughters when he had his own children.

Francis rarely left his side, nor did the two palace guards that Richard suspected someone had specifically assigned to him, as they were always the same two guards, John and Huge. He and Francis had been able to slip most of the guards when they went into the city, but these two were persistent, and eventually they were accepted as permanent shadows, as long as they were willing to participate. They remained watchful, always, but they also all became good friends through the long winter.

Despite always being in constant company, Richard was grateful for his friend, even if he thought Francis was being over protective of him. There were times when Richard felt like he was the younger of the two, but he wouldn't trade his friendship with the young Lovell for anything. He made Richard's first royal Christmas banquet tolerable, the noise and drunkenness astoundingly beyond anything Richard could have imagined. It was Francis' gossip and sarcastic comments that got him through the evening.

Palace meetings resumed late in January and slowly winter faded into spring, when another recess came. Edward left for Windsor, leaving Richard with time to himself while the government dispersed to the countryside. With little else to do, he and Francis escaped to Oxford, and from there to Francis' home at Minster Lovell.

April, 1469

"You don't need to look so glum," Francis said, coming up to Richard where he stood, unfocused gaze somewhere on the tree line in front of him. Richard sighed, but didn't smile.

They stood outside Francis' home, a small estate in Oxfordshire, some seventy miles from London, on the bank of the river that flowed past the house. It was a quiet little place, the estate lands far larger than might be expected from the modest home. Only fifteen, Francis had yet to spend any real time here, so he'd done little but the yearly upkeep and had no plans to expand the place into something larger and grander. His mother preferred one of the other family residences and both his sisters lived with her, which left this home empty of all but servants for most of the year. Francis loved it just the way it was and so did Richard.

Of all the places in the south of England, this was easily Richard's favourite. The country was peaceful, quiet. It felt safe in a way that London never could and the people here still lived with the land, in tune with the seasons, just like they did in the north. With the house right on the bank of the river, Richard enjoyed spending his afternoon just sitting, watching the current pass him by, or reading to the sound of the water gently flowing.

"Richard?" Francis nudged him and Richard sighed, breaking out of his thoughts and back to the reason for his frown.

"Elizabeth Woodville had two sons with her first husband, and she has given my brother three girls," he said after a long moment and Francis shrugged, tossing a rock carelessly into the river.

"She's young enough, she'll make more brats, she has to have your brother's son eventually," he said, tossing another rock. It was April, so the river was low this time of year, slow and meandering. "What does it matter?"

"It means I'm still only two steps away from the throne," Richard muttered, annoyed by the implication of those words. "You know that's the last thing I want. What if he dies without an heir?"

"You speak as if your brother will drop dead any day, God forbid." Francis rolled his eyes. "He's young and strong, Richard, you needn't worry, and there is still George."

"Hmm," Richard hummed. He was concerned about George, and not sure what to say to Francis about it.

George was a puzzle. But, perhaps, that made him the simplest of them all. He was ambitious in a way Richard, and even Edward, weren't, a way Richard would never be. George always wanted more. More money, more land, more titles. More power. His latest move just after the new year was to propose a marriage with Isabel Neville, Anne's sister and the Earl Warwick's elder daughter. Since Warwick and the countess had no

The Last Winter Rose

sons, all their combined estates estate would be inherited by his daughters, split again between them, becoming the property of their husbands. Even half the estates were more land than most nobles hoped to hold in their lifetime. Richard Neville was one of the richest men in the realm after the king, something many rightly thought made him extremely dangerous.

None of that mattered to Richard, though, he wanted Anne regardless. And yet, he hadn't brought up the idea of marriage with his brother. He wanted to see her again, speak to her first. He wouldn't marry her unless she wanted him as well. He cared for her too much to do that to her.

"You're brooding," Francis said, nudging him again gently with an elbow and Richard sighed. "You're thinking about her again, aren't you?"

Richard shook his head at his friend. "I miss her, you know that."

Francis chuckled, grinning. "So, ask for her hand. She's old enough to marry. You can wait to do...all of that." Francis waved a hand and Richard smothered a laugh. He knew for a fact that Francis had been through London's brothels at least once since they'd come to the city, but he was still surprisingly prudish. Though he was also right. There was no rush for intimacy.

Richard shook his head and leaned on his hands, head tilted back to stare at the sky. "You should have seen Edward's reaction when he found out George wants to marry Isabel," he muttered. "He'd already refused Warwick's request for suit the week before.

Besides, this may not be important to anyone else, but I haven't asked her yet."

"Talk to Edward," Francis encouraged lightly. "He knows you're not like George, explain to him that you want to marry Anne for love. Tell him about your friendship while you fostered at Middleham. Tell him I'll stand witness to your friendship. I was there, Richard, I saw how you looked at her, especially the last few days. I saw you holding hands in church after you gave her your gloves."

Richard smiled, caught up in the memory of that morning on the castle wall, the frost and chill, Anne's hand warm in his and her gentle scolding.

"Just like that," Francis teased and Richard laughed, grinning over at Francis.

"I love her," Richard shrugged, because Francis was his closest friend and they had few secrets. "I'll try and find the time to talk to my brother."

"You deserve to be happy, Richard," Francis said, laying a careful hand on his shoulder.

Richard hadn't told Francis about his back, but he suspected Francis knew something was amiss anyway, and probably had for a long time. They'd been inseparable for the last three years, so he must have noticed that Richard was always careful with the way he held himself, careful with how he mounted and dismounted, how he'd started holding his hands clasped behind his back because it took some of the pressure off. He was grateful for Francis in so many ways, for his steadfast friendship, his wry humour, and for the way he spoke his mind and always told the truth as it was.

Richard sighed, closing his eyes and letting the sound of spring wash over him and the sunlight warm him.

They remained at Minster Lovell for another month before returning to London in late May, and within a month even greater trouble was stirring.

May, 1469

Richard got the news before Edward. The stewards didn't even have a chance to reach for the door handles before Richard shoved them in, striding into Edward's favourite audience chamber without so much as a greeting.

"George is riding with Warwick," he said, registering that Edward's surprise was mild as he practically threw the letter at his brother.

George had already tried to gain himself more power by petitioning to marry Isabel Neville, but now he'd taken the men of his retinue, men who rode under the York banner of the Duke of Clarence, and together he and Richard Neville had crossed the channel to France, sowing disobedience and open rebellion.

Richard was beside himself with fury, so much the more so because he was so rarely angry. Since they were boys, only George could really infuriate Richard. It was something George had prided himself on when he had realised, and their mother had often been too busy, or distraught, or simply too tired to stop him.

"If he goes against my command," Edward said, breaking Richard out of his thoughts, "then I will have no choice but to disinherit him, possibly even brand him a traitor to the crown. Him and Warwick both."

He seemed calm about it, but Richard could tell Edward was just as furious. His eyes were hard and the lines around his mouth had deepened when he clenched his jaw.

"You think he'll do it?" Richard asked and Edward scowled. "You think he'll marry Isabel?"

"I think of all my brothers," the king said tightly. "George is the one who will dig his own grave."

It was two weeks later, dawn on the first warm July morning, and Richard was barely awake when there was an urgent knock on his door. He found himself summoned to an unplanned council meeting in Edward's private dining room. He was still tugging his doublet into place as he entered the room and found Edward seething, pacing the head of the table.

"What's happened?" Richard asked when no one spoke immediately. All the members of the council seemed stunned into silence.

"George has married Isabel Neville," Edward shouted, furious. "He has disobeyed my express order and now they sail for England with an army at their back to depose me! Warwick, that traitorous bastard, wants to put George on the throne instead of me!"

Richard felt a cold chill go down his spine. He wanted to ask about Anne but he didn't dare, not in front of everyone. He felt sick knowing she must be with them, trapped in her father's schemes. He didn't want that for her, he wanted her safe and happy, he wanted to protect her. And for the first time in his life he felt the desire to hurt one of his brothers. No, not just hurt, he wanted to kill George. His ears were roaring and he closed his eyes, forcing himself to breathe. When Richard could concentrate again, the room was in chaos, everyone talking at once. He could barely make out what was being said, until Edward roared over all of them and there was silence. Edward ordered the army readied and then stormed from the room. Almost at once the shouting began again, even louder than before.

Richard snuck away quietly after listening to the councillors argue for close to an hour, though a few had left to follow Edward's orders immediately. He didn't see Edward for three days, and then it was only to chase him down after Richard found out that he'd been ordered to remain in London.

"I should go with you," Richard argued, hurrying after Edward as he stormed through the palace. His rage had only increased when they'd had word that Warwick's fleet had landed and were rallying men through Kent.

"No," his brother said, glancing back at him before striding across the great hall though a flurry of activity. "I need you to stay here and keep the realm from falling to pieces."

"But there must be someone else who can do that," Richard protested. "I don't know anything about, well, any of this!"

"Richard," Edward said, as he turned and stopped, laying his hands on Richard's shoulder when they nearly collided. "I don't trust anyone else to protect my family and my crown."

"I..." Richard said, then he nodded, taking a breath. "All right. I will do everything I can to be worthy of your trust."

"Thank you," Edward breathed, relief evident. "We leave tonight and we should be back inside a fortnight."

Richard nodded, his stomach churning with terror, but if he could help his brother by staying here, he would do everything he could to make sure Edward had a crown to come back to.

There was surprisingly little to do with the king away from court. Half his minsters were lords who raised their men for Edward and marched with him, and the remainder continued in their roles in London with little interruption. Outside his own duties, Richard was called on twice a week to hear petitions and make judgements, some of which were left for Edward's return, once a week to pass judgement on any criminal cases, and once a week to lead Sunday mass in place of the king. The routine was almost a relief.

Then the news came. They had lost a battle. Edward had been captured. Richard Woodville, the queen's father, and his second son John, had been executed by Warwick without trial.

Suddenly Richard's world turned upside down. Lords descended on London demanding his attention, demanding he act, demanding he march the army north to free Edward. Only, Edward's letter had arrived the day after the news of his capture, instructing Richard to do nothing, and carry on running the government as if nothing had happened.

Richard spent long minutes staring at the letter, a headache forming behind his eyes. He'd only been standing in as proxy for Edward for a few weeks and already he swore, never again. If, God forbid, something happened to Edward before he had a son, and George was killed or barred from taking power, he would refuse the crown. He was not a king, he would never be a king.

Clenching his jaw Richard raised a hand for silence and slowly a hush fell over the chamber.

"My brother, the king, has instructed that in the event of his capture we continue on as if he is simply absent from the capital, and not held in captivity against his will."

There were a few nods, a few protests, but once the letter had been passed around for all to see, and they were satisfied with Edward's seal and instructions, they backed down, agreeing to wait and see what happened before taking any further action outside the normal. Richard held in a sigh, determined not to let things fall apart now, not after holding everything together for so many weeks without Edward. He wouldn't fail his brother.

September, 1469

Richard's head was pounding, the never-ending stream of requests and decisions driving him mad. It was late evening and he was nearly done for the day, if he was lucky, and he might get to retire and eat something, finally. He was just signing the last documents when the doors to his private office slammed open and the queen strode in. He stood as she approached, ready to speak, but she didn't give him a chance.

"You will release my mother," she nearly shouted at him and he gazed at her coolly. Her hair was braided back from her face, her dress was plain wool, she wore no jewellery, yet still she looked every inch a queen.

"I did not have your mother arrested," he told her, truthfully, because he had nothing to do with the charges brought against Jacquetta Woodville. They had been made by a lower court, one with its own authority, one overseen by a constable.

"My husband," Elizabeth snarled, "is prisoner of his own brother. My father and my brother were both murdered, their heads put on spikes not a full month ago, and now my mother is accused of *witchcraft*." Her fury was a thing to behold, but Richard wasn't cowed by her. He'd lost his own father and brother the same way, and he understood her pain, and her anger, but that wouldn't sway him.

Though Richard was only twelve when Edward married this woman of little consequence, he'd watched the last five years from afar as she sunk her claws deeper and deeper into his brother, surrounding herself with her own family in positions of power. He'd learned after he arrived in London the previous year that she'd tried to prevent Edward summoning him, but Edward had refused to hear it. He'd known already that Warwick was growing restless, planning something. He may even have suspected George, especially after Warwick brought the first proposal of marriage between George and Isabel. Edward was no fool, he would have known the trouble refusing the suit would cause.

And now Edward was seven weeks in the custody of Warwick and his own brother George. He was, for all intents and purposes, locked in Warwick Castle, a prisoner though they had made no move to have him deposed, as Warwick and Edward had done to Henry ten years before. Warwick and George's rebellion was not about Edward. It was always about the very woman standing in front of him, and her far reaching family, something Richard had come to understand in the last weeks. Something Edward had already understood was a source of discontent with Warwick. The Earl had been embarrassed when Edward had revealed his secret marriage, and it had caused a rift between them, a rift Richard worried could turn to Warwick moving to depose Edward, if one day imprisoning him was no longer enough.

"What are you going to do about it?" Elizabeth asked when he said nothing, her eyebrows pinched with anger and adding years to her face. Richard raised his own eyebrows.

"What can I do about it?" he asked. He was seventeen years old and had been in London less than a year. He was not a member of the judicial court, nor was he keen to interfere in their processes. Until arguments were heard and it was brought before the crown for final judgement, he had no part in it. "It's a matter for the courts."

"You're the brother of the king, you're the highest respected authority in this palace." The way she said it made it clear how much she resented it, as if he should be able to simply sweep all accusations against her mother away. "George is a traitor, he is in open rebellion against the king, he has taken him *hostage*. Do you not understand that you are now the king's heir?"

Richard did understand, but he'd tried as hard as possible not to think about it. He didn't want to be the heir, any more than he wanted George to be king. He didn't want to be acting in Edward's stead here in London, but he'd had little choice. The last thing he wanted to do was help Elizabeth Woodville, but he could also see how the accusations against her mother would blow back against Edward. It seemed once again he was given little choice but to intervene in this, if he wanted to keep his brother on the throne.

The Last Winter Rose

"You're nothing, but a useless child," Elizabeth sneered and Richard scowled at her, anger rising.

"Queen or not, heir or not, I will not be spoken to like that," he said, straightening his shoulders, towering over Elizabeth. "Your blind ambition is what started this trouble. George and the Earl of Warwick didn't begin this plot to remove Edward from the throne, but to remove your claws from him and the realm. I will help you, only because this accusation hurts Edward as much as it does you and your mother, and would make him look weak if it was found you used witchcraft to snare him into your bed."

Elizabeth bristled, but she didn't respond. She had nothing to say because he wasn't wrong. She stood for another moment before turning and sweeping out of the room, shoulders stiff with anger, Richard assumed to return to sanctuary where she had been since Edward's capture. He was surprised she'd dared leave at all.

Richard sighed, staring hard at the floor. He believed in God with all his heart, but he didn't believe in witchcraft. He knew it was just fear that made men accuse the old ways of being evil, fear and lack of education. They were a dying society, held high on the shoulders of religion and superstition and before long it would all come tumbling down.

He knew he held heavy power now, with George a traitor and Edward a prisoner, he truly was the highest authority in London, in England. He could order Jacquetta Woodville released and the whole mess buried and it would be done. If it had been Elizabeth who had been accused, not her mother, he would have let it play its course, but to his knowledge Jacquetta had done nothing more than urge on an already ambitious daughter and possibly send a curse on Warwick for her husband and son. But Richard didn't believe in curses and he understood grief.

There was also the matter of the secret marriage between Edward and Elizabeth, but whether it had been a valid marriage was out of Richard's care, nor did he listen to the rumours being spread around that it was not. That was Edward's business, and he trusted his brother. Besides, with no male child born from Elizabeth, it didn't matter anyway.

What had been done to Richard and John Woodville was a breach of justice from Warwick that would be addressed, but right now there was nothing he could do about it. Warwick was doing everything he could to attack the Woodvilles, but crying witchcraft was a step too far. Perhaps he didn't even realise how it would come back on Edward, if his wife's mother was found guilty of such a charge. He would appear weak, if people thought he'd been bewitched. Maybe Warwick didn't care anymore, maybe he wanted Edward gone, maybe he wanted the throne. Maybe ambition and power had finally blinded him to principle and honour.

Regardless of the reason, the trial of Jacquetta Woodville could not go ahead, if Edward hoped to have any chance to remain king. So, as uncomfortable as it made him to wield such power, Richard ordered her release, the case sealed, and all who knew about it sworn to secrecy.

Edward rode in to London the first week of November with little fanfare, cowled and cloaked and with only two men. Word had come from the north the week before that he'd managed to escape Warwick Castle and gone to York, before riding on to London, where Richard had managed to keep the city free of Warwick's men and influence for the last four months. It hadn't been easy, but Warwick hadn't made a direct move on London, finding his removal of Edward had been highly unpopular. The rumours also said that Edward had simply been let go, or allowed to escape, but he wouldn't know until he saw his brother.

Richard was exhausted, counting the very seconds until Edward returned and he could hand control of the realm back to the rightful ruler. He had enough of his own duties that had been pushed to the side since Edward's capture, things outside London that needed his attention. It wasn't long before Edward arrived at Westminster and Richard hurried to the courtyard. He grinned when Edward raised a hand in greeting as he rode through the inner gate. The king dismounted and came straight to Richard, embracing him as Richard returned the gesture.

"It's good to see you," Richard said quietly against Edward's shoulder. His brother nodded, tightening his embrace for a moment before stepping back to look Richard over, hands on his shoulders.

"You look well," Edward said, apparently pleased. Richard gave him half a smile because the same could not be said of the king.

"You look awful," he told Edward and Edward chuckled. "You look like you've slept in a barn the last few months."

"I feel like I've slept in a barn," Edward muttered, dropping his hands and then running them through his overlong hair. "I was certainly not mistreated, but nor was I treated with even the respect of a valued guest. We give messengers better quarters, and Warwick Castle has a horrible draught."

Richard shook his head, just glad that Edward had returned to London.

"You should eat and rest, and see your wife," Richard said and Edward nodded with a sigh.

"She's well? And the girls?"

"All well. I've made sure of it."

"Thank you," Edward sighed, clapping Richard on the shoulder before he turned away toward his own rooms. Richard would hesitate to describe his brother's gait as a trudge, but he could think of no other word as he watched Edward walk away, shoulders slumped and each step slow.

Taking a breath, Richard realised he might have to manage matters for just a few more days, while Edward rested. Shaking his head, he summoned over the boy who followed him everywhere with a stack of messages that needed attention and opened the top letter as he climbed the steps back inside, already reading as the door swung shut behind him, blocking out the November chill.

March, 1470

After Edward returned to London, life was briefly quiet and uncomplicated. Richard was able to return to his own duties and little more, which came as a welcome relief after months of turmoil. Snow settled over the city and Christmas was a sedate affair while the country seemed to hold its breath. There was something of a stalemate now, between Edward and Warwick, after Warwick's failure to gain support for deposing the king. Everyone knew that more trouble would come, likely before the snows had fully melted. The new year turned and Richard spent as much time as he could with his mother, visiting two or three times a week, sitting in her sun room with a book, talking quietly about anything and everything.

It was an afternoon of long silences when Richard found out that his mother had been exchanging letters with George. She hoped to reconcile them and finally, after months, George had agreed to meet. Richard didn't hurry on his way back through the city. This was not news he particularly wanted to bring to Edward, since he knew it would likely only make Edward mad. Nevertheless, he entered the palace and made his way

The Last Winter Rose

directly to Edward's council chamber, pushing the doors open and interrupting the session.

"Richard?" Edward looked up, face surprised when he entered the room, voices falling silent as he approached his brother's seat.

"I must speak with you," he said quietly. "It's a matter of some urgency."

Edward nodded. "Speak."

Richard glanced around then looked directly at Edward. "It is a family matter," he said and Edward nodded, his mouth tightening.

"Give us the room, please," he said with a jerk of his head, and the others bowed and trailed out, the door finally shutting as Edward frowned.

"George wants to see you," Richard said, watching Edward's frown deepen. "If you will see him, I suggest meeting at our mother's residence, with her to mediate. Else I'd half expect there to be bloodshed."

"A wise choice," Edward muttered, his tone making it clear that if he had the chance, he'd certainly shed George's blood. He fiddled with a dagger absently, digging a chunk out of the table top. "Does he say when?"

"Three days from now," Richard said tightly and Edward just nodded. "Our mother will send him a time when we agree to it." Again, Edward said nothing. "Are you well?" Richard asked after a long moment of silence and Edward sighed, slumping back into his chair.

"I suppose," he sighed. "For having traitors and enemies everywhere I turn."

47

Richard nodded, taking a seat and reaching out to pour them both wine. He'd been attending more and more council sessions and he knew as well as Edward how divided the lords were.

"If the factions split, who will be on our side?" he asked quietly and Edward shrugged.

"I'm not sure anyone will be on our side," he muttered.

"Edward," Richard chided, because his question had been a serious one.

Edward sighed, head dropping back against his chair. "It's easier to list the people I trust," he shrugged. "You, Anthony, Hastings, Lovell, for all he's still a boy. Our mother, our sisters."

"Certainly we know Warwick and his brother are against us," said Richard. "The Percys are unlikely to get involved since it's not a northern matter, not without a direct order."

"The Percy boy is too busy learning his estates to be a bother or a help anyone," Edward said and Richard nodded. The young Henry Percy had only been granted the return of his family lands a few months before and had left for Northumberland immediately.

"What about the Earl of Oxford?"

"He's already sided with Warwick," Edward dismissed with a wave of his hand. "If not with a public declaration, then with his actions. He's been following Warwick's trail for weeks now."

"Do you think they'll seek help from France?"

Edward snorted. "No doubt. We must assume he'll have it, at the very least from Margaret of Anjou. You've never met the woman, but let me tell you she'd do anything for power, and she gains power if she puts her husband back on the throne."

"You think that's what they'll try?" Richard asked, contemplating his brother. Edward was quicker and smarter than he ever let on, and the only time it ever really showed was in moments like this when they were alone, and especially when they played chess. Richard was good, he could beat almost anyone, but Edward beat him three times of four. He was always three steps ahead.

"I'm sure it's their first plan," Edward nodded, sighing deeply. "Now the question is will we be ready for them by the time they attempt it? And what is our dear brother George going to do?"

Silence fell for a moment before Edward spoke again.

"I have one piece of advice for you, little brother," he said, meeting Richard's eyes squarely. "Never trust a Stanley."

Richard remained silent, but he nodded, turning Edward's words over in his mind after they parted ways for the evening and long into the night.

March - April, 1470

They had meant to arrive early, but George was already there when they were shown into the large audience room, not, Richard couldn't help noticing, the same room where he and his mother usually spent a morning or an afternoon. This room was informal, for visitors, not for family. The expression on George's face said he didn't miss that fact, either.

"Mother," Richard said, crossing the room and kissing her cheeks in turn, hands resting gently on her elbows. She smiled at him, touching his face and hair, and squeezing his shoulder as a whole conversation passed between them in a single look. He squeezed her arms before he let his hands drop and stepped to her side, turning to face his elder brothers.

Edward had paused not far inside the room, eyes on George, who stood by the large fireplace, watching his eldest brother. They stared each other down like two wolves ready to fight over a kill and Richard felt an unpleasant twist of fear in his stomach. He'd thought being here in a neutral space would curb both of them from violence, but now, seeing their faces, he wasn't so sure. It seemed that to George, Richard and their mother might as well not even be there.

The Last Winter Rose

"Make me understand, George, why did you go against my express wishes?" Edward said finally, his voice quiet.

"I love Isabel," George said easily, and Richard wondered if anyone in the room believed him. He certainly didn't. George loved her lands, her wealth, and her father's ambitions. He saw in Isabel his way to the throne.

"Try again," Edward muttered. "You have been given everything. Lands, wealth, comfort, you are the brother of the King of England. Before this farce you were my heir until Elizabeth gave me a son, what more could you want? Are you really so greedy? Do you really want my crown, too?"

Richard saw George's eyes flicker, his fists clenching. Edward, it seemed, had hit the preverbal nail on the head. George wanted to be king, he resented being the younger brother, resented that he'd be put aside if Edward had a living son, and it didn't matter the chance that Elizabeth may never have another son. That resentment made him dangerous, Richard saw it, he thought Edward saw it, but he wondered if Edward would allow himself to acknowledge it, or if he would continue to give George the benefit of the doubt.

"I care for Isabel, I promise you," George said, his face clearing as he shifted, clasping his hands behind his back, copying Richard's neutral stance. Richard narrowed his eyes, but Edward didn't seem to notice. "I wanted to make her my wife, more than anything,"

George continued earnestly and Richard felt a deep pit opening in his stomach.

"You swear that's all?" Edward asked after a long moment and Richard suppressed a sigh. He felt his mother's hand on his elbow and he leaned into the touch slightly, feeling her resigned breath next to him.

"I promise, brother," George smiled, and Richard knew Edward was the only one in the room who believed him.

They managed to pass the afternoon cordially enough after that, sharing a meal and talking, though each word was stilted and eventually George made his excuses and took his leave. Richard let out a sigh as the door shut behind him and he reached for his mother's hand, gripping tightly as she wrapped both of hers around his like a vice.

"Do not trust him," she said softly and Richard pressed a grim smile on his lips.

"I haven't for a long time, mother," he responded and she glanced at Edward, who was standing by the window, shoulders stiff and hands clasped behind his back. Even from here they could both see his knuckles were white.

"I fear if your brother forgives George, it will not be safe for you," Cecily whispered, and this time Richard's smile was more genuine as he covered both her hands with his other one.

"I can take care of myself, mother," he assured her and she sighed, reaching up to brush a lock of hair out of his eyes. Richard brought her other hand up to his mouth and kissed the back, leaning into her touch slightly.

"See that you do," she said. "And remember, you are always welcome here."

Richard nodded, not trusting his voice. They sat silently for another long moment before Edward turned and all but stomped from the room, not even bothering to bid their mother farewell. Richard and his mother shared a glance before he rose, kissing her on the cheek and making his goodbyes before he followed Edward back to the horses.

Three weeks later they sat in council when the letter came. It wasn't unusual to have letters coming and going throughout the council session, and Richard paid it no mind when a man brought in a letter and handed it to William Hastings, who held his hand up for silence as he read.

"Warwick and George have fled to France," Hastings said after a moment, passing the letter to Bishop Stillington. "Warwick has taken his wife and both daughters with him as well."

"Isabel shouldn't sail," Richard said, reaching for the letter. Edward, to his left, leaned closer to read over his shoulder. "The child must be due any time, is he really that callous? He'd risk his own daughter and grandchild crossing at the worst time of year?"

Isabel had fallen pregnant almost immediately after George had married her and it felt like they had been holding their breath ever since. Edward still had no son, though Elizabeth was with child again herself, and if George were to have a son first it would muddy the waters of the succession even further.

"Warwick values his own head above everything, even his family," Edward muttered, his face grim. "George might truly care for Isabel, but Warwick will not be denied. You know this," he said, glancing at Richard, who nodded as the others broke out into rapid conversation around them.

Warwick was a hard man, determined and fierce, but Richard hadn't thought him capable of turning his back on his every loyalty, on his family. They were cousins with the Neville family, Richard and Edward's mother was the sister of Warwick's father, but none of that seemed to matter to him anymore. It didn't seem to matter that he had sworn his loyalty to Edward when he took the throne. That he'd been instrumental in putting Edward on that throne.

"I cannot believe this of Warwick,"Richard said quietly. "He has ambitions, yes, but I fear his thoughts have turned to madness. I would never have thought this from him. He was a good friend, a mentor."

"He has turned our brother against us and seeks to dethrone me and put George in my place. George would be a terrible king," Edward pointed out and Richard couldn't help but laugh at that, because it was true. George was selfish, he thought first of himself, not the

The Last Winter Rose

people, not how to make things better. Edward was sometimes absent of thought and a bit too fond of wine and drink, but he was kind and devoted to his family and to the people.

"Then, we shall simply have to remind him of that fact," Richard said, handing the letter to Edward, voice like steel.

"Are you ready for that?" Edward asked, his own voice low, though no one else was listening, too absorbed in the implications of Warwick returning with a French army.

Richard glanced at his hands, rubbing the tips of his fingers together. He'd been eight years old when Edmund was killed, and too young to even remember Thomas, who had died when Richard had been only a few months old. Henry, William, and John he'd never even known, all of them gone before he was born. The only brothers he'd ever really known were Edward and George, and of the two of them Edward was ten years his senior. Somehow though, that didn't matter, because Edward had been a better brother than George ever had.

"If I'm not," Richard said quietly, determination on his face. "Then I will be."

September, 1470

R ichard was settled in front of the fire, reading a new book from the low countries, when a loud knock startled him. He stood quickly, pulling the door open to reveal an out of breath page boy holding out a note.

"You're summoned to council, lord," he said at once and Richard frowned, taking the note. There was no council meeting today. Something must have happened.

"Thank you," he said, dismissing the boy, who disappeared quickly down the corridor.

He pulled on his doublet and laced it as he left his rooms, walking quickly through the palace halls. There were guards hurrying along the corridors and Francis was waiting outside the council room, a frown on his face. He looked relieved when Richard appeared and pulled open the door, following him in and closing it behind them.

"What's happened?" Richard demanded, as he stepped into the room, but only silence greeted him. The council was assembled and they were all staring at a single piece of paper in the centre of the table. Edward's seat was empty and the wine pitcher had been smashed on the tiled floor.

The Last Winter Rose

Francis moved forward, plucking the letter off the table and scanned it quickly before he handed it to Richard. It was dated the 14th of September, two days ago, and it contained disturbing news.

"Three days, ago George and the Earl of Warwick landed an invasion army," he read, more to himself than to the room. "They have the support of Margaret of Anjou, Jasper Tudor, John de Vere, Earl of Oxford, John Neville, Marquess Montagu, among others."

"And Thomas Stanley and Henry Holland have joined them, the weasels," Francis spat. Something in the words stirred the council and after a moment everyone started talking at once.

Richard winced. The Stanleys were known for their questionable loyalties, but Henry Holland was the husband of his eldest sister, Anne. They'd been separated for years and Holland had remained in exile in France, until now. He glanced around the room again.

"Where is Edward?" Richard asked but no one heard him. "Where is my brother?" he shouted and the chamber fell into an uneasy silence once more.

"The king has retired," someone finally said but Richard wasn't sure who, because as soon as he spoke, chaos broke out and a dozen voices covered each other. Richard knew he'd get no more sense out of them.

"I must speak with Edward," he said to Francis and Francis nodded. Together they left the council of chaos to search for the king.

An hour of roaming and questioning servants led them outside to the quay, no guard in sight, just Edward sitting on the end of one of the docks, feet dangling toward the water and shoulders slumped in defeat.

"I'll go," Richard said softly and Francis nodded, falling back and keeping his eyes on the water upriver of hem, watching for any threat.

Richard approached Edward tentatively, sitting next to him in silence, his own feet hanging over the edge.

It was a Sunday, so the river was quiet, few people moving around or working. Every once in a while, a boat would pass as they sat in silence, but as far as Richard could tell no one realised they were looking at the king and his brother. Edward was dressed plainly today and Richard's face wasn't well known enough to be recognised.

"I have to kill him," Edward said finally.

"George?"

Edward grimaced. "Warwick. And George, if he holds this foolish course."

Richard sighed. Edward wasn't wrong, but he still didn't know how to feel about George. George was his brother, his blood. Warwick had been a father figure when Richard had none, and he was also family. But his actions, both their actions, they were treason. Edward had already had George struck from the line of succession, if not outright branded a traitor.

And then there was Anne. Anne who Richard hadn't seen in almost two years, Anne who had been dragged to France with no choice, Anne who he knew would never willingly support any of what her father had done. And Isabel, though Richard had never been her friend, he felt sorry for her, too. Married to George, possibly against her will, Isabel who had lost her first daughter when the Calais garrison had remained loyal to Edward and refused Warwick entry, leaving his ships trapped in the channel in the worst storm in years. Whether she had been a willing bride or no, she was still suffering for her father's ambitions.

"You know I'll stand beside you," Richard said quietly and Edward sighed.

"I know," he murmured, "Just give me another moment to not be...him."

Richard nodded, knowing exactly what Edward meant. Just one more moment when he didn't have to be king. A moment he could just be a man.

"Take all the time you need."

The next days were a blur of activity. They tracked Warwick's progress toward London and it soon became abundantly clear that his army was growing too quickly and they would not be able to defend the city. The council was convened once more and it was not so much a council as a room full of old men shouting their own terror around the room again and again.

"We're mad to stay here-"

"We cannot raise troops in time-"

"The city will not be able to defend itself-"

"My king, you must flee-"

Edward roared at this last, turning the colour of a ripe tomato as he threw a goblet against the wall, tired of listening to his advisors shrieking like hens. The room fell silent and only the bravest among them didn't take a step back.

"You expect me to abandon my country, my throne, my children, my pregnant wife?" he shouted. A few men muttered quietly, but they suddenly seemed united behind the idea. "You make me a coward!"

Richard had to make a decision fast, because he agreed with Edward, but he also agreed with the others. Warwick had come too fast and too strong and he had more support than anyone expected. They had to adapt to the situation or they'd all be killed outright. Richard knew whatever he advised, Edward was likely to listen. It was a heavy responsibility for Richard, but he knew it would be more sensible to run, so he said so.

"Better to appear cowardly and know when to retreat, than be a head on a pike at the city gates," he half shouted, knowing his words would strike Edward where he'd see sense. Richard hadn't seen his father's and brother's heads mounted on Micklegate in York, but Edward had. The reminder would make him take a step back.

Edward blinked, then sank into his seat with his head in his hands, and Richard sighed, stepping closer and laying a hand on his shoulder. He knew how hard this must be for his brother, especially when the queen was heavily with child.

The Last Winter Rose

"Elizabeth cannot travel," Edward said, echoing Richard's thoughts. "Her time will come in a matter of weeks."

"I'll see her and the children safely to sanctuary," Richard assured him. "But you must leave tonight, within the hour if you can. Warwick's army has too many supporting it now. His brother rides from the north, he has Oxford, Stanley, and Margaret of Anjou coming on his heels. We are beyond outnumbered. We need time, and if you want to remain king, then you must remain alive to take back the throne."

"We can sail for Burgundy, to your sister," Lord Hastings said, and a few others nodded. "There you'll be able to raise your force to return in the spring to route Warwick and the Duke of Clarence."

"I will not leave my wife," Edward said again, but Anthony Woodville shook his head.

"I know my sister, she would rather you live. They will be safe in sanctuary," Anthony assured, and finally Edward deflated slightly, considering.

"You swear you'll see them safe?" he said softly to Richard and Richard nodded.

"I'll stay, if you wish me," he said, but Edward shook his head and took a breath as he stood.

"No, if I'm going, then I need you with me, brother. I need your charm and insight to help raise an army in my name to take back our England. We'll need to borrow money. You are far more diplomatic than I am right now, and have a far better rein on your temper."

Richard frowned, but he nodded. He was good with numbers, and he was good with presenting the logical argument, so he supposed he could see how he would be helpful in securing loans and soldiers. As for temper, well... Edward had never excelled at controlling his anger and it had shown on his face every day for weeks.

Edward's departure from the palace was quick and quiet. Dressed in servants garb he and three guards slipped out of the palace via the water, taking a small boat that was leaving with empty barrels and sailing across the river. Richard watched from the window as they stepped onto the far bank and disappeared into the warren of Southwark, where they would find horses and ride to the coast to take a ship to Burgundy. Edward hadn't even taken the time to say goodbye to his queen and, if the shouts echoing along the halls when Richard walked toward the royal apartments were any indication, she was furious about it.

The doors to the queen's rooms stood open and Richard approached with trepidation, already able to hear the flurry of activity inside. He stepped in cautiously and Elizabeth's eyes immediately fell on him.

"I should have known you'd still be here," she sneered.

Elizabeth was clearly enraged, standing in the centre of her rooms as her ladies-in-waiting scuttled around packing several small trunks that would be taken with them to Westminster Abbey. Along with the queen and princesses there would be four servants, two ladies of the court, and ten members of the palace guard who

The Last Winter Rose

would stand shifts outside the entrance to the undercroft that was used for storage and for those seeking sanctuary. As soon as Richard delivered them all there safely, he'd be making for the coast and sailing after Edward.

"I stayed to make sure you and your girls were safe," Richard said carefully. "I'll see you to Sanctuary and you will be protected there."

"Sanctuary," the queen spat, one hand resting on her back and one on her stomach, which was large and round and, according to the physicians, was holding Edward's first son, the prince, the future king. Richard would believe it when the child was born, they'd said the same thing about the last three and they had all been beautiful, wild girls.

"Don't worry," Richard sighed, catching little Elizabeth as she ran by and lifting her up easily into his arms. She was five and a half, but still quite small. "Warwick won't breach sanctuary laws or he'll risk bringing the church down on him. You'll be safe."

Mary, the second oldest and just four, tugged on his tunic and he crouched down to scoop her up in his other arm, smiling at both his nieces and trying to make sure they couldn't see the worry on the faces of every other person in the room. Cecily, still almost a babe in arms at a year and a half, was crying and screaming almost loud enough to bring the castle down, left in her crib while her nurse packed the children's things into a chest.

Elizabeth was, unfortunately, not as understanding of Edward's flight as Anthony had made it seem she

63

would be, and continued to storm around the room shouting at her maids and, Richard suspected, the world at large, especially her wayward husband. Little Elizabeth and Mary were both on the verge of tears, so he put them back on their feet, scooped Cecily out of her crib, clasped Mary's hand, and took all three girls out of the room and down to the dining hall to play while the queen finished berating the servants to pack faster.

A kitchen maid bought them warm milk and sweet treats with a smile and Richard sat on the floor with all of them while they played with a set of dice and a few wooden sticks, making their own game of it until all three girls were laughing and Cecily was carefully clapping along to her sisters' antics. By the time the sun was low both Mary and Cecily were sound asleep, curled in Richard's arms, and Elizabeth was making patterns with the sticks. Richard sighed quietly, imagining a different life, a simple life, one where he lived where he wanted, with the woman he loved, and they were surrounded by their own children, half a dozen or more at least.

Darkness was fully fallen when the queen swept into the dining hall, pausing for a moment at the sight of Richard and the girls, and she sighed, rubbing her stomach before she approached them.

"We're ready," she said softly and Richard looked up, surprised. He hadn't heard her cross the room, but now he nodded, glancing down at the girls in his arms and wondering how he was going to stand without disturbing either.

The Last Winter Rose

"Bess, take Cecily," Elizabeth said softly and the little girl nodded, taking the baby carefully and holding her close, obviously well practiced. Richard carefully handed Mary up to her mother before he stood, suppressing a groan at the ache from sitting on the hard stone all afternoon. Edward had been gone almost a day now, and soon he'd have Elizabeth and her daughters safe, and he could follow. Perhaps on the crossing he could get a few hours' sleep.

It was a short distance to the abbey from the palace so they didn't bother with horses or a carriage, not even for the heavily pregnant queen. She wrapped a cloak around herself, wrapped Cecily in her arms, and took Elizabeth's hand as they slipped into the night. Richard carried Mary, still sound asleep, and a dozen guards surrounded them as they crossed the short distance and filed through the side door to be greeted by the bishop.

The undercroft was well lit, the guards already in place, and within half an hour all the chests had been moved from the palace, along with a large bed, chairs, and a writing table. It was cold, but several braziers were lit to help warm the space, and Elizabeth tucked all the girls into the bed under the warm furs.

"Thank you," she said softly when they were all settled, and Richard just nodded, touching her arm gently. He could see she was exhausted and her pregnancy weighed heavily on her, as heavily as the events of the last week, double the burden along with every other she carried.

"I'll keep him safe," he promised softly. "I'll bring him back."

She just nodded, her anger and tears used up, and he left her alone to rest.

He closed the door and nodded to the guards before he climbed the stairs into the main aisle of the cathedral. He paused, turned toward the altar, and took just a moment for himself. The midnight watch had called, and it was now the 2nd of October, his eighteenth birthday. He was fully and truly a man now, in all views of legality and maturity, but he didn't feel it. He still felt like the helpless young boy who watched his mother dragged from the room by her hair, who had listened to her screams while he clutched his brother and prayed. George had been his best friend then, and now he was an enemy. Richard felt like he barely understood the world, like he would always be waiting for that wealth of knowledge that you were meant to have when you became a man.

He still just felt like Richard, brother of the king, now his heir until a son was born, brother of a traitor who had turned on his family for the chance of a crown. He missed seeing his mother every day, he missed his sisters, although he'd see Margaret soon enough now. He missed Anne, the woman he loved.

Every single day he thought of her and now she was somewhere in France with her father, with George, with Margaret of Anjou. She was in danger every moment and there wasn't even one tiny thing he could do about it, short of raising his own army, marching to wherever they were, and taking her away at the point of a sword, an action he knew was impossible.

With a sigh Richard turned away from the altar and left the abbey. Edward was over a day ahead of him and he had work to do.

November, 1470

Richard landed in Calais in the middle of the night almost two weeks later, the only passenger on a small fishing boat that had barely made the crossing. Winter had set in fully and the seas were roiling the entire way, threatening to capsize them at any second. Setting foot on solid, if not dry, ground was a relief like Richard had never known, and within the hour he had hired a horse and was riding to meet Edward and the others at the agreed location. He only hoped they were still there, that they'd arrived safely and that the seas hadn't claimed them on their own journey a month before.

The sun lightened the thick clouds as he rode and many hours, and a fresh horse, brought Richard to the inn where he was supposed to meet Edward, Hastings, and Anthony Woodville. He didn't expect he'd be recognised here, but still he kept his hood up as he handed a boy a coin to stable his horse and entered the tavern on the ground floor.

He glanced around the room, sighing with relief when he spotted Anthony sitting in a corner and he pushed his hood back as he made his way to the table.

"You made it," Anthony said, as he rose to greet Richard. "My sister?"

The Last Winter Rose

"Safe in sanctuary," Richard nodded, accepting a cup of ale and drinking deeply, grimacing at the taste. He hated ale, but it was better than nothing.

"Edward is upstairs," Anthony nodded to the staircase and Richard glanced around the room.

"This place is safe?" he asked, willing to trust, but still remaining wary of their surroundings. "Is there word from my sister?"

"Safe enough," Anthony said as he downed the last of his ale and turned, leading Richard up the stairs. "The Duke will not see Edward, but your sister asks you to visit when you can."

Richard frowned, but was prevented from asking any further questions when they reached the rooms and Anthony pushed open the door for him. Edward was inside, sitting at a small table covered in papers, letters, maps, and three different coloured inkwells.

"There you are," Edward half glanced up at Richard. "I expected you three days ago."

"The crossing was difficult," Richard scowled, tossing his gloves on the bed and taking the empty chair across from Edward. "Good to see you too, brother."

Edward smiled, glancing up. "Yes, it's good to see you. Elizabeth? My girls?"

"Safe," Richard assured him.

Edward nodded. "There is news," he said, digging through the papers and then holding out a stack of letters. Richard frowned, taking them and opening the first, reading through them as Edward continued the letters he was writing. Anthony returned briefly with food, then they were left alone in the small room. Richard was exhausted, not having slept in almost two days, but he persisted, forcing his eyes to focus on the dense writing. The letters didn't say much, rumours of what happened in England, but nothing from a source that could be completely trusted. All of them were dated before Richard had sailed.

"And Warwick plans to marry his daughter Anne to Henry's son," Edward said when Richard set the stack on the table, unaware of the weight of the blow his words had just delivered to his brother's chest.

"You're not serious," Richard said after a long stretch of silence, recovering himself enough to speak, but still staring at Edward in shock. He felt like an axe had just cleaved his chest in two.

Edward glanced up at him, face puzzled.

"Why wouldn't I be serious? It's a smart move for Warwick, aligning himself with Margaret by marrying their children to each other. It gives him some shield from the sword I have aimed at his heart."

"But," Richard stammered. "That's not… I…"

"Brother, I don't believe I've ever seen you this lacking in loquacity in all my years," Edward said, a sudden mischievous glint coming to his eyes. He knew Richard was often quiet by inclination, but when he did speak he was never at a loss for words. "Do I sense there was something between you and her? More than friendship, I mean."

Richard stood and walked to the window, staring out at the darkness a he recovered himself.

The Last Winter Rose

"No," he said after a moment. "There was not."

Edward waited, but Richard didn't speak again, his shoulders stiff and his hands linked behind him. His back ached to hold the position, but it was better than letting his brother see how his hands were shaking in anger and eventually Edward looked away.

"Anyway, it's only of consequence to us if France throws their support in. Margaret of Anjou doesn't have many friends left, but it may be enough to tip the scales in Warwick's favour," Edward shrugged, looking back at the table and forgetting about whatever was troubling his brother.

Richard scowled at Edward's head, cursing George inside his own head, cursing Warwick for betraying them. He'd been a friend, a mentor, a supporter, he'd been as close as Richard could remember to a father, could have been his father by marriage, if he'd been able to wed Anne. Now Richard wanted to kill Warwick with his own hands.

He didn't believe in killing for vengeance without just cause, but Warwick, he'd betrayed them, used his own daughters as pawns, caring nothing for their happiness. Richard doubted Isabel wanted anything to do with his brother, and she'd been married to George anyway, sold off like cattle, and for what?

And George, his loyalty swung like a pendulum and Richard felt sick to think about it. That George could be bought by a beautiful wife and empty promises of the throne was sickening. Of the three of them, only George had the ambition to be king. Edward hadn't wanted it, but he accepted the responsibility. George wanted it, because he wanted to feel important. And Richard... now he was legally his brother's heir while Elizabeth had yet to produce a son, and he prayed daily that she would, because he had no desire for the crown, even less so than Edward had when he was Richard's age.

Six more months, if he had just had six more months before being summoned to life as part of his brother's court, he could have arranged for Anne's hand in marriage and they could have lived the lives they wanted. He could have protected her, kept her safe from the political intrigues and the dangers of being so close to the throne of a country in constant turmoil. If they weren't at war with France, they were at war with each other. Sometimes they were both, as now, when Warwick, once sworn to them and the only reason Edward was on the throne, was raising an army to restore the Lancastrian king with the help of Henry's French queen and her supporters.

For now though, there was nothing to be done. They were in exile, and unless they could find themselves the support to take back their country and Edward's throne, there would be nothing for them to do, but remain in exile for the rest of their lives.

Curling his hands into fists Richard silently swore he would not allow that to happen. He would not let this be the end of them, he would not let Anne be bargained away to a cruel boy and a loveless marriage. It seemed Edward had done little since he arrived, and he was a poor diplomat on his best day. So it fell to Richard to find the support to put his brother back on the throne, and he would work day and night until their goal was achieved.

January, 1471

The night was dark and the streets were more than wet, they were a veritable bog. The rain had been pouring for almost a week and the streets of Utrecht were ankle deep with mud and other filth. Any drainage system had become completely blocked days ago, leaving a horrible cesspit of human and animal filth right on the street.

Richard grimaced with every step, thankful for his sturdy boots that kept his feet dry and clean. His cloak was heavy wool oiled with lanolin to repel the rain, and it was lined with supple leather to stop what the wool did not. It had been an exorbitant expense, but for once Richard didn't care about spending Edward's money on himself. He was going to put his brother back on the throne, but he wasn't going to drown in the streets of Utrecht to do it.

He knocked on the door when he found it, the sound muffled by the rain and the damp wood, and after a minute the door swung open and he was ushered inside.

The man Richard had come to see, William Herbert, the Earl of Pembroke, was sitting by the fire in the main room. The house was dark except for the flames from

The Last Winter Rose

the grate and two candles that burned on a dresser off to one side.

"My lord duke," Pembroke nodded, but didn't rise. Richard frowned, but handed his gloves and cloak to the man who'd shown him in anyway, taking the seat opposite Pembroke and stretching his hands to the warmth of the fire.

"William," he said, eyebrows raised, and Pembroke chuckled.

"Richard," he said. "I know you're not here on a social call."

"Obviously," Richard scowled. "Who would come out in this to be sociable?"

Pembroke smiled, but it was strained. "I don't know if I can help you," he said, staring into the fire.

Richard accepted a cup of hot wine from a serving girl and took a drink, shivering as the hot liquid hit his stomach. He eyed William for a long moment in silence. It had been two or more years since he'd seen the earl and time had been kind to him. His hair was shot through with grey, but he looked healthy, if tired. Richard had always liked him, he was a congenial man, always with a joke or a laugh, but it seemed even he had run out of laughter now.

"Edward has offered great rewards," Richard pointed out, because Edward had offered a king's ransom in gold and lands, wealth to be stripped from Neville and his followers and passed to those who helped Edward back to his throne. He'd offered it loudly across the continent, and there was no way the offer hadn't reached Utrecht.

"And does your brother have the money he's promised in return for this help?" Pembroke asked and Richard bristled.

"My brother is the King of England," he said sharply and Pembroke laughed his full laugh, nearly curling over himself as he shook.

"You brother is a king without a crown, a country, an army, or any money," he said harshly and Richard would have been more angry if it wasn't true.

It was the crux of every issue, the truth. Edward was a king without a throne, without a kingdom, without an army, and without money. It was a truth Richard had been trying to talk around for weeks, a truth he couldn't change.

"He promises to make you rich-" he tried.

"I'm already rich," Pembroke waved a hand dismissively.

"And my brother keeps his promises," Richard finished stubbornly.

"Hmm," the earl hummed, leaning back and considering Richard in silence for a few long moments. "I have no reason to trust your brother," he raised a hand to forestall Richard's protest. "I don't know your brother. He doesn't come here himself asking for my help. Instead, you come, and I don't think you come at his behest. I think you come because you would restore him, because he is your brother. Do you truly believe he can take back his throne?"

"I do," Richard said, face like stone. His last chance, it seemed, was the respect he himself carried with the nobles. Not Edward, but him. It was a strange thing to Richard, but he would take any advantage.

The earl was silent for another minute. "Then I am with you."

With a grim smile, Richard finally felt the knot at the base of his skull begin to loosen.

He grimaced as he stepped back into the night, immediately sinking ankle deep into the mud and other refuse. He swore colourfully, then muttered an apology to the sky, though he imagined if God himself had to walk the streets as fouled as they were, he too would swear. The sooner they were back in England the better. Not that it didn't rain in England, but it was rain Richard was accustomed to. Lighter, most of the time, even if it rained more often, but this constant heavy deluge was going to drive him mad.

He headed toward the stables, debating. He should ride back to Edward tonight, but the thought of riding three hours or more in the dark and the rain? He shook his head, turning right at the cross street and heading for the closest inn, where warm lights were doing their best to shine through the rain.

The door clattered behind him as he stepped inside, the din of noise hitting him like a wall and he sighed. At least it would be warm.

He'd brought no luggage, guards, or servants when he came to see Pembroke, thinking to be there and gone the same evening, but he hadn't counted on the rain being even worse in the city than it had been at the small country house where Edward and Hastings were waiting. He approached the long bar against the back of the room, trying to recall what little he knew of the local language.

"A room?" he asked haltingly, but it must have been clear enough because the man at the bar held up three fingers, and Richard handed him three silver coins in exchange for a key with a tag on it, the number 9 painted in bright red on the back.

He nodded his thanks and pushed through the crowd to the stairs and climbed to the third level where he found a small door with a brass number plate on it. The key turned easily and he pushed the door closed behind him with a sigh, the din of the crowded tavern well blocked by the heavy wood.

The room was small, but serviceable, and Richard was confident he could rest in safety here. The door locked and bolted from the inside, though he still set the single small chair in front of it before he hung his dripping cloak from the peg and tugged his muddy boots off. There was a pitcher of fresh water and a plain copper ewer, allowing him to wash his face after he'd tossed aside his heavy doublet and unbuttoned his shirt part of the way. He debated his trousers for a long moment before sighing and removing them as well, slinging them over the end of the bed to dry, leaving him in just his shirt and plain wool leggings.

It was cold, but the blankets were warm and the straw stuffed mattress was freshly filled and clean, and within moments of laying down, he was fast asleep.

February, 1471

Richard paced.

More than four months they'd been in Burgundy, exiled from England and living at the court of their sister Margaret. Christmas had come and gone, there had been little news from across the channel, and every day Richard grew more and more restless. What little news there had been, had been bad.

Anne had been married to Edward, son of Henry VI and Margaret of Anjou in early December. Richard Neville had succeeded in selling both his daughters, one to a lout, and one to a would-be tyrant. Richard was furious. He'd never been so angry in all his life. He thought of Anne's smile darkening into pain and sadness and he swore to himself he would see her safe, no matter what.

They'd lingered, or rather Edward had lingered, while Richard had been travelling, finding support for them to cross with an army and retake the throne. They had been ready to sail for a week, but Edward remained in his cups and distracted by his two mistresses, women he didn't think Richard knew about. Edward also didn't think Richard knew about the illegitimate children he'd had already fathered, but that was beside the point.

Edward had been avoiding Richard since he'd arrived in November, and enough was enough.

His decision made, Richard went to his brother's room and knocked loudly, pushing the door open when Edward made a sound that could be considered an invitation, determined to have this conversation now.

"I need to speak to you," Richard said bluntly, closing the door and turning the key in the lock, both to deter interruption and to prevent Edward from escaping this conversation again.

"I'm in no mood, brother," Edward muttered, reaching for the wine jug, but Richard snatched it before Edward could close his hand around it.

"I've put this off for long enough," Richard told him, setting the jug aside and taking the seat across the table from Edward. "I need to speak to you about Anne Neville."

"What about her," Edward huffed into his cup.

"Edward," Richard snapped and Edward finally looked up at him, surprised. Richard had never taken that tone with him before, had never raised his voice, and his eyes were deadly serious. "I didn't say anything before because of what George did when he married Isabel, but I've been in love with Anne for years."

Edward blinked, then sat up straighter, pushing the cup away as he stared at Richard.

"Are you serious?" he asked and Richard nodded.

"If it hadn't been for all this," he said with a sweeping hand, "I'd have asked for her hand months ago. But then George and Warwick, and now they've forced her to marry Margaret of Anjou's bastard and I will get her back, I swear it to God."

"I had no idea," Edward shook his head, amazed. Richard sat back with a sigh, running a hand over his face.

"Tell me we're sailing for England soon," Richard begged. "Tell me we aren't just going to sit here in exile until George puts himself on your throne."

Edward sighed, rubbing both his hands over his face. "We need support, we need-"

"What do you think I've been doing for two months?" Richard half shouted, suddenly angry again. "Burgundy is behind us, there are ships waiting for us in the harbour, there's money to hire an army. The only thing we're waiting on is you, and I'm done waiting."

Richard had never stood up to Edward like this about anything, he hadn't needed to, but he was out of patience. He wanted peace and he wanted Anne safe, and if Edward wouldn't take his responsibility as king seriously, then Richard would lead an invasion into England, never mind that he was only eighteen years old and had never fought in a battle.

"You're right," Edward said morosely, staring at the table. "I haven't had my wits about me, and for that I am sorry. I had no idea you cared for her that way, you should have said."

"When?" Richard asked dully. "She's not yet fifteen and I never expected Warwick or George to betray us and start a rebellion that dragged her and Isabel into the midst of a plot they have no control over."

The Last Winter Rose

It still stung him to think that Warwick would treat his girls the way he had, when he had seemed to care so much for them in those years Richard had spent at Middleham. They deserved better than a father who treated them like things to be bargained with.

"Richard, you are my brother, and you know I never wanted this," Edward said quietly. "I never wanted to be king, that was our father's ambition. I grew to accept that one day I may be king after him, but this…"

"I know," Richard sighed, reaching for the pitcher he'd put aside and filling both their cups. "I never wanted to be your heir."

Edward snorted a dry laugh, taking his cup and staring at the wine. "I never understood George," he admitted. "He was always so different from you, and from our sisters."

Richard nodded. "We were friends once, I think," he said quietly. "But the older he grew, the more distant he became."

"Our mother and sisters have been in contact with him," Edward revealed and Richard raised an eyebrow. "They're trying to convince him that all will be forgiven if he returns to the family. Not Anne, but Elizabeth and Margaret have both written to him."

"And will he be forgiven?" Richard asked, fiddling with his cup, unsure what answer he wanted to hear. Edward shrugged, running a hand through his close shorn hair, something he had done when they fled. Richard thought it looked awful, but it was none of his business.

"I suppose it depends on what he does when we land in England," Edward said and Richard let out a sigh of relief at the spark in his brother's eyes. It seemed Edward had finally found his motivation again.

"Edward," he said, wondering suddenly. "Have you stayed here in your cups because you fear your wife has given birth to another daughter?" They'd had no word of the queen at all since they'd fled.

Edward chuckled and shook his head. "Not that, no, but I fear something may have gone amiss, that she or the babe didn't survive. I don't know how to face that kind of pain."

Richard was silent for a long while before he held out his cup and waited until Edward raised his own to rest against it.

"You face it like a man, brother," Richard said gravely. "You face it like a king."

They sailed for England two weeks later with twelve hundred men on thirty-six ships. They weren't a large force yet, but there were men in England who would join them when they landed, and Richard knew they were pinning all their hopes on the people wanting Edward back on the throne. If the support in England didn't come to fruition, then this ambition would over before it had a chance to begin.

Richard's ship sailed close behind Edward and Anthony, while Lord Hastings sailed after them, the fleet

The Last Winter Rose

nominally split into three equal groups, each following a lead ship across the channel. They made good time, but the night before they were to land, a storm blew up, nearly obscuring the coast and making it impossible to bring the ships in. Richard had been asleep when the ship rocked violently, nearly spilling him from his small bed, and he struggled up on to the deck and into the driving rain to find Edward and Anthony had crossed to his ship, despite the high swells, and Richard joined them near the prow.

"We can't make land in this!" Anthony shouted over the noise of the wind. "We must keep going north!"

"What do you suggest?" Edward asked, frowning at the horizon. Not only was the wind strong and the sea harsh, as likely to crush them on the rocks as not, but the letter tucked inside his tunic which had arrived minutes before they'd launched only made it more impossible. Their planned landing was now in enemy territory, held and garrisoned by the Earl of Oxford.

"We could make for Ravenspur. We should face no opposition there and the landing should be easy," Anthony said.

"York won't be with us," Richard pointed out over the noise of the ocean, drawing his cloak tighter around him. Edward frowned, then his face brightened.

"We don't say we've come for the crown," he said, turning to them. "We tell them that we've returned to claim back the Dukedom of our father, and that is all."

Anthony and Richard looked sceptical, glancing at one another. The rain had already soaked Richard

85

through and the others looked like drowned rats, and all he wanted was to go back inside and change into dry clothes.

"You think they'll believe you?" Richard asked and Edward shrugged.

"Do you have a better idea?" he shouted over a crack of thunder.

They were silent for long enough that Edward nodded, turning back to the bow of the ship and with one more glance at the coast, turned to stare north.

"I'll tell the helmsman to alter course," Anthony said, walking away and leaving the brothers alone.

"We're likely to encounter George soon after we land," Richard said, not quietly because of the wind, but quietly enough it wouldn't be overheard by the men on deck. Most of the soldiers were crammed below to avoid the storm, but there were still a few dozen working or sitting around the ship.

"If our mother has had any luck, I'm confident he won't be a problem," Edward said. Richard didn't ask what he meant. He wasn't sure he wanted to know.

Edward and Anthony returned to their ship, leaving Richard awake and dwelling on his brother. George was only two years older than he was, so much closer than the ten years that separated him and Edward. They'd been close, for a while, as boys. They'd been best friends, once, before Richard went to live at Middleham and Anne became his best friend, while George stayed at Ludlow. But that had been years ago, and since then he'd grown closer to Edward and further from George, until he hardly knew George at all. He knew his mother and his sisters had been trying to persuade George to turn back to their family, but Richard wasn't sure it was possible. He wasn't sure he wanted it to happen.

They reached the coast of Yorkshire on the 14th of March and Richard was glad to set his feet on land again. He wasn't fond of sailing, though it didn't make him desperately ill like it did some of the men with them, but he preferred solid footing and a horse under him. Anthony rode for York immediately with ten men to bring the news of Edward's landing, and see if they could find any support in the north, though Richard suspected there would be little.

Edward, it seemed, had regained his spirits, and could be found at all hours pouring over a map or a list of nobles, or dictating letters. Messengers streamed to and from the camp for two days until Anthony returned to tell them there would be no opposition if they came to York peacefully.

Men had come, much to Richard's surprise, and more were coming. A few were left to direct any late comers while the camp struck and split, Edward, Richard, and a retinue of just over fifty riding to York, while the rest of their forces camped ten miles south of the city, ready to march toward London, George, and Warwick.

They stayed in York only a day, before heading south toward Coventry, where Warwick was thought to be. Edward wanted a battle, but Warwick was dug deep and refused to engage with them, so they laid siege to the city instead. They knew Warwick was waiting for George to come, but then something happened that surprised them all. On the fifth day of the siege a messenger came galloping into the yard, as out of breath as his horse. George's army, such as it was with little more than a thousand men, had pitched camp near Banbury, and George wanted to talk.

March, 1471

The sun had set by the time Richard and Edward finished with the makeshift council meeting two days later. George's messenger had been sent back to the camp across the valley to tell him the meeting time, and Richard shrugged on a cloak before he left Edward's massive tent, his brother following silently.

George wanted to speak to him alone, before he spoke to Edward. Why, Richard couldn't be sure, but Edward had agreed to the request immediately, and so Richard was going.

"If this is a trap," Richard started, voice quiet, and Edward shook his head, keeping pace easily with his younger brother as they crossed the open space to where Richard's white mare waited.

"If he tries anything, the guards have their orders," Edward said and Richard clenched his jaw, frowning.

"Why must our family always be at the centre of turmoil," he asked, not really expecting Edward to answer.

"I'll be waiting," was what Edward said instead, clapping Richard on the shoulder.

Still frowning, Richard swung onto his horse, gripping the reins hard as he nudged her into a gentle trot, down the slope from their camp and out into the wide field between the two tent cities where George waited alone with his banner and a white flag. Over a hundred yards behind him were five guards, holding out of hearing range. Richard's own guards stopped at an equal distance at his gesture and he crossed the last space to meet George by the light of a single tall torch planted in the ground, casting a bright circle of light around them, the last of the sunlight long gone.

"I have come to pledge my loyalty and renewed faith to our brother, Edward, King of England," George said formally. "I have made an error in judgement and would beg his forgiveness."

"The king will accept your fealty, if you acquiesce to his terms," Richard returned, keeping his tone formal as well.

They should have witnesses, but Edward had agreed to George and Richard meeting alone and perhaps he was right. George would shy away from them like a spooked colt if they gave him nothing and a meeting on his terms was simple enough, if it made George feel like he was being treated as he thought he deserved. In the end it didn't matter much anyway, George would have to repeat the declaration to Edward and the king would have to accept it.

"Name them," George nodded and Richard took a breath.

"First, you will cede command of your men to Edward. They will become a part of his army, and fight against the traitor, Richard Neville, Earl of Warwick, and against the invading forces of Margaret of Anjou. Secondly, you will, personally, act in defence of the king in any battle, remain at his right arm and serve as his shield. Thirdly, you will forfeit one third of your lands as the king sees fit, as well as all incomes from those lands, plus another quarter of the remainder, to be paid to the king every year for ten years as recompense for the distress caused to His Majesty the King, Her Majesty the Queen, and the realm at large."

George grimaced, but nodded his agreement. The silence stretched between them.

"Is there anything else?" George asked finally and Richard's hands tightened on his reins.

"Tell me one reason, just one, why *I* should forgive you," Richard said coldly. This wasn't about alliances now, this wasn't about the crown, or Edward, this was about them, about Richard and the brother with whom he had always been so close. George had agreed to Edward's terms, but Richard had his own, and that was understanding George's motives.

"I'm your elder brother. I don't have to justify myself to you," George sneered, shifting in his saddle.

"No," Richard said, voice quiet in the still night. "But you will, brother, or I will go back to Edward and tell him that you would not meet terms."

"I've met every term," George snapped, spine going rigid as he grit his teeth.

"You have not met mine," Richard said, voice deadly quiet, and George fell silent, perhaps surprised by the harshness in Richard's voice. It didn't escape either of them that any alliance between their forces was entirely in Richard's hands.

"Does the promise of power not intoxicate you, little brother?" he asked finally and Richard shook his head, one hand reaching to lay along the mare's neck to calm her. She could tell he was agitated and it was making her nervous. Around them there was little sound, too far from both their camps to hear much of the noise of the men, their guards too far back to disturb them.

"You know it doesn't," he said and George sighed, looking away.

"Then you're a stronger man than I," he admitted quietly.

Richard watched his brother quietly for a long time, but George didn't speak again. Finally, he nodded and turned his horse away, riding back to Edward's camp. He half expected George to follow, to call out, but there was silence.

"Well?" Edward asked, as Richard dismounted in front of his tent. He was tired, he was filthy, his back was screaming, but Edward would not be put off, not so close to a coming battle. His brother was jagged, restless, as if he were itching for bloodshed.

"He has agreed to all terms. His army will join ours and we will march against Warwick," Richard said, handing his horse off to a waiting groom and wincing as he stripped his heavy gloves off.

"Good," Edward nodded. "I'd hate to have to face my own brother across the field."

The Last Winter Rose

His attention was already gone as he went inside, absently muttering and making calculations in his head. Richard knew his brother was unlikely to sleep that night, but he had no such desire to stand hunched over a map table into the darkest hour of the night. He wanted a bath, a meal, and some rest.

Dawn came too quickly and it seemed as if he had only just laid down to sleep before he was being shaken awake by a young page boy who had brought him a heel of stale bread and a bowl of hot porridge. Richard hated porridge, but it was the morning fare in an army camp, even for the king, so with a mild grimace he ate his meagre fare quickly and set about readying himself for the day.

By the time the sun broke the horizon he was dressed in his armour and mounted next to Edward, the army assembling behind them as the tents were hastily broken down and stowed on wagons.

They rode to the place where Richard had met George the night before and dismounted, striding forward across the field. Richard hung back as Edward drew ahead, the sun quickly burning away the morning fog, revealing George's army standing ready, but at ease as George also crossed the space between them to meet Edward in the middle. Only after they had embraced for everyone to see did Richard join them, though somewhat reluctantly. He had no desire to speak to George or even be near him. He hadn't yet fully forgiven his brother and he might never.

"Come," Edward said cheerfully, clapping them each on a shoulder. "We will ride together." Richard bit his tongue to stifle a wince, but Edward wasn't to know. He still hadn't told Edward, or anyone, about the strange twist in his spine. He wasn't weak, he wouldn't be, couldn't be, seen as weak, and if people knew he could only imagine the ridicule.

They rode together, the three of them at the head of two armies joined, George on Edward's left, Richard on his right. As they rode Edward made clear that George would not resume his title of heir, and, not wanting to lose his head, George agreed as graciously as possible to step out of the line of succession permanently. Richard wondered if Edward would really have carried through with the threat, but George seemed to believe he would, and that was all they needed.

It bothered Richard, because it meant he was still the next in line, but he also didn't want to let George near that kind of power and influence, so he kept his thoughts to himself. He hoped when they reached London there would be some news that somehow, miraculously, the queen had given birth to a son.

The gates of London were open.

There was smoke rising from the city, but no more than normal from the hundreds of cook fires and smithies and guard posts. There were no extra men posted along the walls, no obvious disturbances of an occupation. London was as it always had been, trade wagons rolling in and out and horns blowing at the docks as ships came and went, people crowding the streets as they went about their lives.

"There's no resistance," George muttered from Edward's left, shifting in his saddle as he squinted at the walls a mile away. "They haven't even shut the gates."

"It's likely a trap," Richard said with a frown to match Edward's. It was some trick, it had to be. He could not believe Warwick would have abandoned London.

"We proceed," Edward said finally, after deep consideration. "But with caution."

They met no resistance as they crossed the last distance to London and passed through the gates, approaching the cathedral of St Paul's, where a man in fine robes was hurrying out to them as they rode closer.

"That's George Neville," George said with a heavy frown. "Warwick's brother."

"Greetings!" the aforementioned Neville, the Archbishop of York called, as he descended the stairs, hands raised in peace. "The city is yours, my king, you'll find no resistance here. We have no desire for war."

"Where is Henry?" Edward said sharply, drawing up his horse and dismounting in one smooth movement. Guards clustered around him as he approached the archbishop.

"Inside," Neville said, jerking his head over his shoulder. "His mind is in no fit state, he'll return with you to the Tower quietly, that I can promise. You have news of my brother?"

"Marching toward us as we speak," Richard said, still atop his horse. "He has refused offers of peace." Neville frowned at that, but Edward waved it away, impatient.

"The queen?" he asked, for he'd had no news of Elizabeth in weeks, and despite what he'd said to Richard he wanted desperately to know if she and their child lived.

"Safe in sanctuary, your highness, and there is news. She brought forth the babe in November last. A son."

Edward's entire face lit like the sun bursting through the clouds on a grey day and a cold relief washed over Richard, knocking the breath from him as he slumped in his saddle. He was no longer the next in line for the throne, no longer his brother's heir. He was free. Of course there was a chance the boy might not live, but Richard staunchly refused to consider the possibility. All of Elizabeth's other children had been healthy and lived, there was no reason this son shouldn't also.

George mumbled something under his breath, but Richard paid it no mind, straightening himself up again, taking stock of their surroundings. Neville seemed to have spoken the truth, there were no armed guards, no soldiers besides their own men. It seemed that London truly didn't want to fight. There were a handful of people gathered around, watching them curiously, but that was all. It seemed Warwick was not so much liked by the people of London, nor was there much support to

The Last Winter Rose

return Henry to the throne. Richard idly wondered what had happened while they had been in exile, if there was anything at all of import, or if the city had simply carried on with no mind to what was happening between the lords.

They returned to the Palace of Westminster that night, after seeing old king Henry back to his lodgings in the Tower. Richard thought perhaps they should all stay there, in the safety of the high walls, but Edward was too eager to see his wife and children in Westminster Abbey, only a stone's throw from the palace. Indeed, he did not accompany them to the palace itself, but turned right and rode for the Abbey at the first chance, disappearing through the doors before Richard turned back and rode through the gates of the palace.

His rooms were surprisingly undisturbed and he shut himself inside and locked the door, sliding down against it to sit on the floor and put his head in his hands. Their first step had been taken, they had returned and captured London without resistance. Now they simply had to survive the coming battle, and he had to find Anne and spirit her away from their enemies.

He was shaking, the last week catching up to him, and he was only slightly surprised to feel hot tears rolling down his cheeks, quiet sobs shaking him. He wasn't ashamed to admit he had been terrified, he still was, and within days they would be leaving again and riding to a battle, his first real battle. He was eighteen years old, a man by all rights, and most days he still felt like a boy who barely knew what he was doing. All he could do was carry on and hope one day the feeling inside his chest matched the calm and steady demeanour he'd built for himself. Somehow, he suspected it never would.

With a sigh, he forced himself up to shed his clothes and crawl into his bed for a few hours' sleep, because he knew it would be a precious commodity, and he was right. Two days later they once again marched out of London, toward Barnet, where Warwick and his army were camped. They arrived as the sun sank, and pitched their tents in the growing dusk as they readied themselves for the coming battle. With the dawn, they would attack.

April, 1471

It was just before dawn and the camp had risen early to prepare for battle. They'd sat through morning prayers, but Richard could hardly hear the words. His stomach churned when he forced himself to eat, and his back ached from sleeping so many nights in rough conditions. He'd been surprised when Edward had entered his tent while two pages helped him into his armour and waved them away, helping Richard buckle the heavy chest plate himself.

Richard wore mail over felt and leather, like most foot soldiers, with a solid plate chest and back pieces, and plate graves and bracers. He had a light helmet, his sword, and two daggers, and still he felt naked as he tried to recall Thomas' training.

"Do you trust George?" Richard asked, his face twisted in a frown as he turned to let Edward reach the buckles under his arm.

"Stay close to me," Edward said in lieu of answering Richard's question. "The press of battle is a confusing and disorienting place. I don't want to lose you."

"I'm to command the flank," Richard reminded his brother, touched by his words. "If all goes well, I'll see you after."

Edward tightened the last straps and Richard lowered the arm he'd been holding out of the way, turning to his brother.

Edward was ashen, his eyes vacant. Richard didn't think he'd ever seen Edward afraid, and he wasn't sure that was what he was seeing now. Warwick had been their friend, their mentor. He was almost like a father to Richard and would have been there for Edward after their own father, and Edmund, were killed. His betrayal stung them all, but Richard suspected Edward felt the hurt and anger even more deeply than he did, though he was unlikely to admit it. This wasn't fear. It was devastation.

"Just be careful," Edward said finally, and in a move that shocked Richard, Edward embraced him tightly before turning and leaving the tent without another word.

Richard stared at the tent wall, mind suddenly blank, unmoving until he heard the horn sound to assemble, then he took a breath, pulled on his gauntlets, and went to kill his countrymen.

The fighting was over and Richard's ears were ringing. Years later when he looked back on his first battle, he could barely call to mind a single clear memory from the time he commanded his line forward to the time he found himself standing beside Edward in the ruined aftermath of blood and bone.

The Last Winter Rose

"The *Kingmaker* is dead," Edward said, staring straight ahead, hands clasped below his chin and elbows on his knees. It was a strange way to see a king, even more so because he was still wearing his full plate and was covered in dirt and blood. His words brought Richard out of his own battle stupor and he took a breath.

"And Anne?" he asked, fingers still tight around his sword. His own armour was heavy, he hurt everywhere, and his padded wool doublet was soaked with sweat and blood. He was injured, somewhere, but he was still too taut from the battle to know where, other than it was clearly not a mortal wound or he'd be dead already.

"She's not here," Edward shook his head. "Neither is Margaret, or her upstart of a son. I'm told the weather delayed their crossing and they're still in France."

Richard frowned, taking a step back and leaning heavily against a tree. Around them, the sounds of men dying and being taken prisoner filled the air. No two battles were ever much alike, but the aftermath was always the same. Soldiers, women, even children combed the battlefield for survivors, for weapons, to make lists of the dead, sometimes to rob valuables. The last was unlawful, but most were too stunned by the horror of fighting and let it pass. No matter how many battles you fought, the shock always set in afterward. This was Richard's first true battle, but he'd seen enough brawls and skirmishes to know that there was no difference, only the scale of the destruction.

He felt a deep conflict at hearing that Warwick was dead. Relief, on the one hand, but disappointment on the other. Relief was easy enough to understand. It meant the threat to Edward, to all of them, was lessened now. The disappointment was harder, because it was twofold. With Warwick's betrayal he'd lost a mentor and a father figure. Warwick was dead, gone forever. Yet while he mourned, Richard also wished he'd had the chance to kill Warwick himself, to avenge the injustices done to Anne, to Isabel, and to anyone else who had been hurt by Warwick's ambitions.

"What are you going to do with George?" he asked quietly and Edward sighed.

"Pardon him, I suppose, if he survives his wounds, " he said tiredly. "He fought with us bravely, or so I'm told. They said he took a blow to the head, which oft times can be fatal, but it's in God's hands now."

Richard sighed heavily. The last thing he wanted was to lose another brother, but he felt a horrible sense of foreboding about George, as if the trouble he could cause wasn't yet over. George was ambitious in a way none of them were, and Richard worried he'd never be satisfied unless he sat on the throne. He wouldn't let the death of Warwick simply put an end to his aspirations, and now both Edward and his son stood in George's path to the throne, not to mention the old king Henry, his queen Margaret, and their son. Though Margaret and her son were delayed, they were still on their way to England. There would be another battle before long, and Richard wondered if George would stay true to his

The Last Winter Rose

brothers and his family, or flee to Margaret of Anjou with his tail between his legs.

It didn't bear thinking on at the moment, though, George was injured, as were hundreds of others, and there were the dead to bury or burn.

"Are you hurt?" Edward asked and Richard looked back at him in surprise.

Edward wasn't callous, or unfeeling, but he was so often in his own head, so taken up with being king that he didn't have much time for those around him. He'd certainly been distant with Richard since this whole mess had started.

"I'm fine," Richard said with a smile and Edward sighed. "Hurt somewhere, but I'm still standing."

"Your hand," Edward said and Richard blinked, looking down at his sword hand. His sword was bloody, not only from killing, it was dripping from his hand to the hilt, onto the blade and down to the ground. He couldn't even feel it.

"Oh," he said, and Edward heaved himself up from where he was sitting and took Richard's sword, helping pry away fingers that had been clenched so tight they refused to open.

"Let's get you cleaned up, little brother," he said kindly, holding Richard's arm as they made their way across the battlefield and toward where soldiers were setting up a tent to treat the wounded.

May, 1471

Richard grimaced as he curled his fingers, pain making his hand and lower arm throb. It had been a week since Barnet and he still couldn't grip his sword properly.

They'd returned to London to the news that Margaret and her ships had landed in Wales the same day as the battle and Edward had called for a fresh muster of troops to be assembled at Windsor in three days' time. He'd briefly tried to persuade Richard to stay in London and finish healing, but he'd quickly given up at the look on his youngest brother's face.

Richard was even more determined than ever to rescue Anne. He knew she was with Margaret's army. Their scouts and spies had identified nearly everyone of any import who had arrived with the former queen and her ships. He was going with Edward and he would make sure Anne was safe.

Four days later they left Windsor, riding at the head of over five thousand men. George, contrarily to Richard, had been ordered to come despite his injury. Edward didn't trust him, and neither did anyone else. When they fought, and they would fight, George would stay under Edward's eye while Richard had asked to lead the vanguard. Edward had been hesitant at first,

The Last Winter Rose

because of the injury to Richard's sword hand, but by the time they reached Cirencester on the last day of April, Richard could hold his sword steady and Edward gave him command of the vanguard.

They chased Margaret's struggling army north and west, toward the Severn crossing at Gloucester, where she was rebuffed by Richard Beauchamp, governor of the city and cousin, in some way, to Anne and Isabel's mother. From the closed gates she fled another ten miles, before her army, overworked and exhausted, was forced to camp near Tewkesbury.

The night of the 3rd of May, Edward camped his army within striking distance, planning to attack at dawn. Their men, fresh from riding most of the way instead of being afoot, were eager for a fight. Little sleep was had at the camp that night while Richard paced, and prayed.

He wanted to sneak across the valley and into the enemy camp, he wanted to fetch Anne to safety before the battle, but there was no way to know where she was in the disorganised mess of Lancastrian troops. He would be caught and either ransomed or killed, if he attempted it. So, once again, he was forced to wait. Richard hated waiting, and as he paced his tent, he imagined the life he wanted, rather than the one he had.

It was a quiet thing, his fantasy life, filled with warmth and family, Anne at his side and a few children, three, maybe four at the most. They would be happy, live somewhere they could make a home, and have no greater worry than the disputes between local farmers.

Richard knew no matter what happened, he would never have a simple existence filled with the hard work of a peasant farmer, turning his own soil, and growing his own food, but some days he wished for it all the same.

He knew, of course, that a life like that was hard, brutal even, with fears of crops failing, disease in the animals, raiders, but at the same time it was a simple existence. He'd been among the folk of Yorkshire often when he was younger and, for many of them, the most they cared for who was king in the south was if this king would raise their taxes or take their sons to war. There was no need to care who married their daughters to their rival's sons in a quest for power, no need to worry about who held a throne across the sea in France, or Naples, or Florence, or who sat in the highest seat in the Vatican. Most would never go more than ten or twenty miles from where they were born, unless they took up trading or soldiering, or their craft brought them to a larger city. Richard often wondered what it would be like to be ruled by the sunrise and the sunset, not by a host of servants who told him when to rise, eat, dress, who dictated his every move. It was part of why he disliked London, although it hadn't been like that so much since Edward's exile. He'd mostly been left to fend for himself, and the strict royal protocols had yet to be fully enforced again, and wouldn't be until they won their war.

Richard didn't think about what would happen if they lost, he wouldn't tempt fate like that. Instead, he paced, stared at the golden cross hung over a small altar on the north wall of his tent and prayed.

The battle was won, but it would be hours before the field was silent, free from the roiling mess of men and horses and bodies. Richard had seen Margaret of Anjou flee when her son was cut down and he knew Anne must be here somewhere. He'd seen her before the battle, standing next to Margaret. He'd wanted to ride across and steal her, bring her back to their lines and keep her safe. He had no choice, but to leave her and fight his way through Margaret's forces instead.

"Anne!" he shouted now, pushing through the throng of men taking prisoners or putting down wounded horses, toward the side of the field where the fighting had been thin. "Anne!"

He'd marked what she was wearing earlier, a dark burgundy dress that clashed horribly with her hair, no cloak despite the chill of the morning. He looked everywhere for a flash of red and finally spotted it among the supply wagons and he started running. He heard her scream followed by the roar of a man and he ran faster.

"Anne!" he shouted again, but there was no answer.

She couldn't hear him. Nor did anyone else, too busy rounding up enemy soldiers, separating out the dead from those who might be saved, picking over the corpses for anything of value. Edward had ordered that no one who didn't raise a weapon was to be harmed, but something had made her scream. There were always people around a battle, women, children, craftsmen, all manner of folk followed any army, no matter its size, and it wasn't always safe for them in the aftermath.

He finally broke through the last of the battlefield and ran toward the wagons where he'd seen her, gaze sweeping around. He saw no one, then he heard a sound and he dropped to his knees and started looking under the wagons, eyes peeled for her burgundy dress. He found her finally, under one of the larger grain wagons. Her dress was filthy, her hair tumbled from its pins, her arms wrapped around her knees and her eyes stared straight ahead, but she was alive. Next to the wagon a man lay with a knife in his throat, the blood still flowing out around the blade, his eyes wide with surprise and death.

"Anne," he said quietly, carefully reaching out a hand. After a long moment she turned to him, her eyes roving over him as if she couldn't quite believe it. She didn't believe it, he could see it on her face, too shocked to understand what her eyes were showing her. He knelt on the soft ground, shifting to take the weight off his right side as he pulled his helmet off and tossed it aside, pushing sweaty hair out of his eyes.

"Richard?" she croaked, her voice breaking in the middle of his name.

"I'm here," he said softly, holding his hand out for her. She looked at it for a long time before she finally moved, sliding her fingers across his palm. She sighed at the touch, as if reality was slowly coming back, and she gripped his hand tight.

"How did you come here?" he asked, knowing she shouldn't have been this close to the battle. She shouldn't have been here at all. He couldn't imagine she'd wanted to see this.

"She made me come," Anne said, as she slowly shifted toward him, clutching his hand as he stood carefully and helped her out from under the wagon to stand. Her head came up to his chin now, though he wasn't sure if it was that she'd grown taller or that he'd grown shorter. Her face was thinner, her cheekbones sharper, and there was a small cut long the line of her jaw.

"The battle is done," he said, wanting nothing more than to draw her into his arms and comfort her, but he wasn't sure how that would be received. Neither one spoke of the dead man lying on the ground less than two feet away.

"The... queen?" she asked, glancing around as if Margaret of Anjou would spring from the ground. "Edward?" her voice was barely a whisper and his hand tightened on hers. He struggled with how to phrase what he had to tell her, before finally settling on the simple truth.

"Your husband is dead," Richard said and she finally met his eyes. Her gaze hardened and she drew herself up, no longer scared, now standing tall and proud in the midst of all the carnage that surrounded them. He had the nearly overwhelming urge to close the short distance and kiss her.

"Good," she said, her hand gripping his tightly. "I will pray he finds forgiveness, though I am not optimistic."

"Anne," Richard chided gently, but he had to smile at her audacity. She smiled slightly at that and he chuckled, eyes roving over her face, catching on the scrape.

"I'm not hurt," she said softly, suddenly shy under his gaze and he reached up to push back a tendril of her hair that had come loose and was hanging in her face.

"I'm glad," he whispered. "I've missed you."

"I missed you too," she said, tears welling in her eyes and he didn't resist any longer, pulling her forward and wrapping his arms around her tightly. She clung to him as she wept against his shoulder, their embrace made awkward by his armour, but neither of them cared, too glad to be together again to care about any of it.

He would have stayed with her the rest of the day, forever, but within minutes they were torn apart and he was forced to carry on his duties in the aftermath of the battle, while she was taken into custody as a noble of the Lancastrian forces, no matter how unwilling her part had been in any of it. He wished he'd had more time, he didn't know when he'd see her again, or where they would take her. He needed to speak to Edward as soon as possible.

June, 1471

It was nearly a month before Richard saw Anne again. After they returned to London there was a council called to decide what to do about the people that had been forced to march with Margaret of Anjou because of their status or because their relatives had been held hostage. Anne, having been married to the former Prince of Wales, was unlikely to have any blame placed on her, but there was still the decision of her future, now that she was a widow and her father was dead.

The meeting had already started when Richard slipped into the room, eyes automatically searching. Something in his chest released when he found Anne and his shoulders relaxed, seeing she was safe. She glanced his way and their eyes met, as if she could feel his gaze on hers, and a tentative smile brushed her lips. He smiled in return, nodding and slipping around the side of the room to take his seat next to Edward.

He was late, and it seemed that whatever was to be decided about Anne's future already had, for now she was sitting with George and Isabel, and George seemed inordinately happy about something. Richard frowned, reaching over and sliding a piece of paper out from the stack in front of Edward. His brother glanced at him, then freed the page, handing it over and returning his attention to the man in front of them.

Richard felt rage boiling up as he read. With no close male relative, and her mother, Anne Beauchamp, living in confinement and declared legally dead, Anne was to be made George's ward, as the husband of her elder sister. He had access to the entire Neville fortune though her, as well as all their lands and incomes, not an insubstantial amount by any means. He was a greedy, manipulative bastard, and Richard knew he'd never let Anne marry unless it was to his benefit. And there would be no benefit to George if she married Richard.

The rest of the day's session passed in a haze and the council adjourned. Edward disappeared almost immediately and Richard quickly made his way through the people to Anne's side, noting she'd moved away from her seat just as quickly and was standing in a small pocket free of people at the end of the benches.

"Are you well?" Richard asked softly, hand just touching her elbow, out of sight of the others, yet she could feel it through the velvet of her dress and it gave her strength as she nodded. The noise of people talking around them masked their quiet words and it was the first time he'd been able to speak to her since the battlefield.

"I'm well," she said just as quietly, with a soft smile just for him. It was so good to see him again after so long.

The Last Winter Rose

"Did they... hurt you?" he asked. His frown deepened when he saw the shadow that crossed her face before she could stop it and tuck her emotions away behind the courtly mask, and he took half a step toward her.

"They did nothing that time and prayer won't heal," she assured him, holding his gaze. She didn't think he believed her, and why would he, when it wasn't true, but she needed him not to make a scene of it here.

He opened his mouth to speak, to ask what he could do, when his brother interrupted them rudely.

"Ah, there you are, dear sister," George said brightly, Isabel's hand tucked into his arm as they approached. "Shall we?"

"George," Richard started, but his brother cut him off with a steel smile.

"Richard. As my lady wife's sister, the Lady Anne has been given into my care," George said. "She will be residing with us, and all choices of who she associates with henceforth are to be made by me. For her safety, you understand. Come, Anne."

Furious, Richard had no choice, but to watch as George led Anne away. He shook his head when she glanced back at him, face desperate. He would solve this, somehow. He would get her away from his brother, he would be the one to protect her, like he always should have been. He would have married her already if it weren't for George's poorly timed foray into rebellion, for which Richard still hadn't forgiven him. He loved her, and nothing was going to change that. George

113

would not stand in the way, not this time. His greed would not keep Richard from Anne, not when she was here, in the same city, so close and only just out of reach.

"I want to see Anne," Richard said, falling into step with George. His brother sighed dramatically and Richard grit his teeth, knowing what was coming. It had been the same answer now for six months, every time Richard had asked, ordered, and demanded to see Anne.

"I'm sorry, brother, but she doesn't want to see you, or anyone," George said, just as he had every other time Richard had asked. "She is overcome with grief at the loss of her father and husband. I fear she may retreat to a nunnery soon, she's such a fragile little thing, isn't she?"

Richard nearly growled aloud. George knew absolutely nothing about Anne, nothing at all. She was fire wrapped in steel, encased in stone. Fragile was the last word anyone would use to describe Anne Neville, if they knew her at all.

"Where is she, George?" Richard asked, stopping in the middle of the hallway and forcing his brother to stop walking with a hand on his arm.

"She doesn't want to be disturbed," George said, tone patronising. "I'm sorry, little brother." He pulled his arm out of Richard's grip and disappeared around the corner. Richard was sorely tempted to see if he could

The Last Winter Rose

chip the stone wall with his dagger, but he took a breath and clenched his fists, letting his anger go as he breathed.

If George was going to be like this, if he thought he could hide Anne away from him, keep her secret somewhere, then he would find her himself, even if it took him a year. Not for a single moment did Richard actually believe she wouldn't want to see him, or believe a word George said.

Resolved, Richard spent the next few weeks following George, making note of who he spoke who, who he saw, where he went, the people he acknowledged in the hall, the people he paid. He followed him out of the palace and into the city, to different homes of friends or associates, and to one house where he returned every three weeks like clockwork. He always stayed outside the house and spoke to the housekeeper, handing over a large bag of silver before disappearing into the night and Richard strongly suspected this is where he was hiding Anne away.

He waited until George visited the house and spoke to a rotund woman with a ring of keys weighing heavily on her leather belt, keeping to the shadows, too far away to hear what they were saying. When George left and the woman went back inside, he snuck around the back of the house, looking for a way in. There were no windows at ground level, but there were a few at the level of the street, looking into rooms built below ground. Unlike most of the surrounding houses the street went all the way around the property and no part of the house was joined to another. George clearly hadn't thought he might want to be subtle and use a building that wasn't clearly the product of money, but then Richard wasn't sure his brother knew the meaning of the word subtle.

Crouching to peer into each window, Richard couldn't see anything until he came to the fourth, and then he could just barely make out a lit hearth in what he imagined was the kitchen. There was a young woman standing at the table, but he couldn't be sure it was her, not with the poor quality of the glass and the soot coating it. He'd have to take a chance.

"Anne," Richard hissed through the window and she glanced up, squinting at the sound.

"Who's there?" she called, unable to see with the light behind whoever was crouched awkwardly at the window, which on the outside was only a few inches above the surface of the street.

"I'll give you a guess," Richard muttered, trying to pry the window open, heart hammering. Even muffled he knew her voice and he was going to get her out of here, tonight.

"Richard?" Anne gasped, throwing aside the towel she'd been using to wipe her hands and rushed to the window, dragging a rickety stool over to stand on as she reached up, tugging the inside latch. Richard grunted, pulling the small window open, its hinge creaking, and reached inside, grasping her hand tightly as she reached for him.

The Last Winter Rose

"Are you all right?" he asked, his fingers warm around hers and she didn't even care about the tears running down her cheeks or the flour and soot on her hands and dress. This was her Richard, he was here, he'd found her.

"I'm magnificent," she sniffed with a smile and he laughed, smiling softly at her. He was almost lying on the street, twisted awkwardly to reach for her hand, but he didn't care. What was a little pain when he could finally look on her face again and see her smile?

"I'm getting you out of here," he said, squeezing her fingers. "I'm taking you to sanctuary, away from George and Isabel."

Anne didn't have words, standing on her toes to press her lips to his hand, the only thing she could reach. "I prayed you'd come," she whispered and he shifted so he could tug his hand free and touch her face, brushing her tears away with his thumb.

"I will always come for you," he said softly and she smiled. "Get your things, whatever you have or that would be of use. Where is the servant's door?"

She wobbled on the stool and let go of his hand with reluctance as she stepped down, telling him how to get around the house to the servant's entrance. When he nodded and vanished, she reached up to shut and lock the window again. She glanced around the kitchen before she took a bag and piled some food in it, then snuck through the hall to her small room, packed the only other clothes she had and pulled her cloak on, not lighting a candle for fear of someone seeing her.

117

The door was bolted when she reached it, but she'd managed to steal the key from the head kitchen woman, who'd been tipped back in her chair in the hall, snoring loud enough to wake the devil himself, and within moments the lock was in her hand and she lifted the heavy bar, wincing as it crashed to the floor.

Richard didn't wait, pushing the door open and pulling her out into the small alley and his waiting arms, holding her tight for barely a moment before he took her hand and they vanished into the darkness. There were no sounds of followers, so perhaps they were lucky and the crash hadn't woken anyone. They heard the midnight watch call just as they reached the Church of St. Martin, the door opening for them with a gentle push as they slipped inside and to safety.

Richard glanced around the church, but all was quiet. There were only a few candles lit along the walls and one torch near the door for anyone who came in the night to pray or, as in their case, seek sanctuary. He sighed, relieved, pushing the door shut again and turning.

Anne was leaning against one of the pillars, hands hidden behind her back. She was half smiling, her eyes wide, her cheeks flushed and her breath heavy from their quick flight. She looked happy, despite the circumstances he'd just plucked her from or, perhaps, because he had. Her dress was simple and marked with soot, flour, and grease, her hair tied under a length of cloth to keep the red-brown tendrils out of her face. There was a streak of

The Last Winter Rose

soot on her cheek, but despite all of it she had never looked more beautiful.

"How did you find me?" Anne asked when she'd caught her breath, but Richard remained silent, just looking at her.

"Anne," he whispered quietly, at a loss for anything else to say. She bit her lip, hesitating, but her eyes were so full of hope that Richard couldn't stop himself from crossing the short distance and wrapping his arms around her.

She gasped gently and her arms came around his waist, holding him tightly, but carefully, and he buried his face in her hair, so in love he could barely think.

"I'm so glad you're safe," he whispered finally, forcing himself back to take in her face, brushing at the soot streak with his thumb as she smiled at him, tilting her cheek into his palm as her hand came up to cover his, her eyes fluttering.

"I missed you," she whispered, gazing up at him, tears in her eyes. "It's been so..."

"Shh," he hushed when she didn't continue. "You never need to tell me anything you don't want to."

"I do," she whispered. "I do, I just..."

"When you're ready," he said softly, drawing her into his arms again and just holding her, the silence surrounding them, the world far outside the walls and a universe away.

"How did you find me?" she asked again, quietly, words half muffled in his shoulder. Richard chuckled and pulled back again, taking her hands in his and stepping back, putting some space between them.

"I've been following my brother for weeks," he admitted. "He kept coming back to the same house, the same time, every three weeks. Tonight, I took a chance."

Anne's eyes widened in shock, then she laughed, wild and free, trailing off into little giggles as she imagined it.

"Did you sneak through shadows?" she teased and Richard's mouth quirked.

"I'd do worse than sneak through shadows for you," he smiled, face serious. Her breath caught, her hands tightening unconsciously in his.

"Richard…" she whispered, breathless.

"Marry me," he said softly.

"It won't be simple," she said, her hands shaking where his fingers held hers carefully, worry evident on her face, but at her words, Richard smiled.

"Nothing about you is simple," he said, taking a step forward and pressing his forehead against hers. "That's why I love you."

"I love you, too," she whispered, tears escaping her eyes as she reached up and brushed a hand through his hair. "I have for years."

"Is that a yes?" he teased and she laughed, pulling her hands away and wiping her eyes, smiling at him and shaking her head. He settled his hands on her waist, unable to let go of her, but he was smiling too.

"Yes," she whispered, beaming with joy.

He knew he should wait, but he also knew they had both already been through so much, and he didn't want to wait a moment longer. He cupped her cheek in one hand, tilting his head, making sure she knew what he intended. When she rose on her toes a little, brushing her nose against his with a shy smile, he pressed his lips to hers and kissed her like he'd wanted to since he saw her on the battlefield, her hair wild and her clothes covered in blood and muck, her eyes burning with such defiance it had taken his breath away. She sighed against him, kissing him back, and Richard thought this must be what heaven felt like.

April, 1472

It took three days for George to find out that Richard had spirited Anne away. Richard was surprised it had taken that long, he'd have thought a message would have been sent to George as soon as they'd realised she'd vanished right from under their noses.

He was with Edward late in the evening, playing chess, when George burst into the room, rudely sending the door crashing against the wall. Edward looked up at his brother with a raised eyebrow and Richard hid his smirk behind his hands. They'd been expecting this confrontation.

"She's gone!" George shouted and Edward leaned back in his chair.

"Who's gone?" he asked, though he already knew. Richard had already told him everything and Edward was well aware of his intentions to marry Anne as soon as possible.

"Anne Neville!" George shouted. "He took her!" he said accusingly, pointed a finger at Richard, who just smiled at his brother.

"Perhaps she ran away," he said, voice deceptively soft. "Perhaps she doesn't like you, brother."

George paled, suddenly understanding that Edward would do nothing for him, understanding that Richard was the favoured one here.

"I will find where she's hiding," George threatened. "And drag her back by her hair."

Edward raised an eyebrow as George turned and stormed out while Richard shook his head.

"You're sure she's safe?" Edward asked and Richard nodded.

"I've taken her to a sanctuary, no one knows where."

"Not even me," Edward nodded. "Smart. It may be several weeks before our messenger returns from Rome, but I will support you wholeheartedly. I'm sorry I couldn't intervene at the tribunal last year on your behalf."

Richard smiled, glancing up at his brother, noting the lines that had grown deeper around Edward's eyes and the light flecks of grey already making themselves known at his temples.

"This isn't the last we'll have heard from George," Richard warned, because he knew his brother well by now. If anything, they would hear a great deal more from George in the coming days and weeks.

Edward just sighed, nodding as he frowned at his pieces and knocked over his king with a look of disgust. Richard had won again.

"He stole her from my house in the dead of night!" George shouted and Edward looked ready to strike him, having heard the same thing no less than a dozen times now over the last few weeks.

"So you've said," he muttered, teeth clenched, and Richard glared at his brother, arms crossed in front of his chest. He was as tired of listening to this as Edward was.

"I was made her guardian, she is my wife's sister!" George continued even though again, all this had been said.

"Yes, George," Edward said, raising his gaze to meet George's, quelling him with a look. "Richard would marry her, he made that quite clear several weeks ago. You may be her guardian, but you cannot dictate if and who she will marry, that now falls to her own choice. She has agreed to marry Richard, and I will bless the union and that will be the end of it."

"I will take legal action," George threatened, not for the first time. "It is within my rights."

Edward sighed, turning away from them both and reining in his temper with every bit of willpower he had left. They'd been arguing for hours, days, weeks, ever since Richard had spirited Anne away from the house where George had hidden her. The arguments had resumed today, because the messenger carrying papal dispensation for the marriage between Richard and Anne, close enough cousins to make it necessary, had arrived. The union, much like George and Isabel's own, had been blessed by His Holiness and could proceed.

The Last Winter Rose

"If it matters so much to you, I'll cede a portion of the Neville estate to Isabel," Richard said finally, tired of the fighting. He wanted to marry Anne and be done with it, and if he had to give George more land as some sort of a bribe, he was willing to pay the price.

"I want half her Neville lands and titles that come with them," George said immediately, pulling a list out of his doublet and throwing it on the table.

Richard frowned in disgust. He'd once been close to his brother, but those days seemed further and further away with every new scheme George pulled, and Richard began to wonder if their friendship had ever been real, or if he'd imagined it. George's distasteful actions the last few years had hardened Richard to him and he felt little sympathy now. George had his wife, seemingly the only person he truly cared for, and she seemed to have developed some affection for him. He had retained his own lands and titles despite his treasonous actions against Edward. He had a full half of the Neville estate already through his own marriage, and now he was doing everything he could to stand in Richard's way, because he was so greedy that he didn't want to give up the lands he'd been granted custody over as Anne's guardian. The titles he wanted just to say they were his, and Richard was sure he'd shirk any responsibility that came with them. Not that it mattered, that would only give Edward the excuse to revoke them again later.

"Richard-" Edward started, but Richard held up a hand, reading the list. They were mostly lands in the south, near where George already had property. Middleham wasn't on the list.

"No," Richard said. "I want this done. I love Anne, I want to marry her as soon as possible, I want to take her home to Middleham, and I want to be finished with this. If it takes these lands remaining with George, then so be it. After all, I take my tithe percentage from the entirety of Northumbria and much of Yorkshire."

Richard wanted to smirk when George frowned, because even with the larger portion of the Neville lands, Warwick Castle and its estates, and his own lands, George's income didn't even come close to matching Richard's, and Richard took only a small tithe, far less than he was owed as a royal duke. But now George had been outmanoeuvred and he had no further argument. Richard watched him struggle for a long minute, satisfaction heavy in his chest, and finally George nodded.

"So be it," he spat. "Marry the girl."

Richard wanted to shout with joy, but he simply forced a neutral smile on his lips and bowed his head.

"My thanks, brother," he said and George's face flushed red with anger as he spun on his heel, slamming out of the room without even bowing to Edward. Silence followed before Edward sighed.

"He grows more vexatious at every turn," the king said tiredly. "I'm sorry."

"I have what I want," Richard said with a genuine smile for his brother. "I'd like to take the news to Anne."

"Go on," Edward smiled. "Go tell your woman you're to be married. Find the Bishop and tell him, he'll make the arrangements."

"We only want a small wedding," Richard warned and Edward nodded, waving his hand.

"You'll have it," he said. "Go! And don't forget to tell our mother!"

Richard laughed as he bowed and hurried out of the palace, waiting only as long as it took to saddle his horse before he was on his way to St. Martin's to find Anne and tell her the news.

She was sitting at the end of a bench to the left when he came into the small church and she didn't turn until he was nearly next to her, then she looked up and saw him, her face lighting up as she stood and hugged him.

"I have news," he whispered against her hair, arms tight around her. She held him a moment longer, then pulled back, pulling his hand so he sat next to her.

"Good news?" she guessed from his jubilant expression and he nodded.

"We can be married as soon as you want," he smiled broadly. "Nothing stands in our way. The dispensation came this morning."

"And George?" Anne asked, pleased, but still worried. George was not one to back down easily and she knew he had been against this marriage from the start. He'd been fighting with Richard ever since she'd escaped from his house two months before.

Richard sighed and held her hands lightly. "I gave him more, most, of the Neville lands. I know they're yours by right, but he wouldn't be budged, and I wanted to be done with it, I wanted us to be happy."

"We still have Middleham?" she asked and Richard nodded.

"I'll never let anyone take that from us," he swore, and she smiled. "Middleham and most of the northern lands. He's taken everything to the south and the Warwick estates and titles."

"Then I have everything I need," she assured him, unbothered by the loss of the other lands. Let George have them, she had Middleham, she had the north, and she had Richard. She needed, and indeed wanted, nothing else.

They were married less than a fortnight later, in a small ceremony just as Richard had asked. There were few guests, George and Isabel standing to one side, George frowning and Isabel beaming. The sisters had reconciled before the wedding and Richard was glad to see Isabel there for Anne. Anne had almost no one left, her mother still in sanctuary and her father dead. She'd never been close with anyone else.

Edward stood at Richard's side and Cecily had even left her home to see him married, a soft, almost sad

The Last Winter Rose

smile on her face. Francis was there, as was Richard Ratcliffe, who had become a close friend of Richard's in recent months. There were a few other lords and ladies there, but Richard had eyes only for Anne as she entered the small chapel.

She was beautiful in a blue gown borrowed from Cecily, from when she was newly wed herself, with flowers woven in her braided hair and wrapped around her head like a crown. She was shaking as she walked along the aisle and Richard held his hands out for her, gripping hers tightly when she slid them in his. He was shaking as well so she squeezed his fingers and smiled, her shoulders straightening as she found her confidence.

The Bishop's words were a blur until the very end when they were pronounced man and wife. With a grin Richard swept her into his arms and kissed her, the sounds of happy cheers surrounding them. Edward hosted a feast for them back at the palace, full of laughter and cheer, and they danced together until they were breathless, eyes only for each other. Richard had never been happier in his life.

The night wound down eventually and Edward embraced them both, kissing Anne on the cheek as they left the hall for Richard's rooms, where Anne's things had been brought that afternoon from St. Martin's, and when Richard shut the door behind them and bolted it, he sighed with relief.

"As wonderful as it is that your brother gave us a feast," Anne chuckled, "I'm glad to be alone."

Richard hummed, reaching out and pulling her close, wrapping his arms around her and just holding her. "As am I," he whispered, eyes closed. He leaned against the door, just breathing, and she wrapped her arms around him with a heavy, contented sigh.

"Richard," Anne said after a moment and Richard hummed, not answering. "Richard."

"What?" he mumbled, and Anne pulled back, her smile devious.

"It's our wedding night."

Richard cracked his eyes open and looked at her, feeling heat rising in his cheeks.

"It is," he said quietly, opening his eyes fully.

"So," she teased, and he looked away.

"Anne," he said softly, and she ran her fingers through his hair. "I don't want to hurt you, or make you uncomfortable, or-"

"Richard," Anne smiled, tilting his head up to meet her eyes. "I don't think you could. Please, don't fret about me. It's my wedding night and I want you, in every way."

Her smile was soft and calmed his heart as he leaned down the short distance between them to kiss her, hands slipping down to rest on her waist as she stepped back away from the door, leading him toward the bed.

He helped her with the laces on her dress when she turned, slowly pulling the fabric apart to reveal the thin shift beneath it. She shrugged her arms out of the sleeves and the whole mess of blue cloth tumbled to the ground around their feet. She turned back to him and her shift was so fine, so thin, he could see all of her through it and his breath caught. She reached up and pulled a dozen pins from her hair, shaking it free to fall over her shoulders, so long it nearly touched her waist. Flower petals tumbled around her and Richard couldn't help but wrap his arms around her and pull her close, just holding her as he breathed her in, kissing her softly.

Her fingers were less nimble as she worked at his clothes, but between them they were soon tossing his doublet aside and she tugged his shirt until he chuckled, pulling it over his head and tossing it away as well. Her fingers were curious on his chest, then she slowly turned him, eyes on his until he had to look away. He shuddered when her fingers met his back and he could hear her breath as she traced along his spine, gently touching the curve that was far more pronounced now than it had been five years before, the only other time she had seen it.

"Does it hurt?" she asked softly and he didn't want to tell her, to make her sad, but he had sworn to always speak the truth to her.

"Every day," he said, his voice just as soft, and her palm pressed over his shoulder blade before her arms wrapped around his waist and her whole body pressed against his back, holding him gently, but tightly, just as he'd held her. He laid his hands over hers around his waist and laced their fingers together.

"I love you," she said against his shoulder and he turned in her arms, catching her face between his palms and kissing her softly.

131

"I love you with everything I am," he whispered back and she smiled, tears leaking from her eyes. He hastily wiped them away and kissed each eyelid, each cheek, and then her lips again, softly, gently. "And I always will."

Part II - Lord of the North

June, 1472

They left London soon after the wedding, escaping to the countryside to be alone and away from the politics of the city. They went first to Oxford, then to Minster Lovell to stay with Francis. Their time was their own, and evening often found them hidden away in their room, spending time as happy newlyweds did.

"Tell me about Barnet," Anne asked quietly one evening, tracing her fingers across Richard's chest as she lay in his arms.

Richard sighed, his arm tightening around her back and he hid his face in her hair, not sure what to say. The last of the light was fading from the window and they had long since eaten and retired, curling in bed together to talk quietly, like had become their routine most evenings.

"It was a battle," he finally settled on and Anne huffed.

"Obviously it was a battle," she muttered. "Was it horrible?"

"You were at Tewkesbury," he said quietly. "You saw how horrible it is."

"But in the centre of the fighting, it must be so much worse."

Richard was quiet for a long time, fingers running through her red-brown hair idly where it splayed over her back like a waterfall. It was so much longer now, he'd been amazed when she'd pulled the pins from it and let it cascade down her back on their wedding night, and every night since.

"I imagine it's actually worse outside the battle. You can see it, hear it, smell it, fear it, but you can't do a thing about it. In the middle of a battle all you can do it look for the next man to kill, for the next sword or knife or pike coming at you. You don't have time to think, only to kill and stay alive. You don't have time for fear."

Anne was silent, though Richard felt a shudder run through her.

"You're not wrong," she said quietly. "It was horrible, not knowing what was happening. I saw you, before the battle, but I couldn't do anything. I wanted to run out across the field to Edward's army, to escape. Instead, I hid in the only place I thought might be safe from them."

"I looked for you," Richard said, kissing her hair and holding her closer.

"You found me," she smiled, tucking her head under his chin and tightening her arm around him. "I don't know what I would have done if you hadn't found me. I was so scared. I've never been that scared before in my life, not even on the boat to Calais…"

She trailed off and Richard knew she was thinking of the storm, the night Isabel lost her child. They must have been so afraid, Isabel in labour, the ship refused berth at the port, and the storm threatening to take them down to the bottom of the channel. He couldn't even imagine, and he'd known his share of fear in his life and at a younger age than her.

"You're stronger than anyone I've ever met," Richard said, catching her chin gently with his fingers and tilting her face up to meet his eyes. "You would have survived even if I hadn't come."

Anne's smile was beautiful and soft and so full of love it made his heart ache and he only wished he felt like he even began to deserve her.

"I'm not so sure, but I love you for believing in me," she whispered, and Richard didn't resist closing the distance and kissing her softly.

"I love you so much," he breathed. "I will love you until the day I die, I swear it."

"I think you already did that," Anne teased, "when you married me."

Richard chuckled, happier than he'd ever been before in his life. The world seemed far away and there were only the two of them here in this room. They had a few more weeks before they returned to London, then they would leave for Middleham where they would remain free to be themselves, no plots, no personas, just two people in love.

"Richard," Anne said softly, and Richard heard the tension in her voice. "At Barnet... do you know who killed my father?"

He'd wanted to do the deed himself, but he wouldn't burden her with that hatred. Warwick had been a traitor and he'd hurt Anne and her sister, but he had been her father. Still, the truth was nothing horrible, because he honestly didn't know, and he told her as much.

"No, not for sure," he said softly, watching her face. "The first thing I did after the battle was done was ask after you. That's when I found out your ships had been delayed and you were still in France."

"With her," Anne muttered, but she'd set aside her hatred of Margaret of Anjou and her son the day Richard had found her on the battlefield at Tewkesbury. They were gone and she was happy, she had no need of their ghosts hanging over her life.

"That's when Edward told me your father had been killed during the battle," Richard told her.

Anne nodded, her hand clenching and unclenching around the blanket.

"We brought his body back to London," Richard said, voice barely above a whisper. "He was displayed along with his brother, John, in St. Paul's for several days, but Edward spared him a traitor's burial. They were taken to Bisham Abbey and interred with others of their family."

After a long moment he felt Anne relax against him, then he felt dampness on his chest and knew she was crying. He said nothing else, gathering her in his arms and holding her while she wept for the man who had sold her and her sister, who had used them as pawns and bargaining chips. He hated Warwick for everything he'd done, but that still didn't change the fact that he'd been Anne's father, and losing a father was something that he of all people understood.

Their time in Oxfordshire passed quickly and soon they returned to London, where Edward was waiting.

"There you are," Edward said before Richard had even closed the door to his private dining room and Richard chuckled, crossing the room to sink into a chair opposite Edward, reaching for a glass of watered wine.

"Are things well?" he asked and Edward sighed, shrugging.

"Things are as they always are in London," he said, reaching for his own wine. "A nest of vipers chasing their own tails. I'm hoping for good news from you, brother." Edward glanced at Richard and Richard sighed. He knew this would be coming. They'd talked about this before the wedding, but Richard knew Edward wouldn't let it go so easily.

"I'm afraid I have none for you," he said, and Edward shifted, shoulders tense.

"So you won't stay in London?" he asked, a mild frown on his face. "You know I could use your council."

Richard shook his head, meeting his brother's gaze. "I'm of little use to you here," he said. "Besides, this is more your home than mine. I've always felt more at ease in the north."

He had been adamant, before, that he and Anne wanted to go north, that they wanted to be left in peace. Maybe Edward had brought him south to be part of his council, but that was before, when Warwick was a threat. The threat was past now and Richard wanted to go home. Edward had no use for him now.

Edward sighed and shook his head at Richard, but he didn't argue. As much as he wanted Richard here, his brother would also be of great use to him in the north. He had already been appointed Constable of England, a nominal title in peace time, as well as Lieutenant of the North and Sheriff of Cumberland. He'd been granted holds at Penrith, Sheriff Hutton, and Middleham, all lands he'd kept despite ceding portions of the Warwick estate to George, and unlike George, Richard had Edward's unwavering trust. As much as Edward wanted Richard here with him, he could see the benefit of sending his brother to govern the lands that were out of reach to him.

"You'll go to Middleham?" he asked and Richard nodded, picking at a loose thread in the fine embroidery of the tablecloth. They sat in Edward's private dining chamber, the late afternoon sun still shining brightly outside the window. This deep in summer there would be light for hours yet.

"Anne would prefer to reside in her childhood home," Richard said after a moment. Neither had directly mentioned George and Isabel taking Warwick

Castle as their residence since they'd left, directly after the wedding, and Richard didn't expect to hear from either of them anytime soon.

"Then I would have you guard my northern borders," Edward said, decision made. "Be my eyes and ears and authority, be my sword against a Scottish invasion, be my justice in all disputes."

Richard stared at his brother for a long time.

"You're practically asking me to rule," he concluded, and Edward half shrugged.

"You'll do better acting in my name from Yorkshire than I'll do from my throne in London. We were all born to rule, brother, and I think you have it best of us. You may rule in all but name, and you may rule a place you love."

"You do not love your city?" Richard asked, eyebrows raised. He smiled when Edward scoffed.

"I hate London as much as anyone, but it is here I am king and here I must stay," he said, spreading his arms in a gesture of resignation.

"I wish you well, brother," Richard said, and for at least a moment, Edward smiled.

"Never doubt my trust in you, Richard," Edward said quietly, and Richard sighed, nodding.

"And never doubt my loyalty to you, Edward," he smiled, and Edward nodded, reaching out to clasp hands with his youngest brother across the table.

They went north.

The ride was long, slowed by the men and wagons that came with them, filled with supplies and materials, everything they might need that might be hard to find. The steward of Middleham, Geoffrey Frank, was a good, smart man, but he would only have been able to do so much with Warwick gone for so long and little money for repairs. Richard was worried about the state of the castle, but Francis, who rode with them to see them settled before he returned to his own estate where his duties had finally caught up with him, was ever jovial.

When they arrived, they saw the castle was in good repair and riding through the east gate felt like coming home. Richard sighed, closing his eyes and inhaling the familiar smell of the yard, shoulders relaxing.

"The stables will need a new roof," Anne said as they dismounted and stable hands took their horses. She had insisted on riding the whole way from London, rather than travelling in the wheeled cart Edward had provided for them to use. Instead, she'd piled it full of grain and seeds for planting the fields, empty sacks for storage, and bolts of cloth and bobbins of fine thread that came all the way from France.

"That it does, mistress," Geoffrey, the steward of the estate said as he walked up to them, his tone ashamed. "I've done the best I could with the stipend we received-"

The Last Winter Rose

"You've done wonders," Richard said, laying a hand on Geoffrey's shoulder. "I confess I feared it would be much worse."

Geoffrey smiled. He was a short, portly man, and hadn't changed at all in the years Richard had been away, his dark hair and beard neatly trimmed and combed and his eyes kind.

"The kitchens are in good order and the family rooms have been cleaned and made ready," he said, tucking his hands into wide sleeves when a breeze blew through the yard and Richard remembered Geoffrey had always been prone to pains in his hands, especially with how much he wrote to keep up the ledgers and correspondence needed for the estate. "You'll be wanting the Lord's chamber?"

Richard glanced at Anne, who frowned, patting her horse absently. She shook her head after a moment.

"Not tonight, Geoffrey," she said. "That's still my father's chamber and there are... dark things to face. Could we have Richard's old room for now?"

"It's very small," Richard warned with a smile and Anne cast a fond gaze at him.

"I know," she said softly. "But I'll feel safe there. And tomorrow I will start going through my parents' things. I want to make this our home now."

"You don't have to do it alone, if you don't want," Richard said gently, touching her elbow. "I'll always be here for you."

141

Caitlin Sumner

"I know you will," she said, and her smile was as bright and dazzling as the sun rising on a frosted winter morning.

Anne was gone by the time Richard woke the next morning. He dressed quickly, curious where she would have gone without waking him.

He paused in the door of the west range, hearing her laughter ring across the yard. He smiled, slipping out the door and walked toward the sound.

She was near the stables, dressed in a plain brown cotton dress with the skirts tied up to her knees and her sleeves pushed past her elbows. There was a scarf over her hair, which was still loose down her back, and she was laughing as she groomed his horse. Hers was already shining and happily crunching from a bag of fresh oats hanging from the door of her stall.

Richard hadn't realised it was possible to fall more in love, but in that moment he did, and he knew he would always do anything and everything for her.

"Good morning," he said, as he wrapped his arms around her waist, smiling when she jumped in surprise.

"You'd frighten me half to death, wouldn't you," she chided, smacking his arm gently with the brush, but there was no bite to it.

"I woke up alone," Richard said softly, burying his nose in her hair. "Can you blame me if I worry?"

The Last Winter Rose

"Now that's a sight that warms the heart," Geoffrey's voice interrupted them and they turned to see the steward smiling fondly at them. "Young love. Shall we be expecting little dukes and duchesses to grace us soon?"

Richard and Anne glanced at each other. Her face was uncertain, so Richard smiled, pulling her tighter against his chest.

"We haven't discussed that just yet, Geoffrey," Richard smiled. "We've only been married a few weeks."

"Best have that talk then, lad," Geoffrey winked. "Or it'll be happening sooner than later and you'll have no more say in the matter."

Anne blushed, but Richard chuckled. He was home, they were safe, they could be themselves. Everything was right in the world. If there were going to be children, then there would, but only when they were both ready. They were young, Richard was nineteen and Anne was sixteen, they had years and years to add to their family.

The talk turned away from babes to the harvest, which Geoffrey informed them grimly would likely be lean because of the heavy spring rains. How Anne had known, Richard couldn't fathom, but she'd managed to pack enough grain in the cart they brought with them to keep their stores well stocked through the winter, if they were careful. They might only need to travel to York once to buy grain during the dark months, and perhaps not even that.

143

They saw Francis off a few short days later. Richard spent the next weeks reacquainting himself with the castle and the town, greeting old faces and meeting new, and soon everyone knew that although royal blood might run in his veins, Richard didn't stand on ceremony with anyone. He and his lady wife would as happily pass an evening in the small, draughty pub in the town with the everyday folk as they would in their warm hall with soft songs and fine wine.

The stable repairs were completed by the end of July, and both Richard and Anne were up before dawn and to bed well after dusk the first two weeks of August as the harvests were brought in and stored for winter. The yields were better than expected and Richard was relieved that they would be well set through the cold dark months from October to March.

The weather turned chilly and the town and castle bedded down for the winter. Richard spent many nights in the warm hall, fires blazing, while Anne sat with several other women spinning and knitting and laughing. Men were in and out a few times a week with letters and messages from across the north, from York, Carlisle, and Penrith, even the occasional message from London. There were Christmas wishes from Edward, a long letter from Richard's mother, a short note from Isabel, and before Richard knew it, it was almost the new year.

"You're mad," Richard said when he found Anne standing on the east wall on the first morning of 1473, snow falling gently around her in the silence. This time he was the one to wrap an extra blanket around her shoulders and she smiled as she leaned against him.

"I couldn't sleep," she shrugged, tucking herself under his arm. "Besides, this is your favourite spot."

Richard chuckled, wrapping his arms around her, eyes sweeping over the land as the sun rose, shining brilliant golden rays below the clouds at the edge of the horizon. It would disappear behind the storm in under an hour and the day would be dark and dreary as the snow began to fall harder, but this moment was breathtakingly beautiful.

"I love you," he said softly, feeling that he didn't say it enough, even though he told her every day. With Anne it never felt like enough.

"Watch the sunrise," she chided, her mouth curving softly, and he just smiled, holding her close as they listened to the silence.

April, 1473

It was a warm evening, the window open to let in the fresh breeze as the sun set. The castle was quiet, the last noises of the day winding down as the people prepared for bed, still accustomed to rising and sleeping with the setting of the sun. It would be another month before long evenings turned to music and dance in the courtyard or village square.

"You're quiet," Anne mumbled, and Richard sighed, pressing his nose to her hair.

They had retired early, just after dinner, to celebrate the first year of their marriage in their own, private way. Now they lay together under the light covers, warm skin pressed together, the outside world forgotten for a moment.

"Just thinking of spring. I want to see you dance again."

Anne laughed, her breath tickling across his neck where her face was pressed against him. "You'll dance with me this year," she said with a determination that Richard knew better than to argue against.

"I'd dance with you forever," Richard whispered, kissing her smile as she laughed.

The Last Winter Rose

"I'm so happy," she sighed, as she settled back against him, fingers tracing senseless patterns across his chest. "So much happier."

A shadow fell over the room at her words, the careful skirting of her time married to the former Prince of Wales. Richard hadn't asked for any details, he hadn't pushed, but he also saw how she sometimes disappeared, went far away, her gaze lost as she looked out over an empty field and he knew it wasn't the grass she was seeing.

"Will you tell me about it?" he asked softly, his fingers brushing up and down her bare side.

Anne sighed, then pulled away, turning so her back was to him and tucking her hands together under her chin, her eyes far away as she stared at the wall hangings. She didn't put distance between them, though, pressing back against him and his hand settled on her side again where his thumb brushed over a small scar at the base of her ribs, holding her close, anchoring her.

"The queen, former queen, she..." Anne trailed off and took a breath, reorganising her thoughts. "She forbade the consummation of the marriage. She wanted to be able to discard me if it all went wrong, wanted to be able to cast me off as nothing."

She fell into silence for so long that Richard gently prompted her.

"But?"

Anne shuddered, gooseflesh raising along her arms and sides, acutely aware of her nakedness in their bed, of how exposed she was. Yet she didn't feel scared, or ashamed, she felt free and powerful, strong, and it was all thanks to Richard. She'd never shied away from his touch, even after...

"But the prince..." she said softly. "He'd been watched so carefully that he'd never snuck away and had a woman before. He wanted to know what it was like, if it was better than battle." Her words turned venomous as old anger rose. "On the ship, he found an opportunity. When it was over he told me he would test it again after he'd been on the field, that I would take him covered in the blood of other men and scream in ecstasy because of it."

Richard remained silent, still, letting her give him only what she wished. He'd known she wasn't a virgin on the night they wed, but that had never mattered to him. All that mattered to him was that she'd been hurt at another man's hands, and he never wanted to do anything that might make her remember that.

"When you told me he was dead, I knew I was free," she said softly, turning on her back and smiling at him, unbothered that he could see her. Her mother had always told her to remain modest, even with her husband, to not let him see too much of her, but with Richard she came alive when his eyes roved over her naked body and she loved how he looked at her.

"Anne," he whispered, reaching out to cup her face. "May I kiss you, my love?" he asked softly, smiling when her hands came up to wrap around his wrist and hold his hand against her cheek. Her eyes flashed as her

The Last Winter Rose

mouth curled and she slid her foot between his ankles, hooking and pulling him forward and over her.

"My dear husband," she said softly, her voice seductive and thick with joy and love. "I certainly hope you do more than that."

Richard laughed, settling over her at her demand, face falling into a soft smile as he caressed her cheek. She was stronger than any person he had ever known, she laughed in the face of her hurt and she loved him with such an open heart that it humbled him each and every time she smiled because of him.

"I love you, so very much," he whispered and she rubbed her nose against his, her smile untameable.

"And I love you," she breathed. "Even before you saved me, I loved you."

"You have brought me so much happiness," he said, the idea of life without her unfathomable. He never wanted this moment to end, here alone, free and without cares, just the two of them.

"There's something else," she whispered and Richard pulled back, resting on his elbows to throw her a questioning look. She smiled, brushing her hand through his hair. "I'm with child."

Richard's entire world tilted at those three words and before he knew it, he was holding her tightly, laughing and crying at the same time. He pulled back almost as quickly as he'd embraced her, pushing the covers away and shuffling down the bed to lay his hands on her stomach, pressing a kiss just below her navel. She laughed at him, running her hands through his hair as he whispered against her skin and her heart was so full of joy she thought she might burst.

"I love you," Richard said, pushing himself up again and surging up to kiss her. "I love you so much, and I will love our child and they will never want for a thing, son or daughter."

Anne laughed, holding him close as they kissed, sweetness turning to desperation as their skin slid together and Richard pulled her to him, joining their bodies in a passionate embrace.

June, 1473

"Lord," Winton said, crouching next to Richard's bedroll, last autumn's leaves crunching gently under the soft leather of his boots. "Lord, the sun is on the rise."

Richard suppressed a groan as he shifted, sleep sliding away sluggishly. He hadn't slept well, he hated sleeping on the ground, but there wasn't much other choice on a hunting trip.

"I'll just be a moment, Winton," he said, and the boy nodded, rising and heading back to the fire where Gregory and one of the other hunters were preparing the remainder of the rabbits they'd caught yesterday for their morning meal.

Sighing, Richard rolled on his back with a wince and stared up at the canopy of trees, just listening to the leaves rustle and the fire crackle. The others seemed to have left camp already, likely to check the traps and snares they'd set the night before, and the forest was alive with the first sounds of birds. Gentle rays of light were trying to press through the thick trees, despite the early hour. It was nearing summer and the days had grown warm, but that didn't make sleeping on the ground any easier.

It was a struggle to sit up, teeth gritted as Richard tried not to tense against the pain of having to move, but he knew if he stood and walked a little it would ease back into its normal, dull ache, an ache he'd grown used to and most days could simply ignore. He tugged his boots on before he stood up slowly, working the stiffness out of his arms and legs, then he neatened his bedroll and reached for his water skin, splashing some on his face and slicking back his hair as he walked over to the fire.

"Food will be ready in a moment, lord," Winton said with a smile and Richard nodded, yawning as he took his seat on a log.

"All quiet?" he asked, and was met with two nods.

They had left Middleham close to a week ago and they'd been camped in this clearing two nights. They'd be here one more before they moved on to their last camp. Their wagon was growing heavy with the carcasses of close to a dozen deer and twice as many rabbits, all resting between layers of salt from the bags the wagon had originally been packed with, but they had room for a few more kills. They had another day or two before what they'd already brought down started to go bad, and when they returned all but the freshest meat would be cleaned and packed in fresh salt in the storehouses for winter. The rest would be distributed through the village that same night.

Richard had never taken to hunting for sport like Edward or George, or most of the nobility, but he always participated in the practical hunts throughout the spring and summer to put up stores for winter. He'd never been the kind of man who sat idly by while others did the work that kept him alive and in comfort, not since he'd been old enough to help with the spring planting and the fall harvest.

It had been hard, at first, when he and Anne had returned to Middleham. As a boy it hadn't been so strange if he was out in the fields, not even if he'd dragged Francis with him. They'd often been out helping the villagers tend to crops when they weren't in their own lessons in the castle.

Now though, Richard was the Lord and Anne was the Lady, and it had taken a few weeks for people to get used to seeing them dressed in simple clothes, grooming horses, milking cows, moving straw, cleaning stables. Here they were just people, and soon enough they'd been wholly accepted as they were. They were up with the sun most mornings, or at least Anne was, sometimes Richard would sleep half the day because he'd been up half the night sitting in the tavern just listening to the people. It was one of his favourite times, just sitting back and watching the people talk and laugh and joke and, occasionally, fight.

There was a crunch in the woods, drawing Richard out of his thoughts, and Roland appeared, the other four men close behind. They were a party of just nine men, Roland, the senior huntsman, Winton, Roland's apprentice, five men who were among the best hunters in the area around Middleham, Gregory, who saw to their horses and helped cook, and Richard. They'd brought six horses to ride, two for packs, and four to pull the wagon.

"Good size herd a ways east of here, lord," Roland said as he took a seat across the fire from Richard and dropped two fresh rabbits next to his feet. The other four added a dozen pheasants and another six rabbits to those already hanging from the trees. Richard reckoned they'd only be able to take two or three more deer, before the wagon would be too heavy for the horses to comfortably pull.

"We're nearly overburdened," he chuckled, waving a hand at the fresh fowl and rabbits. Roland laughed.

He was a tall man, taller than Edward even, broad shouldered with a loud voice and unkempt long hair, but he was silent in the forest, barely making more than a rustle. He didn't hunt with dogs, just with his own skills, and he taught most boys in the area how to hunt when they were old enough.

"Lord, if we take too many deer, I'll carry three on my shoulders myself," he grinned and the others all chuckled, not doubting it for a moment.

"Of course," Richard grinned. "After all, it's only seven miles back to the village. Most of it up hill."

There was a roar of laughter around the fire, causing a small flock of birds to take flight from the tree their camp was under.

"We've been lucky," Roland said, reaching for a piece of rabbit and accepting half a small bread loaf from Gregory, along with a cup of ale. "Three more hunts like this will lay us in well for winter."

The Last Winter Rose

"Good," Richard nodded, glancing around at each of them. "Let us pray it remains mild. It's already been wet enough, I worry for the grain harvest."

"Aye," Winton nodded. "Not like that spring three years back. I still remember, my father lost nearly all his lambs in a late blizzard."

That had been before Richard and Anne had returned to Middleham, but it was why Anne had brought so many wagons of supplies with them when they came, and between that and a gentle winter there had been little loss of life or livestock through the coldest months, and all had been able to eat well through to spring.

"I suppose we should-" Richard began, but he was interrupted by shouts and a crashing through the underbrush.

"Lord! Lord!"

Richard glanced over his shoulder, standing quickly as a horse thundered into the clearing, a boy barely big enough to ride him half topping off. He knew the horse and the boy both and he grabbed the reins of the large destrier, Hugo, the horse a gift from his mother the year before.

"What is it, Will?" he asked, running his hand along Hugo's nose, trying to calm him as Will tumbled the rest of the way onto the ground, barely keeping his feet.

"Lord, Master Frank sent me, you're needed," Will gasped, taking a skin from Winton and drinking before dumping half of it on his head. "I brought Hugo because he's so fast, Master Frank said to hurry, lord."

155

Caitlin Sumner

Richard's blood ran cold. "Anne?" he asked and Will nodded.

"She's ill, lord, they fear-" He didn't get a chance to finish because Richard was already swinging up on Hugo's back and spurring him through the trees, back to the road and Middleham, uncaring he'd left all his things behind.

It felt like hours, like time has slowed to a standstill as they went. Hugo seemed to know the urgency and he ran fast and steady, barely breaking a sweat. Richard slowed him every mile to let him walk, even though Hugo was as impatient as he was and soon broke into a gallop again without prompting. When they thundered through the gate just over an hour later he didn't know if he'd even be able to stand when he dismounted, but somehow he managed, his legs shaking and his back screaming as he rushed toward the stairs. He saw Geoffrey, but he didn't stop, too desperate to see Anne.

The corridor was quiet and the door to their room was shut and he stopped, catching his breath before he pushed the door open, calling softly for Anne, his heart in his throat.

She was alone, curled under the covers with her back to him, facing the window. The drapes were tied back and the glass was open, letting the fresh air in, but still somehow, the room smelled like death.

"Love?" he said, pushing the door shut and coming to kneel on the bed, reaching tentatively for her. "Geoffrey sent word you were ill."

The Last Winter Rose

Anne was silent, shaking her head and curling tighter around herself and the pillow she clutched.

"Anne," Richard whispered, his heart already plummeting, knowing without her even saying-

"I lost the baby," she whispered and he could feel tears in his eyes and hear a ringing in his ears.

He took a breath then shifted down and took her in his arms, holding her tightly as her tears began and she sobbed. Eventually she turned in his arms and pressed herself to his chest and his stroked his hand through her hair, whispering words he didn't even recall, trying to give her what comfort he could.

His own heart was breaking, but he knew it was would hurt more for her, it was more immediate, more real. He let his own tears fall silently, continuing to hold her until she drifted off to sleep, completely exhausted, and he succumbed to sleep soon after.

The next day, the next days and weeks, were quiet, dark. It was summer, but there was a cloud cast over the town. It seemed everyone shared their grief. There were dozens of candles lit in the church and around the town every night for a week, and the first time Richard and Anne walked through the village a small crowd gathered to offer their sympathies. One little girl ran up to them with a small bundle of flowers for Anne and told them that her little sister had gone to heaven, and that she would look out for their child there.

It brought tears to Anne's eyes and Richard wrapped his arms around her, but something about that small act of kindness helped her begin to heal, little by little. A few weeks passed and Richard did his best to delay his leaving as long as possible. Every summer's end he had to ride to York to handle all the matters that had accumulated over the spring and summer and uphold all the responsibilities that his various positions demanded, but this year he had no wish to go.

They brought in a good harvest at the beginning of August and then they would both go to York at the beginning of September. It had taken most of the summer to persuade Anne to come with him, but finally she agreed and Richard thought perhaps they might stay through Christmas and enjoy the festivities in the city.

It was the last week of August, only a few days before they were set to leave, when a stack of letters came from the south and Richard frowned at the seals. One was George's, but the latter was addressed to Anne, so it likely came from Isabel, and one was from Edward. There were a few other notes for Anne and he separated them out as he climbed the stairs to the hall.

"Letters," Richard said softly, passing the short notes to Anne. She glanced up from where she'd been vacantly watching the fire and took the papers carefully, her lips pursing as she cracked George's seal and read.

Richard remained silent, watching her reactions carefully, and after a moment she passed the paper to him. The note was from Warwick castle, announcing that Isabel had given birth to a daughter named

The Last Winter Rose

Margaret. He grimaced and opened Edward's letter to find similar news. Only three days after Isabel, the queen had given birth to a second son, proudly named Richard after his late grandfather.

It had been several weeks since Anne had miscarried and she'd been withdrawn since, quiet and solitary, though she'd been slowly improving day by day, her smiles coming back in small measures. Richard worried that news of more children might upset her again, but he wouldn't keep it from her either. He respected her too much to treat her like she wasn't strong enough to know, so he passed her Edward's letter as well.

Anne frowned, switching from Isabel's letter to Edward's, then she tossed them both on the table next to her, frowning at the fire before she stood, her face determined.

"I need to see to the kitchens," she said and Richard let her go without protest.

He watched her disappear down the steps to the lower levels and sighed, sinking into the chair she'd left and staring into the fire. It was too warm, really, for a fire, but she'd been poorly since she lost the baby and she liked to be warm. Though he was sweating in only a thin shirt and breeches, Richard didn't mind, and in a moment he would go back out to the yard and carry on with the preparations for the trip to York. He read the other letters in quiet contemplation, none needing any urgent reply. He'd see to them in the morning.

He worried through the afternoon that the news had upset Anne, but when he checked her in the kitchens later she was smiling, laughing with the other women, all of them up to their elbows in flour, and looking more like herself than she had in weeks. She caught his eye as he stood leaning in the doorway and she smiled. His heart jumped and he returned her smile, a weight lifting from his chest to see her joyful again.

That night when she came to bed late, long after he'd collapsed on the soft mattress with a groan of relief, she stripped off her night dress before she crawled beneath the covers. She kissed him, and she whispered that she wanted to try again. Richard smiled, holding her close, and he couldn't stop smiling because this was his Anne, his beautiful, fiery, determined wife, and she was still the strongest person he had, or would, ever know.

September, 1474

It was too early.

Richard paced up and down the hall, feeling like a madman. It was too early, Anne was only seven, maybe eight months pregnant, and she had been so ill the last few weeks. Everyone around him whispered their fear, everyone told him it was too early. The chances of either of them surviving the birth weren't favourable, and yet, the pains had started late in the night and by the time dawn neared, Richard had been banished from their rooms and was left with nothing to do, but pace endlessly.

He'd walked the walls until the sun was nearly overhead, the guards watching him silently, then he'd begun to circle the courtyard, again and again and again. He'd refused to eat, though Will spent nearly an hour following him with a plate of food and a jug of water before giving up. He'd tried to pray for almost an hour, kneeling in the small chapel on the east side of the castle, but he couldn't focus. He couldn't hear anything inside the small room, so he rose and pushed through the door into the early afternoon air. A piercing scream echoed across the grounds and his shoulders slumped in relief. If she could still scream, she was still alive.

He wanted to be there, he wanted nothing more than to be holding her while she fought to bring their child into the world, but the two midwives, stern, older women, one of whom had been present when both Anne and Isabel were born, had bodily shoved him from the room and bolted the door. No matter his protests they hadn't let him back in. He stared up at their room for a long time, then turned away, hands linked behind his back, no options left to him.

And so he paced.

The day grew hot, the last heat of late summer stifling. The castle was near silent as the entire household waited with bated breath. The day's work went about as it always did, but it was obvious everyone was waiting for word, waiting for something to happen. Tasks were done slowly, and in silence, whispers traded now and then, eyes on him as he walked and walked, lost inside his own head as he paced circles around the castle, pausing under the window of their room every time he came to it. It had been opened wide since the night before, despite the fresh chill of late September after the sun had set. The day's temperature belied the fact that the leaves were turning and falling, floating to land in puddles and on stacks of hay outside the stables. It hadn't been so hot since July.

Richard forced his feet to move, away from the window, and he continued to walk. He wished Francis were here, or even Edward. He quickly shook away that thought because Edward's suggestion would be to open the wine. No, what he needed now was Francis' steady

The Last Winter Rose

presence and ability to lighten any situation. He needed his mother. She'd given birth to twelve children, she would tell him plainly if it was all going wrong. He was under the impression it took time, but he didn't know how much time, and the longer he was barred from their room, the more worried he was. He'd only been three when his younger sister Ursula was born, he didn't remember. And she had only lived a year. He cursed silently, swearing that he would find out more about what was going on in their room, especially if everything went well and they had more children, the next time he wanted to be there.

The sun was beginning to sink in the sky, heat turning to chill as quickly as chill had turned to heat in the morning, and Anne's screams were coming more and more often. He'd given up pacing now and was standing below her window, forehead and hands pressed to the stone, eyes closed as he prayed and pleaded she'd survive. No one approached him, and almost everyone had returned to their houses in the village. Only the night guard at their posts bore witness to his terror.

Finally, after one final bloodcurdling shriek, a new sound rang out in the evening, the loud, unhappy scream of a new infant taking their first breath. He sagged against the wall, knees weak with relief, even though he knew the danger wasn't past for either of them. He took a few breaths and recovered his strength, pushing through the door and climbing the stairs, resuming his pacing outside Anne's room, desperate to knock, but knowing he had to be patient and wait until they were ready. The midwife that had thrown him out was terrifying when she wanted to be, and he wouldn't cross her.

A quarter of an hour later the door finally swung open and the stern-faced midwife looked him over, then stood aside to let him pass. He knew he must look terrible after the day he'd spent running his hands through his hair, sweat soaking him as he walked endless circles in the sun, but he didn't care as he finally stepped into the room.

The first thing he saw was Anne, pale, but alive, sitting up in bed with a smile on her face, her eyes locked on the tiny bundle in her arms. His heart nearly stopped and he walked closer softly, carefully sitting next to her and wrapping an arm around her shoulders. She leaned against him immediately, shifting her arms just enough that he saw a tiny, perfect face just visible in the swaddle of blankets, pink and rosy and healthy.

"It's a boy," Anne whispered, and Richard smiled, leaning his head against hers as he watched the little boy, his son, clench and unclench his tiny fist, which he had somehow pushed out of the cloth and was moving slowly, discovering his new existence a little at a time.

"He's perfect," Richard sighed. "And you, my love?"

"Exhausted," she said softly, and Richard pressed a kiss to her hair, not caring that it was damp with sweat. She was trembling against him and was likely desperate to bathe, but they were both here in his arms, alive and healthy and he had never been so grateful in all his life.

The Last Winter Rose

"She'll need rest," the midwife said, no nonsense as she circled the room cleaning, putting dirty cloths and bloody sheets in a basket. "I'll leave you now, but I'll be back early to change her packing and see that she bathes."

She left without another word, the other midwife trailing after her silent as a shadow, and Richard opened his mouth to ask what she meant when Anne winced.

"Trust me, my love, when I say you don't want to know, you don't want to know," she said, and Richard closed his mouth with a frown, then nodded. He did want to know, but he also knew well enough to respect her wish to keep this from him. He thought he might have an idea anyway and he didn't need more details than that.

"Nothing's wrong?" he asked tentatively, and she shook her head.

"It's normal, just... unpleasant," she said softly, and he nodded, pressing a kiss to her hair.

"I'm so glad you're safe," he whispered. "Both of you. I worried. I think I walked to York and back around the walls," he admitted and Anne chuckled.

"I'm sorry I scared you," she said softly, leaning her forehead against his jaw, her eyes dropping shut. "I'm so tired. He's had his first meal, and should sleep soon, then maybe I can rest."

"I'm not going anywhere," Richard said, laying on the bed next to her and gently taking the child, holding him carefully in one arm while he tucked the other around Anne, holding them close while they both drifted off to sleep.

He was exhausted, but he didn't think for even a moment of sleeping, not with his son tucked so carefully into the crook of his arm. He stayed awake long into the night, memorising the tiny, perfect features. He only cried once, and before Richard could even move Anne was reaching for him with a soft groan, bringing him to her breast to feed.

"He'll need to be changed," she mumbled, as she drifted off again, the child sucking happily and Richard fought a moment of panic. He had no idea what to do, he had never been around children so small. He took a breath, carefully shifting off the bed as he made sure there was no way the baby could fall from Anne's arms, even though she was mostly asleep.

Swearing quietly to himself that he was absolutely not ready for this, Richard tiptoed to the door and peered out in the hall, hoping beyond hope his shadow had followed him. Sure enough, Will was dozing at the end of the hall, a basket next to him and the remains of his supper on a plate.

"Will," Richard whispered, and the boy came awake with a start.

"Lord?" he asked, scrambling up and coming to Richard, who pursed his lips.

"You have younger siblings, do you not?" he asked, and Will nodded with a yawn.

"Three, lord, a brother and two sisters."

"And do you know much about infants?"

The Last Winter Rose

Will's eyes lit up with mischief and he nodded. "Do the swaddling clothes need to be changed?"

Richard sighed. "I can only assume that is what Anne means, but she's fallen asleep already."

Will nodded, going back for the basket and bringing it to the door. "You should eat, lord, and sleep. I can show you how to change the swaddling clothes, I'm sure herself left some spares."

"Herself?" Richard raised an eyebrow and Will grinned.

"That's what my ma calls Missus Barns, on account she's so stern," he piped, and Richard chuckled, yawning. He was exhausted.

"Very well, give me a moment," he said, and Will nodded, clearly excited.

Pushing the door close to shut Richard crossed the room and carefully lifted the baby from Anne's arms. He'd finished nursing and was yawning contentedly, and Richard made sure Anne was tucked under the covers before he softly called Will into the room.

Will set the basket on the table and found the clothes in a neat pile, then showed Richard how to lay the baby on the end of the bed and carefully unwrap him, clean him, and rewrap him. He slept through the whole process and Richard was in absolute awe that such a tiny creature trusted him so much already.

"He should sleep till morn," Will whispered, holding the baby carefully. "Eat something, lord."

Richard sighed, ruffling the boy's hair as he walked to the table and poked through the basket for a roll and

167

some cheese, eating them with one hand as he went behind the dressing screen to change into his night shirt. Exhaustion was pulling at him, but he forced himself to pay careful attention as Will showed him how to tuck the tiny baby into a small wicker basket that had been left along with the clothes, and when Richard had climbed into bed next to Anne, Will set the basket in the middle of the bed between their knees, so that they could both reach him easily and he was in no danger of falling.

"I'll be just outside the door, lord," Will promised. "In case you need anything."

Richard nodded, nearly asleep. "Will," he called, just before the door shut. "Take a cushion and a blanket, don't sleep on the cold stones."

Will hesitated for a moment then took two cushions from Richard's chair and a spare blanket and shut the door softly behind him. Richard sighed, gazing one more time at his son before he let his eyes drop closed and he was asleep in seconds.

April, 1475

Edward was full of energy and adventure, but to the worry of both his parents he was sick often, which left him weaker than most children his age. He was approaching a year old, and to Richard it felt like his son had spent more time sick than well. He'd been born as the seasons began to change the previous September, and some days it seemed like a miracle that he'd live through the cold, harsh winter. It had been mild the two years since Richard and Anne had returned from London, '72 and '73 remaining unseasonably warm until deep into December, but the winter of '74 tested them all.

The harvest had been poor, and they'd taken steps to make sure their supplies were well laid in and would last the winter, even if they had to distribute grain to the town. They'd been cut off by snows early in January and it was the middle of March before anyone could get out of the valley and to one of the Roman roads. Richard himself went, and there were dozens of messages, and two messengers themselves waiting for him when he and four others reached Richmond. Among the most disturbing was from Edward, asking him to come to London with all haste.

"Hell and damnation," Richard muttered under his breath as he read the letter. Edward was planning to invade France that year.

He spent a week in Richmond writing letters and judging what disputes he could from the correspondence. There was an issue in Carlisle that he'd need to see to personally, but he made sure every correspondence was answered before he set out to return to Middleham, six extra horses loaded with supplies now included in their number. It wasn't enough, but it had been a hard winter for everyone, and the extra grain and salted meat would see them through to spring.

When Richard reached home, he was relieved to see Anne standing on the wall, waiting for him. Edward was bundled in blankets in her arms and she smiled and pointed to him, bouncing the boy gently. A hand extended from the blankets and made grabbing motions when she tried to show him how to wave and Richard's face lit up, his chest swelling with so much love he felt like he might burst.

"I have to go south," he told her later, as they sat in front of the fire in the hall, Edward asleep in his wicker basket lined with sheep's wool and straw, yawning when Anne dared to stop rocking him. They both chuckled as she resumed pushing the round bottom basket back and forth and for a long time she said nothing.

"What's he planning?" she asked finally, and Richard sighed, running a hand through his hair.

"He wants to invade France," he muttered, and Anne shook her head. "I'll need to attend the council anyway, and Parliament. Perhaps I can talk him out of it. We've no need of another war."

"You'll be gone long?"

Richard sighed, looking over at her. She was staring at the fire, her hair in one long braid wrapped around her head and a heavy shawl wrapped around her slim shoulders. She was beautiful with the light reflecting on her red-brown hair, more beautiful every year. She would be nineteen soon and sometimes Richard could barely believe they were both so young. He himself would only turn twenty-three this year and he felt like an old man already.

"I may be gone all spring and summer," he said quietly, not wanting to lie to her. "If he does invade, I'll have to go with him."

"I wish I could go with you," Anne said, and Richard sighed, reaching out and catching her braid in his hand, fingering it absently. They both knew she couldn't, Edward was too young and weak to travel and neither of them wanted to leave him behind.

"I have to go to Carlisle first," he said, rubbing his other hand over his face, already feeling exhausted. "I'll come back this way when I go south."

Anne remained silent for a long time then sighed, shaking her head.

"That will make it harder for me to watch you leave again," she whispered.

Richard frowned, but nodded, face hard. He hated leaving them, but he had no choice. They'd had three years nearly undisturbed and now duty called.

The ride to Carlisle was mercifully short and adjudication of the dispute even shorter. Richard only took ten minutes to listen to the ridiculous arguments over a stone fence and a stream before he dismissed both farmers and told them to share the water or they could both find new land. They'd scuttled from the hall at his tone and a hearty laugh followed them as the door slammed.

Richard turned to the laugh with a scowl, already in foul mood, and came face to face with Richard Ratcliffe, his hair and beard wild like a Scot and his eyes as bright as ever. Richard relaxed into a grin, temper dissolving as he shook his head.

"That's telling them," Ratcliffe laughed, striding across the room and gripping Richard's offered hand tightly.

"That," Richard said dryly, "did not need me to come all the way here."

"No," Ratcliffe agreed easily. "But I did."

Richard raised an eyebrow and gestured for Ratcliffe to take the seat across from him, offering wine which was declined with a brief gesture.

"What's wrong?" Richard asked, because it was obvious something must be.

"You're heard about your brother's plans for France this summer?"

The Last Winter Rose

Richard frowned, pressing his lips together. "It's the last thing we need right now."

"The French agree," Ratcliffe nodded. "They're already talking about how to win a peace treaty, what they can offer to keep Edward on English soil."

"What support does the king have?" Richard enquired, and Ratcliffe frowned, leaning back in his chair and scratching his bushy beard. "And why do you look like that?" Richard laughed. He'd never seen Ratcliffe anything less than neat and put together.

Ratcliffe laughed again, distracted, tugging on his beard. "I've been playing away across the border, don't ye ken?" he said, his words and accent so entirely Scottish that Richard could only stare before he laughed loudly.

"Did Catesby finally put you to work as a spy?" he teased, and Ratcliffe rolled his eyes.

"That boy thinks he's God's own omnipotent eye some days. I'm here of my own accord, but I do send reports south, if there's some concern."

"And obviously you get news from the south as well, if you know about Edward's plans for France," Richard pointed out, and Ratcliffe shrugged.

"Catesby is far from the only one with a network of whispers."

They fell silent for a few minutes, before Ratcliffe sighed.

"I don't have much information for you, but I thought you should know the French don't want a war. The way I see it, this can go two ways. Either Edward strikes a peace and avoids a colossal waste of life, or he invades and takes territory he's unlikely to be able to hold."

Richard nodded. They had the men, certainly, to win back French lands, but winning and keeping were two very different things.

"I must be on my way," Ratcliffe said, as he stood. "I wish you luck."

They clasped hands again and Ratcliffe was almost at the door before he paused and turned.

"Richard," he said quietly. "He has the support of your brother, the Duke of Clarence."

Richard swore as the door swung shut behind his friend, already feeling the headache coming.

May, 1475

Richard entered London as he preferred to do, under the cover of darkness. He'd sent no reply to Edward, so his coming was not precisely expected, giving him the ability to slip into the city without the fuss of royal guards or an escort meeting him outside the gates. And, secretly, he enjoyed the reactions at the palace when he rode into the yard just before midnight. He refused to let anyone wake Edward and instead asked for his rooms to be prepared so he could rest after the long ride, knowing there would be little time for rest in the coming weeks.

It wasn't long past sunrise the next morning when Richard woke to the sound of his door slamming opening and his name being shouted.

"You've grown no less rude," he told Edward plainly as his elder brother flopped gracelessly across the end of his bed with a jovial laugh. He just managed to pull his feet back in time to avoid them being crushed by Edward's large bulk. He'd gained weight the last three years, but with his height he wore it well, still.

"When did you arrive?" Edward demanded, and Richard sighed, leaning back against his pillows. He'd had maybe five hours sleep all told.

"A little before midnight," he yawned. "I didn't feel like a formal arrival."

"Hmm," Edward hummed. "I didn't think you were coming, my summons went unanswered."

"We spent most of the winter snowed in," Richard told him, as he tried to gather his thoughts, still muddled by sleep. "I heard George is here," his voice grew hard as he met Edward's gaze and Edward sighed.

"Does that mean I won't have your support?" he asked, and Richard looked away.

"Convince me," he said quietly, because he could be convinced, he was sure, but only if Edward showed him there would be more benefit than just the glory of saying he did. If there was benefit to the people, to trade and commerce. He wouldn't support another of Edward's endeavours, if all it did was put more money and land into the coffers of the already rich and titled.

Edward nodded, resigned. He knew Richard wouldn't just follow blindly, he never had. But they would have time to discuss France later.

"How is Anne?" he asked instead. "And your son?" He hoped the mention of his family would bring a smile to his dour brother's face and he was rewarded when Richard's face softened.

He told Edward everything they'd done the last few years for the town and the castle, his face growing sad when he spoke of the child Anne lost and the worry he felt over little Edward, who was always sick, despite his happy nature and seemingly boundless reserve of laughter. He spoke of the nights they prayed for another child, and yet none came.

They talked long into the morning, just two brothers who hadn't seen one another in years, and eventually Edward left to begin his day. Richard lay in bed a while longer before he rose, knowing he'd have to face George sooner or later, and not at all looking forward to it.

They sailed for France at the height of summer. Edward seemed convinced he had the advantage, but Richard knew better. He kept his thoughts and information to himself, since Edward wouldn't listen anyway, but he knew all that was waiting on the other side of the channel was a peace treaty that would change effectively nothing.

Ratcliffe had been right, the French didn't want a war, nor did they want to surrender territory, so instead they simply planned to pay Edward and George to go home and not bother them. Richard didn't even see the point in getting involved, but he went with Edward anyway.

When they landed they were met with envoys of King Louis, rather than troops from their brother by law, the Duke of Burgundy, to everyone's surprise but Richard's. While Louis drew Edward into negotiations, and George made his indignation known to anyone who would listen, Richard travelled to Bruges to visit his sister, Margaret. They passed a pleasant visit and by the time he returned to Amiens, Edward had taken the French bribe and already sailed home.

By mid September they were back on English soil and Richard was on his way north, glad to put the whole mess behind them with only a slight blow to Edward's dignity and no loss of life. He was ready to be home again.

November, 1476

"This place is bleak," Francis said, and Richard smiled, not taking any offence.

"You loved this place as much as I did when we were boys," he told his friend with a chuckle.

"I've become used to the warm winters of the south," Francis groused, staring bleakly at the fire. "I take the children along the river on the coldest days and they're full of laughter. Here I'd be terrified to let them more than a half dozen feet from a fire for fear they'd catch their deaths."

Richard nodded because he was sympathetic to that. Poor little Edward hadn't been out of doors since early October. Though, at only two years old, he wasn't yet aware there was a world outside his warm and comfortable nursery, so it wasn't so bad for him. Francis, despite his own time in the north and the relatively new holdings he now toured, had never grown accustomed to the perpetual chill.

"How are the children?" Richard asked, and Francis brightened a little.

"Well," he said with a proud smile. "Thomas, the eldest is almost sixteen, he wants to leave in the spring to go to London and join the guard. Jane, she's the youngest, you remember, she's been taken in by one of my tenants and his wife after they lost their own daughter last winter and she's happy."

Richard nodded, remembering the children from the last time he'd visited the Lovell estate. Jane had been just three, orphaned in a fire in a nearby village and brought to the estate by one of the kitchen maids. Richard thought she might be six or seven by now. Aside from Thomas there had been his sister Eliza, and two other boys, John and Benedict, all orphans that Francis had taken under his care rather than see them starve with no one to support them.

He admired what Francis did for them, when so many others wouldn't go further than gifting a sum of money, usually small, to the church to care for orphans. More often than not, though, the money didn't seem to make it to where it was intended. Richard and Anne funded the care of orphans by directly sending money and supplies to three local nunneries and an orphanage, making sure there was no way it got lost along the way.

"Still no prospects of a wife?" Richard asked, and Francis glared at him balefully. He raised his hands with a chuckle.

"You know I'm not one for marrying," Francis said quietly and Richard shrugged, because he didn't care that Francis didn't find an interest in women, he only cared for his wellbeing. Technically Francis had married a girl when they were both young, barely more than children, but Richard knew Francis hadn't seen her in years and the marriage was all but dissolved. It would

The Last Winter Rose

take almost nothing to annul it if he did find someone else, since the short union had produced no issue.

"It might do your image well," he pointed out, not for the first time. "And give the children a mother figure. She doesn't have to be rich or powerful or political. She could just be a friend."

Francis snorted. "They have a mother in Maude," he grumbled. Francis might have been the Lord of his land, but Maude the housekeeper had run the estate since the time of Francis' grandfather, and she did it with an iron ladle in one hand and a rug beater in the other. She had practically raised Francis and his father.

"Is there anyone?" Richard pressed gently, because he hated to see his best friend alone. Francis shrugged, gazing distantly into the fire.

"There was, for a time," he said softly. "But you know how these things are. Nothing lasts. People move on. People die."

Richard nodded, letting the topic drop. He'd often talked to Francis about Anne, but he wasn't going to push his friend for things he didn't want to share, he respected him too much for that.

Talk turned to things other men found mundane, crop harvest and the price of wool exports and taxes, among other things, until an hour or so later Anne breezed into the room with Edward on her hip. She deposited the boy in Richard's arms and told him to mind their son if he ever wanted to see another meal from their kitchens, before she left as fast as she had come.

Confused and curious, Richard and Francis shared a look before they followed her, pausing just outside the kitchen to find it in complete chaos.

"I'd better see if I can help," Richard sighed, not even able to discern what the cause of the problem was.

Wordlessly Francis held out his arms and took a cheerfully fascinated Edward while Richard waded into the chaos. Leaning against the doorframe with the boy in his arms, Francis watched as his two closest friends lost themselves in the working of the castle kitchen, something that felt a lot like happiness curling around his heart. He laughed when someone thrust a spoon at Richard and he hastily traded his doublet for an apron and was put to work while Anne chuckled, up to her elbows in flour and sticky pastry dough. Edward clapped his pudgy hands and Francis just sighed. He never did find out what had thrown the kitchen into such pandemonium that night, but it was one of the best evenings he ever spent at Middleham.

December, 1476

The letter came two days after they celebrated Christmas and Richard hesitated at the sight of George's seal, a heavy weight of dread settling over him. He broke the seal and sat, reading the contents numbly.

Isabel had given birth to a son in October, but she had never recovered properly and three days before Christmas she had died. The child, named Richard for both his grandfathers, was sickly and not expected to see the spring.

Richard scrubbed a hand over his face, feeling the heavy weight of his twenty-four years. He had to tell Anne, but he was loath to bring her news that her sister, the last of her family, was gone. She had cut the last ties with her mother the year before and Anne Beauchamp was as dead in the eyes of her daughter as she was in the eyes of the law. Knowing that delay was pointless, Richard pushed himself out of his chair and went in search of Anne.

He found her in the hall, her favourite room, adding logs to the fire, and he just watched her for a moment. She smiled when she saw him in the doorway, but that smile faded as she took in his expression.

"What's wrong?" she asked, her stance already hardening, bracing for bad news.

"I'm so sorry," Richard said softly, handing her the letter.

She sat heavily as she read, one hand covering her mouth as tears gathered in her eyes. The letter dropped from her fingers and she sobbed, clutching Richard when he wrapped his arms around her.

"I should go to her," Anne said after a while, still crying softly. "She was my only sister. I should see her before... if he hasn't already put her in the ground."

"I'll send a messenger to delay the burial," Richard offered, and Anne nodded, wiping her eyes.

"Will you come with me?" she asked, and he hesitated, wary of leaving their son alone.

"Will Edward be safe?" he asked, knowing the boy was particularly attached to his mother and missed Anne desperately when she was only away from the castle for the afternoon. They would likely be gone for at least three weeks, and that was if the weather held.

"Safer here than on the road," Anne said softly.

Richard nodded, still frowning. Their son was two now, still in the delicate age where any illness might snatch him from them, and he was ill often. It tore at Richard's heart every time Edward cried, and he'd spent long nights walking the corridors with him, telling him about England and France, words the boy wouldn't understand, but Richard's voice seemed to sooth him.

"It's your choice," he said finally. "I'll come with you if you think Edward will be all right without either of us."

Anne sighed, shaking her head. "I don't know," she whispered, tears welling in her eyes. "I need to see her and I don't... I can't..."

"You don't want to face George alone," Richard concluded, and she nodded. He understood, he'd rather be at her side for that. "I'll come," he said, thinking of a solution, and she gripped his hand hard, her shoulder relaxing.

They left early the next morning after sending a messenger to fetch Francis, who was staying in Penrith and could ride to Middleham in two days or less. They trusted Geoffrey and Edward's two nurses, but they both felt better knowing Francis would come and watch over their boy, having no doubt he would not refuse them when he read Anne's letter.

George was drunk, though Richard couldn't find it in himself to be surprised. It had taken them almost a week to reach Warwick Castle and they'd passed the new year on the road, arriving the second day of January to find out that the child had passed away the night before.

Anne's face had crumbled when she heard, but she stoically asked to see her sister.

Isabel was in her coffin, the small bundle of her child wrapped and placed carefully next to her, her hands folded around a silver rosary. The coffin was in a small room under the window and the fires hadn't been lit for days. The room was freezing, but it kept the decay of death from setting in, even two weeks later. Outside, the ground was too hard to dig a grave, but several men were at work softening the earth with small fires that allowed a few more inches to thaw and be dug.

Richard left Anne to sit with her sister and nephew and found George slumped over the kitchen table, empty wine jugs surrounding him and the critical eye of the cook watching him. The cook, a surly man in his forties if he was a day, acknowledged Richard with a curt nod that Richard returned. Sighing, he shook George's shoulder, then levered him up from the table when George just grunted. He'd lost weight, but he was still heavy enough that Richard struggled as he all but carried his barely conscious brother to his rooms, dumping him gracelessly on his bed. He stood for a moment, but George was well and truly unconscious now and likely would be for some time, so Richard left him to his sleep and went to find Anne.

She was no longer with Isabel, but Richard found her in the nursery with their niece and nephew, Margaret, a girl of three, and Edward, not yet two.

"George is asleep," Richard said, as he sat beside Anne and wrapped an arm around her. Margaret was asleep in her lap and Edward was awake, but quiet in his cradle at their feet. She nodded, leaning against him with a sigh.

"The grave is almost done," she told him quietly. "They only need to thaw a few more inches. We can bury them on Sunday."

Richard nodded, pressing a kiss to her hair, not knowing what to say to comfort her. But this was Anne, strong, brave Anne who didn't need his words, so Richard kept his silence and comforted her with his presence instead.

"Get out," George snapped, and Richard looked up from his plate, one eyebrow raised.

George was leaning in the door to the dining room, hair a mess and his shirt soiled. He could barely stand upright, likely still drunk.

"We're not going anywhere," Richard said, voice even. "Not until Isabel is properly buried."

"I said get out!" George screamed, and Richard sat back in his chair, face hardening.

"And I said no," his voice rang clear and George growled as he stumbled into the room, leaning against the table.

"I don't want you here, *brother*," he snarled. "You or that bitch of a wife. I know what she wants, she wants Isabel's land and money, land and money that belongs to me!"

"We are here," Richard said, slowly as he stood, "so that my wife can bury her sister, and her nephew. You lost the right to dictate what Anne can or cannot do years ago, George, and if you ever speak that way about her again, I'll make sure you lose the ability to dictate anything about anyone ever again."

Richard fingered his dagger and George's eyes dropped to the blade before he made a gruff noise and stumbled back out of the room without another word. Sighing, Richard sat back down, staring at the empty doorway vacantly. He would have to write to Edward soon, more than the note identical to the one he received about Isabel's death, which, it turned out, had come from the house steward with George's seal. George had already been too distraught and drunk to make any kind of effort. Richard worried that losing both Isabel and the child would push George over the edge and that he'd become dangerous, perhaps even deranged. His schemes had nearly cost Edward his crown once, they didn't need trouble like that again.

After, Richard decided. They'd see Isabel buried and then Richard would write to Edward, before they left to return home.

October, 1477

Nearly a year passed in relative quiet before more trouble began to encroach on them once more, in the form of George rapidly losing his mind.

"George has been arrested," Richard said one day, handing Anne the letter that had just come from Edward, summoning Richard to London. She pursed her lips as she read, then shook her head.

"My sister not even a year in her grave, he's tried to remarry twice already, and now this?" she asked, waving the paper. In it, George was once again being accused of seditious and treasonous acts against the crown. Bad enough he'd already had one of Isabel's ladies falsely accused and put to death, using his position and power to circumvent the process of law, but now he was once more after the crown for himself, and seemed to care little for the consequences. He'd already been detained once during the summer, but this felt far more final.

Richard was silent for a long moment, willing away the headache that always seemed to follow any mention of his elder brother. "Should we take the children?" he asked finally, referring to the young Margaret and

Edward who had remained in their father's dubious care after Isabel died and now had no one.

Anne frowned, then nodded. "I mislike the idea of them alone at Warwick," she said. "They're barely two and four, and I don't trust that someone might not try to harm them."

"We'll go to Warwick first, then," Richard said, pulling a sheet of paper toward him and reaching for a quill. "You can see them safely back here, while I continue on to London."

Anne wrapped her arms around herself and nodded. "I'd rather not go to the city," she admitted, though she knew Richard would have to stay in London for a time. "I'll bring them back and get them settled. You'll come back as soon as you can?"

Richard frowned, pausing as he wrote. "It may be some months, if George has a trial, but I'll return as fast as I can."

Anne knew there was little choice, but a part of her was loath to face the winter alone. They were well stocked and it seemed to promise mild weather once again, but caring for three young children without Richard was not something she wanted to imagine. It didn't matter though, how much it unsettled her, they were her niece and nephew, and Richard had his duties in London to attend. They would have another few days, and then they would see one another again in the spring.

Their son, they determined, would once more have to remain at Middleham. Being only three years old he

The Last Winter Rose

would slow them greatly and the weather was already too cold for his fragile health. Little Edward didn't seem bothered this time as he watched them ride away, and both his parents prayed he would remain well and happy until Anne returned with his cousins.

They made good time, better than their trip the year before, and soon they were being welcomed to Warwick Castle by servants who seemed all the happier for George's absence. They were settled into well-appointed rooms quickly and taken to the nursery to see the children.

"They've been lonely," their nurse told Anne and Richard, smiling sadly at the children who were playing with some wooden toys in the middle of the carpet. "I've done what I can, but they miss their mother, and their father..." Her face darkened into a scowl before her eyes flicked to Richard. "Your pardon, lord, but your brother isn't a well man."

Richard's eyes were on Margaret and he nodded. "I'm not sure he ever has been," he said quietly, and Anne put her hand on the woman's arm.

"You've done admirably, Jane," she smiled. "You're welcome to come with us, if you wish. I plan to take the children back to Middleham and raise them in a happier house from now on."

The nurse, Jane, smiled, her face lighting with relief. "Oh lady, that would be wonderful. I've nothing for myself here now, not since my sister left to marry a farmer away the other side of the county. I'd be so happy to stay with the children."

191

"I'm sure they'll be glad of your company as well," Anne said, and Jane dropped in a low curtsy before leaving them alone.

"How you already remember everyone's names," Richard teased, because it took him an age to match a face to a name, and Anne just chuckled, shoving him lightly.

Richard hung back as Anne went over to the children, sitting on the rug near Margaret and smiling gently.

"Do you remember me?" she asked, and the four year old girl nodded, thumb in her mouth. Her brother, Edward, was too young to remember Anne, having been not quite two when they had last been to Warwick for Isabel's burial the year before, and now not quite three.

"How are you?" Richard asked, crouching next to Anne and smiling reassuringly at Margaret, who watched him with wary eyes. "Are you well?"

Again she nodded, but didn't answer. Anne sighed softly.

"Margaret," she said, reaching for the girl's free hand. "Would you like to come live with us at Middleham? You can meet your cousin, he's also called Edward, he's just a little older than your brother. You can have your own room in a year or two, and the boys can share, and you can learn to read and write and ride horses, and whatever else you'd like to learn."

Margaret frowned around her thumb, glancing back and forth between them, then slowly she nodded her head. Anne smiled and held her arms open, offering, and

The Last Winter Rose

after a moment Margaret stepped into them, curling close against Anne's chest as Anne held her, tears shining in her eyes as she pressed a kiss to dark hair, so like Isabel's.

That afternoon seemed to break a wall. The next few days Anne was rarely without both children right on her heels while they went through Isabel's things, still in their place despite a year. Richard took time to look into the accounts and settled many of George's numerous debts from the frankly obscene amount of money he had hoarded. If he ever did return to Warwick he would find himself with a significantly lighter purse, but no debtors trying to knock down his door for a pound of flesh in lieu of coin. Within a week they had a wagon packed full of things that had either belonged to Isabel and were now Anne's, or that were for the children as they grew. Just like that, they were ready to set off north.

"Are you coming with us?" Margaret asked Richard, as Anne was settling Edward into the carriage, her voice so quiet he almost didn't hear her. He crouched down to her level, hiding a wince as it made his back ache, and shook his head.

"No, I'm sorry, but I must go to London first. I'll come in the spring, I promise. The roads may be too hard to pass soon, it's meant to be a wet winter." He glanced up at Anne, seeing the pain twisting on her face at the thought of being apart for so long and it was the same as the pain in his heart. "I will be home as soon as I can, I promise," he told the little girl. "You'll be warm and safe and happy at Middleham, and when I come from London, I'll bring presents."

"Lemon candies?" Margaret asked shyly, and Anne sucked in a breath. Lemon candies had been Isabel's favourite.

Richard nodded with a smile. "Lemon candies," he agreed, then stood, lifting Margaret into the carriage where Jane fussed about her and tucked her under a heavy blanket. The woman clearly loved the children and Richard was glad they'd had someone since Isabel had died, and Jane was eager to stay with them. He doubted they'd had any love from George, if they had ever even seen him.

He turned to Anne, who had finished settling Edward, and for a moment Richard thought of his own son and his heart hurt. He gathered Anne close and held her for a moment before he pulled back with a smile, brushing a loose piece of hair back and cupping her face in one hand. "We'll have to find something to call one of them," he said softly. She leaned into his touch, even though his hands were cold, and he pulled her cloak tighter around her. "This confusion of Edwards will cause chaos."

Anne smiled, resting her forehead against his chin as her arms slipped around him, holding him close.

"Be safe," she whispered. "Don't let the king or George lead you into any more wars."

Richard smiled against her hair, holding her tightly. "I will. If the snow starts, you find the first inn and you stop, you wait until the roads are clear, I don't care how much it costs. Don't try to travel if the weather turns."

"I promise," she said, and Richard pulled back again, tilting her chin up and kissing her deeply as the sunlight winked in the frost around them and made the world sparkle.

"I love you," he said against her lips, and she smiled, combing a hand through his hair.

"And I you," she said. "Now let me go, or I'll never have the strength to leave you."

With regret, Richard stepped back and helped her up into the carriage, making sure they were all secure before he tied the heavy canvas shut over the window and waved the driver and guards on, the whole party rumbling out of the courtyard and up the road to Middleham. He sighed, running a hand over his face in exhaustion before he turned and strode to his own horse, mounting with a grunt that was covered by the horse snorting, and he jerked his head to the rest of the men milling about the courtyard.

Out of the gate he paused to watch the carriage until it was out of sight over a hill, then he turned south and spurred his horse for London

November, 1477

He didn't go see George. Certainly, he debated the whole ride from Warwick and spent a good amount of time paused at the Tower gate, but Richard found he didn't have anything to say to his brother, and he didn't need to hear anything George might have to say either. He was tired of half-truths, false justifications, and excuses.

He turned his horse away finally, sending most of his men ahead to Westminster with his things and the spare horses, and he went instead to see his mother.

He was showed in with no fuss, but she didn't come to greet him like she usually did. Instead, he found her in her bedchamber, still in her night things, staring blankly out the window.

"Mother," Richard said quietly, but Cecily raised a hand to silence him gently. She didn't even seem surprised that he was there.

"Richard, your brother has chosen his own fate," she said softly. "He is my son and I will always love him, but I cannot become involved again, not this time. I forgave him before, but we both know bringing him back won't be possible again."

"So you won't speak to Edward on his behalf?" Richard asked, curious. His mother was one of the strongest people he knew, but now she looked as tired as he felt most days.

"I will not," she said, and all Richard could do was nod. It seemed they were all at an end, and George had finally gone too far.

Richard sighed, pulling a chair over from in front of the fire and sitting next to his mother, reaching for her hands. He winced when he found them ice cold and he rose again, fetching a blanket from her bed and draping it over her lap before he built up the fire. When he sat again, she smiled sadly at him, eyes finally looking somewhere other than the window.

"My sweet boy," she said softly, reaching out to touch his face. "You and Margaret, you are the best of my children."

"Mother," Richard muttered, but Cecily shook her head.

"It's a mother's prerogative to have favourites," she smiled.

"Anne has taken the children to Middleham," Richard said, changing the subject. "I don't know if there was any legal provision made for their care, I've certainly found none so far, but we want to raise them."

Cecily sighed and nodded, clasping Richard's hands tightly. "I'm so sorry you were never able to have more children of your own. It must be so hard for both of you."

"It has been," Richard nodded. "But I can only imagine how much harder it's been for you, losing so many, over so long."

She hummed, but didn't say anything else and they fell into silence.

After a while Richard took his leave, extracting her promise that she would eat something and spend time in her reading room, and leaving his own promise to visit again as soon as he was able.

Outside Richard stood almost frozen, staring up at the cloudy sky for a long moment, praying for fortitude, before forced himself to move and mount his horse. Now it was time to see Edward.

January, 1478

Edward was furious, to no surprise of anyone who knew him. He'd kept George in well-appointed solitude well into the new year before a trial was brought and the result, again, was no surprise. Guilty. Now they debated what would be done with George, and while the council was split, the final decision ultimately rested with Edward.

"I can see only one outcome from all of this," the king muttered darkly, digging into the table with the point of his dagger.

He and Richard were in Edward's private rooms, late in the evening, the remains of their meal pushed aside and a jug of wine between them. Richard hadn't wanted to have this discussion with Edward, but it seemed his opinion was still valued by his older brother, and they'd been in heated debate for most of the evening.

"He's our brother," Richard said finally, when all the arguments had been exhausted for or against George's execution and Edward glanced at him.

"I'm surprised to hear you defend him," he said, settling back in his chair, fingers fiddling with his wine cup. "By any measure, especially after everything he has done."

"I'm not," Richard muttered, voice laced with frustration. He pushed himself out of his chair paced the room. "I'm not defending him, but I don't... I would not see him executed and his head put on a spike. Whatever he's done, he's still our blood."

Edward's face was hard as he looked away, into the fire. Richard hadn't seen what he'd seen after their father and Edmund were killed, but Edward had been there. He'd seen the heads in York, nearly unrecognisable as men he'd once known. He had no desire to do that to George, but the law was the law, and George had been found guilty of treason, the same as he would have seven years ago, if Edward hadn't pardoned him. He didn't know if he could pardon him again.

"What would you suggest?" he asked tiredly, the weight of everything heavy on his shoulders. He had an entire kingdom to run, a demanding wife, seven young children, and a brother who threatened to destroy everything yet again.

"Imprisonment," Richard said, pausing his pacing, "in the Tower, for the rest of his natural life."

"And if he has support outside the Tower? If they try to take him like they did Henry and put him on the throne?"

"Who does he have left?" Richard reasoned, spreading his hands. "Warwick is dead, Isabel is dead. George has never been popular with the nobles, he's never been popular with the people. He's too petty and power hungry to advance anyone else in return for supporting him, and he thinks the people that really keep this realm on its feet are beneath him. Even our own mother won't speak for him."

"Only you," Edward sighed, and Richard pursed his lips and nodded.

"Only I say don't kill him, and some days even I wonder why," he admitted quietly and Edward shook his head, draining his wine.

"I'll think on it."

It had been nearly three weeks since their conversation and they sat together late into the evening, like they did most days. Edward was concerned about the northern border and the threats of Scottish invasion, and was taking the time while Richard was in London to discuss every aspect of repelling the raids and planning a campaign. They had nearly finished for the night when a knock came on Edward's door and he called to whoever was outside to enter.

"What is it?" Edward asked, not even looking toward the man standing in the doorway, who hesitated before he stepped into the room and bowed, but Richard easily recognised his livery. He was a guard from the Tower, one whose face Richard didn't recognise.

The man stood stiffly, looking straight ahead, he wouldn't have met the king's eye even if Edward had turned, and he certainly wouldn't meet Richard's gaze even though Richard was watching him openly, standing by the fire with his hands behind his back, fingers of one hand around his other wrist in the only stance that eased the pain in his spine.

"I've been sent from the Tower, sire," the man said, clearing his throat, "with news of the Duke of Clarence."

Richard suddenly had a sinking feeling deep in his stomach, like someone had ripped the ground out from under him, and he saw Edward stiffen.

"Speak."

"The duke was found dead in his rooms an hour ago, when the servants brought his evening meal," the guard said, spine stiff and eyes staring straight ahead at a spot on the wall.

Dead. The word rocketed around Richard's head as he clenched his hands. He would have given George a final mercy, life confined, but now even that had been ripped away.

"Does the constable suspect foul play in my brother's death?" Edward asked, voice quiet and sharp like steel. The guard was almost trembling.

"The investigation has only just begun, but there has been no strange activity, nor anyone unknown or unusual allowed entry to the Tower within the last days," he reported, still staring straight ahead. "Only three besides myself know of this event, and we are already investigating the kitchen staff and servants quietly. A physician has been summoned to... examine the body for signs of foul play. The warden will come to see you personally as soon as he knows anything further."

Edward flicked his hand, dismissing the guard, who all but fled, sweat visible under his cap as he turned and hurriedly closed the door behind himself. Richard and Edward looked at each other, then Richard sighed, collapsing into a chair and reaching for the wine.

They passed the night in silence, a strange kind of limbo where nothing seemed important while they waited for any other word. It seemed like the world around them had paused, dropping away and leaving them in a void until finally, an hour before dawn, the warden came, pale in his livery and anger pinching around his mouth and eyes.

"Sire, I have little more to tell you," he said tiredly, as he bowed. "There are still servants and guards to interview, but those with any immediate contact with the duke, and every member of the kitchen staff have been questioned to my satisfaction."

"How did he die?" Edward asked. His voice was rough with exhaustion and his shoulders were slumped.

"He was found in his bed and it appears that he choked on his wine," the warden sighed, pulling off his cap and rubbing his bald head. "It is possible he drank so much that he passed out and the contents of his stomach rebelled. He may have choked to death. The doctor has taken samples to determine if there was poison involved, but there were no marks of struggle or bruising on the body."

Richard winced internally, but otherwise had no outward reaction. His hands tightened in his lap and he forced himself to remain stoic.

"I will have your report in writing," Edward said, and the warden bowed before leaving the room, understanding he was dismissed.

"Do you believe it was an accident?" Richard asked after a long moment, and Edward shrugged, despondent. "You don't think he... took his own life?"

"Drowned himself in wine?" Edward snorted darkly. "I wouldn't put it past him, just to spite us."

"What will you do?" Richard pressed when the silence had descended again. Edward shrugged, scrubbing a hand over his face.

"What can I do?" he asked bleakly, and Richard sighed.

Outside he heard the watch called the hour. The sun would rise soon on another day. With a barely suppressed groan he stood, crossing the room.

"Get some sleep," he said quietly, resting his hand on Edward's shoulder for a moment. His brother tilted his head, something like acknowledgement, and with another deep breath Richard left him to his thoughts.

He returned to his rooms to find them warm, the fire built high despite the early morning hour. He sighed as he barred the door and bent to pull his boots off, leaving them on the rug as he sank into the chair in front of the hearth, setting his dagger on the table next to the chair and reaching for a glass of wine. He drained it in one drink before he leaned back into the cushions, staring at

The Last Winter Rose

the fire with his fingers steepled together. He didn't know, he didn't have proof, but in his heart, he was sure. *She* was behind this. Edward's wife, his queen, Elizabeth Woodville was the reason George was dead.

She wouldn't have been, Richard thought. George had gotten himself arrested and tried for treason all on his own, his stupidity and short sightedness rearing its head in the wake of his loss of Isabel and their infant son. But Edward had agreed to commute George's sentence at Richard's urging, agreed to keep him imprisoned for the rest of his life, rather than having him executed.

Richard frowned harder, his mind whirling. Edward might suspect foul play, he might not. He might believe the report from the Tower that George had overindulged in drink to the point of his death, whether by accident or deliberately, but that wasn't what mattered in the first instance.

Even though the decision had been made, the sentence hadn't been publicly commuted yet, which meant Edward was faced with a choice. Announce that his brother had been executed for his crimes, as the law demanded, or say that he'd died while in royal custody of natural causes. The councillors would tell him the former would show strength. And it would, but it might not be popular either. Edward hadn't ordered George's death, so there was no weight on his consciousness in that respect. The question was would he choose to lie about it to show he upheld the law, that no one, not even a prince, was above it? Or would he tell the truth,

205

that George had been granted life only to die of unknown causes?

Richard didn't care about any of that, not really, he didn't care what the public knew or thought. He cared that he himself knew with every fibre of his being that George had been murdered.

Obviously, the queen hadn't done it by her own hand. He knew that, and he knew he had no way to prove it, no way to accuse her. Edward would never believe it, but she was behind it, he could feel it in his bones. Maybe it was Anthony who had actually done the deed, or even Elizabeth's son by her first husband, Thomas Grey. He could find out, but what would it matter? She had achieved her goal and he couldn't touch her. All he could do was build the walls around his family higher in the hope of protecting them from her machinations. They weren't a direct threat to her, so perhaps he could keep Anne and his boy safe.

And George's children. Anne had already taken them back to Middleham when George was first arrested and Richard would hear no argument about them taking custody of the young boy and his sister. He wouldn't have them raised somewhere he couldn't see them, to meet with an accident or some other tragedy. It didn't matter that they'd been struck from the line of succession by George's actions, they were still his blood. Edward hadn't cared what happened to the children, which had relieved Richard only insofar as he didn't have to fight over their custody and care.

The Last Winter Rose

He wondered what Elizabeth thought now that he held control over all the Warwick lands. Anything left of George's money after his debts had been settled, along with all his other estates, had been forfeit to the crown, but the Warwick estate had been rejoined and reverted to Anne, and thereby Richard. Richard sighed, rubbing his temples, because perhaps they were a threat to Elizabeth Woodville after all, at least in her eyes.

All he wanted was to return home, see his wife, hold his son. They hadn't been blessed with another child since Edward, though there had been some false hopes, and once, a real hope that turned to sorrow, and now Richard ached for his family, wishing they were closer.

He would stay for George's funeral, however large or small it might be, then maybe he could escape this hell of London and go back north, go home. He wanted nothing more to do with it than he ever had, not with the scheming and plotting that surrounded his family and the crown, not with the politics of a kingdom. If only his father had lived, things would have been so different.

Richard was exhausted, the winter chill eating at him even in the south. He rubbed his face and gazed at the fire for a long moment before he hauled himself out of his chair with a grunt, wincing as pain shot across his back and he had to take a moment to breathe before he crossed the room and crawled into his cold and lonely bed, still fully dressed except for his weapons and boots, and prayed for sleep to come and relive some of his weariness.

207

1478-1479

It was early April by the time Richard managed to ride north. He'd meant to set out almost a month earlier, but heavy snows had blocked the roads for three weeks, and even once he was on his way, the journey took twice as long as it should have. To fuel his foul mood, the sun was shining the day he finally rode into Middleham and it was the warmest day of the year yet.

It was just before noon when the horn singling approaching riders blew and Anne was running before the sound had even faded from the air. Richard was barely inside the town square when he saw her running from the castle with her skirts pulled up and he drew up his horse, dismounting and holding out his arms, every frustration vanishing as she crashed into him with a measured restraint, ever careful of hurting him, but he didn't care as he pulled her tightly against his chest and held on, her face buried against his shoulder and her hands fisted in his cloak. He knew she was crying, her sobs shaking her, and his own eyes were wet as he breathed in the beautiful scent of her hair.

"I missed you," he whispered, and her arms tightened around him. "I'm here, Anne, I'm here."

The Last Winter Rose

She pulled back and smiled, wiping her face as she took him in with a critical eye.

"Have you been eating enough?" she asked, and Richard laughed loudly, unable to deny himself the joy of sweeping her up in his arms and swinging her around and around as she cried out in surprise. It made his back hurt to lift her, but she wasn't so very heavy and she was smiling so beautifully at him, making it well worth it. The men around them chuckled and raised a light cheer as they pulled apart and Richard grinned, jerking his head toward the castle, and the line of horses proceeded past them.

"I've been eating just fine, my dear wife," he said with a chuckle, as he set her back on her feet, holding her hands tightly. "How are the children? Edward?"

"Ours is strong and cantankerous," she smiled. "Isabel's is... he's quiet. And Richard, we have to find something to call him, we cannot keep calling him Edward, it confuses everyone, and he's not an infant so he needs to be called by his name."

"I'm sure we'll think of something," he smiled, tucking her hand into the cook of his arm. "Take me to see them."

Anne smiled and leaned her head against his shoulder as they entered the castle, talking quietly about what had been happening at Middleham. He'd tell her about London tonight, when they were alone. They walked to the castle slowly and Richard nodded greetings to various men as he passed. It was clear the people were happy to see him returned and he was happy to be home. They'd just passed through the gate when there was a shout.

"Father!"

Richard stooped to catch the blur coming at him and he laughed as he lifted Edward into his arms. He was slight for three and a half years old, but there was more colour to his cheeks than when Richard had last seen him.

"My boy," Richard smiled. "How are you?"

"I'm well, father," Edward said slowly, pronouncing his letters carefully like a grown up. "Mother says I may ride a horse after my birthday."

"Does she now?" Richard chuckled, raising his eyebrows at Anne, who shrugged.

"I learned to ride at four," she said, and Richard shook his head. In fairness he'd been much the same age.

"Hello, uncle Richard," Margaret said, as she stood up from the blanket spread in the sun, tucking her doll behind her skirt.

"Hello," Richard smiled, as Anne took the youngest of the three from the nurse watching them and bounced him on her hip. "Have you been well?"

Margaret nodded shyly.

"And do you enjoy it here at Middleham?" he asked, crouching down to her level and she nodded again.

"Margaret, we were talking about what we might call your brother, since he and your cousin have the same name," Anne said, and Margaret's face scrunched in thought.

"Ma called him Ned," she said after a moment, staring at her brother. She was not quite five, and Edward was only three, but there was a dark wisdom in her face that told them she'd seen things no child should see. "She didn't like the name Edward," Margaret whispered, and Anne sat on the blanket and wrapped her free arm around the girl.

"And what about you, my dear niece?" she asked. "What shall we call you?"

Margaret whispered something and Anne leaned closer, tilting her ear so the girl could whisper again.

"Maggie," Anne smiled, as Margaret nodded. "I think that's wonderful. Edward, Ned, and Maggie."

"Perfect," Richard said softly. "Don't you think?" he asked Edward and the eldest boy nodded.

"I missed you," he said, and Richard hugged his son tightly.

"I missed you, too," he said, smiling at Anne over Edward's little shoulder.

"It's almost time to eat the midday meal," Anne said, and that brought smiles to all the children's faces.

"And sweets?" Ned asked, words not quite clear yet in his mouth, and both adults chuckled.

"And sweets," Anne promised, taking Maggie's hand as she stood and the five of them went to spend their first meal together as a family.

Richard frowned, tossing another letter into the ever-growing pile. There had been another raid by the Scottish across their northern border, the seventh now since the beginning of the year. They'd lost cattle by the dozen and whole crops had been burned by the roving raiders, who didn't seem at all deterred by the local authorities response. In fact, they'd grown bolder, and so far no one had seemed inclined to do much about it. It came as a relief, then, to find the next two letters on the pile were from Francis and Ratcliffe. Francis was on his way with two hundred men and would meet Richard in Penrith and Ratcliffe had raised five hundred from Carlisle. Richard had another four hundred waiting in the east for word of a meeting place, and then they would make their way along the border and see if they could catch the thieves in action.

It had been nearly a year since Richard had returned from London after George's death, a year of quiet, country life, with nothing much worthy of note happening. They'd spent part of the summer in York and the winter comfortably installed back at Middleham. There was work to be done on the castle, so they decided to remain there for the spring and summer the next year, but then news of the raids had started.

He'd moved to raise troops immediately, hoping Edward would retaliate, but his brother didn't seem particularly interested in what was happening on his border. In March, Edward's youngest son, George, barely two years old, had died, Elizabeth was once more pregnant, and this would be their ninth child in fourteen years. He couldn't even begin to imagine what both of them were going through with such a dichotomy, one child gone and another on the way.

Richard was torn about what action to take, wanting desperately to stay with his family and not get involved, but the north was his territory, the border his responsibility, and he would do all he could to protect the people, every last one of them.

He rode out from Middleham in early June, leaving his family behind despite Anne's protests. She had wanted to come with him, but he didn't want her or the children closer to danger, so he insisted that they stay removed from the area of conflict. Anne had extracted his promise to be careful and that the next year, provided there was no war, they would spend the summer touring their northern holdings.

They stood on the wall as the men rode out, the children watching with fascination as fifty men and horses fell in line behind Richard as they marched down the valley and east, toward Darlington. Anne raised her hand in farewell just before they'd dropped out of sight and Richard had paused a moment, bringing her face to his mind, so he wouldn't forget.

By the time they reached the city they were almost two hundred, with another four hundred waiting to join them. They turned west, and by the time they reached Penrith the company had swelled to almost a thousand. Angry farmers, most of whom hadn't soldiered in years, but who all wanted revenge for their losses and the injustices done to those around them. When they were

Caitlin Sumner

joined by Ratcliffe and Francis' men they numbered close to two and a half thousand and most of the men had to be billeted outside the town, Penrith being far too small for so many.

"They're getting bolder," Ratcliffe said, as he ducked inside the castle hall, out of the rain, pulling his sodden leather gloves off and shrugging his cloak into the hands of a footman. "They took fifty cows and beat the farmer near to death last night."

"Where?" Richard asked, and Francis reached for a small flag on a pin, piercing the map laid out on the table when Ratcliffe pointed to a spot.

A line of flags had been assembled since Richard arrived, and the trail of raids and destruction was obvious, coming down from the west and heading east along and across the border.

"We'll send larger patrols to that area," Richard said, after some consideration. "Ratcliffe, I'm leaving you here to watch over our western flank from Carlisle while Francis and I go east. Francis, I want you to camp your men near Hexham and send patrols east and west from there, while I continue on to Northumberland. Henry Percy has started to raise men after a large raid into his lands and he wants to speak about joining all our forces together."

"Has there been anything from London?" Francis asked, and Richard shook his head.

"Edward says we're not to cross the border until war is officially declared," he muttered. "And apparently

214

The Last Winter Rose

James has made an offer of marriage between his sister and Anthony Woodville."

"While his raiders cross into our lands and steal our food and hurt our people," Ratcliffe fumed. "That seems like the Scots."

"It's too late in the year to declare war," Francis sighed, shaking his head. "He'll accept the marriage offer or it will be war next year."

It was July already and less than a month until the crops would be brought in. After that it would be too hot to march without high risk of disease sweeping through the men and on the heels of that it would be too cold. Edward would have to declare his war at the very start of the year and be ready to march by April.

"We can only hope if my brother is serious, he acts early next year," Richard sighed, already mentally preparing for a long winter.

"I fear your brother no longer remembers how to act decisively," Ratcliffe said, and Richard stared hard at the map, frowning. There was truth to his words, too much truth, and Richard prayed he could keep hold of the fragile pieces of his life, keep them together, when he already felt them unravelling in his grasp.

1480

Richard rode east again as soon as Christmas was over, having returned to Middleham to spend a few weeks with his family.

Once more, Francis had become his unofficial shadow, and they were on their way to meet Edward's man, Alexander Legh, who had spent the last several weeks in Scotland, attempting to negotiate reparations for the raids that had continued throughout 1479. There had been no more intervention other than what the northern lords could provide on their own, and again there had been no help from the crown, with Edward remaining indecisive and silent far to the south.

"Have you ever met him?" Richard asked on the afternoon they were approaching the meeting place, and Francis shook his head.

"I wonder if he'd managed to get the Scottish king to agree to anything," he pondered, gaze trailing across the landscape in front of him.

Francis had grown more serious in recent years, though he still always had a joke to hand when the situation needed diffusing. Now, though, he often spent long hours in contemplative silence. Richard had often

asked what he was thinking, but so far Francis had yet
to reveal what seemed to plague his mind.

"I doubt it," Richard snorted. "James is a stubborn,
stubborn man."

"Hmm," Francis hummed, and they fell silent until
they reached the inn where Legh had said he would be
waiting.

"Is that them?" Richard asked, pulling up his horse
with a frown. There was a group of mounted men
arguing outside the town gate and one of them was
carrying Edward's banner.

"It's them," one of the men behind Richard said. "I
met Legh last year, I remember his face."

"Thank you," Richard nodded to him, then took a
breath. "Let's go."

They spurred forward and the argument died as they
approached, horses and men turning to meet them.

"My lord Gloucester, it's an honour," Legh said,
bowing from his saddle. "We were just leaving, I hoped
you would catch us on the road, but all the better you're
here."

"Good to meet you," Richard nodded, reaching out
to clasp the other man's hand in greeting, their horses
stomping in the mud. "We'll travel with you, if you've
no objections."

"None at all, lord," Legh said, and he seemed to be
telling the truth, rather than speaking from courtesy.

They joined parties and turned south, heading
toward London.

217

"Have you made any progress?" Richard asked as they rode, bringing his horse in step with Legh's. Legh frowned and shook his head.

"Some, perhaps, but I don't know how much good it will do with the king. I'll present my report to him in full, but I can only pray he'll be more responsive than last year."

Richard nodded with a frown. The support from Edward had never materialised, leaving him, Francis, Ratcliffe, and Percy to try and maintain the border from incursions alone, without retaliation. He hadn't been too happy with his brother and the half a dozen unanswered letters he'd sent.

The ride to London was uneventful, despite the winter weather, and they arrived late in January. As usual, the first thing Richard did, even before seeing Edward, was go to visit his mother.

He sighed as the door swung shut behind him. It didn't matter where his mother lived, wherever she was had always felt like an escape from the rest of the world, and the relief of being able to have a few hours away from everything was palpable.

"The Lady Cecily is in the front reading room," he was informed by her head of house as he handed over his cloak and gloves to the older man whose name he'd always struggled to remember. He nodded politely, able to find his own way, and the man disappeared quickly, though Richard caught the smile on his usually dour face and he chuckled to himself. It was nice to know he was at least warmly welcomed somewhere.

The Last Winter Rose

"Hello, Mother," he said, as he entered her reading room and she smiled, putting her book aside and rising to embrace him. She'd known he was coming, but not the exact day he would arrive.

"Oh, my darling," she said softly, holding him close. "I've missed you."

Richard smiled, catching her hands and holding them tightly as he pulled back. He was glad to see her again, but so many things were weighing on him.

"I'm sorry I haven't come to see you," he said, chuckling when he saw she'd had his favourite chair moved into the room and he sat gratefully, sinking into the soft cushions that supported his back and helped relieve the constant ache.

"You've been busy," Cecily smiled, taking her seat again and watching as Richard slowly relaxed, sighing when he opened his eyes again.

She'd always been so fond of him, her youngest boy, the one with bright curious eyes and dark twisting hair, he looked more like her uncle than his father, and she'd doted on him as much as she could when he was just a child. She'd had to send him away too young, and she'd never really gotten him or George back after that fateful year.

"Mother?" Richard said gently, seeing the expression on her face, and she sighed, forcing a smile.

"I was just thinking about your brothers and sisters," she admitted, clasping her hands. "I had twelve children, and now only four remain to me. I rarely see

219

your sisters, not unless I were to travel and I'm far too old for that."

Richard grimaced. "I'm sorry about George," he said, and Cecily shook her head.

"Your brother... he chose his own fate," she whispered. "I tried all I could with him, but it was never enough."

They were silent for a few long moments, then Richard sat up, clutching his hands together and staring at the carpet. He knew Edward had never told her the truth of George's death, she only knew what they'd said publicly, that George had been granted a private execution and had been buried quietly next to Isabel. He debated now and decided she deserved the truth.

"George wasn't executed," he said quietly, and Cecily's eyes shot to his. "I had just persuaded Edward to allow him to live, albeit imprisoned for the rest of his life. Only a very few knew that his sentence would be reduced to imprisonment, and then we had word he was dead."

Cecily looked away, out the window at the river, a deep frown on her face. Richard watched her profile now, seeing the years and what they had done to her. The losses of his father, of Edmund, of Anne who died only two years before, of Henry, William, John, and Thomas, brothers who had lived and died before Richard was born, of Ursula who had lived only a year when Richard was three. He had felt so much loss in his young life, but it was nothing compared to his mother.

The Last Winter Rose

"What happened?" she asked finally, and Richard sighed, slumping back in the chair and looking out the window, one hand rubbing his chin lightly, scratching through stubble he hadn't bothered with that morning.

"Edward has accepted that George drank himself to a stupor and choked to death on his own bile," he told her. "But I don't believe that. I believe he was murdered because he would have been allowed to live."

"You mean she killed him," Cecily said, voice hard like the edge of a new sword. "Edward's whore of a queen."

"She's the mother of your grandchildren," Richard reminded her, but she waved a hand.

"I don't blame the children for their parentage," she said. "But she cannot be allowed to have such power. I know that was the start of Warwick and George's rebellion eight years ago, it wasn't a war against Edward, it was a war against her."

"It began like that, yes," Richard said tiredly. "But that wasn't how it ended."

"I know," Cecily said, and she did. It had ended with her nephew the Earl of Warwick dead on the battlefield, Edward back on his throne, and George tentatively forgiven, until he'd started on his schemes for power once again.

"I cannot be certain of any of this," Richard said, because it was only a suspicion. He had no way to prove that Elizabeth had been behind his brother's death. He couldn't even be certain that it hadn't been George's own doing, or even an accident. But he'd needed to tell someone. He hadn't even told Anne.

"This crown will be the ruin of us all," Cecily said softly, and Richard was silent, because in the face of such words, words he felt to be truer than most that had ever been spoken, he had nothing to say.

"I wish father had left well enough alone," he said finally, a rare moment of pure truth, words he never shared with anyone else. "I wish he had been content with what he had, this family quest for the throne has brought us nothing, but pain."

"Nothing?" Cecily smiled gently. "You have your Anne, you have your boy. She writes to me about him, tells me he's a good child. She's told me how you've taken in George's children and would raise them as your own. You're a good, kind man. Are you truly so unhappy?"

Richard sighed, suddenly so angry at his father and his brothers that he wanted to stand and hurl a stone through the window just to hear the sound of the expensive glass shattering.

"My happiness has come at such a price," he whispered. "And I fear it will not last. I fear there will be more blood to pay before the end. More loss, more pain. There are days I cannot reconcile my belief in God with the pain we've all had to live with, and those days shake me to my foundations."

"You're not alone in that, my son," she said, reaching for his hand and Richard smiled, feeling closer to his mother than he ever had before in his life with those few simple words.

Richard remained in London until June, listening to Edward dither and hum. He was appointed to a military leadership, Lieutenant General of the Scottish Campaigns, in May, and left soon after to return to the border, where Francis' troops were worn down and wearing thin as they chased the raiders back and forth across the country. He arrived to news that the Earl of Angus had raised a substantial force and was making for Bamborough. Richard gave chase, but wasn't in time to stop the town being put to the torch. Percy was furious and, in September, the English crossed the border with their troops and raided through the border towns, taking livestock back and burning. Richard ordered that they try and avoid bloodshed if at all possible, because these weren't the people who were attacking them, these were farmers, and they could go north and rebuild, away from the border. There was no need for them to die.

The counter raid seemed to deter the Scots for the year, with the weather turning cold early, and Richard left his men spread along the border towns, well paid to stay there and guard through the winter while he went home, though not for long. Edward's summons came at the end of October with an invitation to Richard's whole family to come stay in London for Christmas, so they packed what seemed like half the household into three wagons and went south, the children's excitement growing with every mile.

Council sessions started almost as soon as they were settled and Edward seemed to have finally found his determination to fully invade Scotland the next spring. Richard wanted to be relieved, but he wasn't going to expect Edward to actually go through with it, this being the third year in a row he'd made the threat. They would stay until April, making preparations and gathering men, and then Richard would return north with the army, with Edward to follow. It was a good plan, if only it came to fruition this time.

"I don't like this," Anne said softly, and Richard held back a sigh. He didn't like it either, but this was what Edward had asked of him, this was the duty he would do. He ruled the north in all but name, and their borders had been threatened and encroached on for years.

"I know," he said quietly, laying a hand on her shoulder. "But if we don't act now, if we don't push the Scots back and reclaim our lands, they'll gain a foothold here in England and then it will be all out war."

Anne frowned, staring at the map on her small writing desk, arrows marking the Scottish advances of the last few years, small red X's marking where towns and villages had been burned.

The Last Winter Rose

"Do you think you can take Berwick?" she asked softly. She knew her history, she knew how a hundred and fifty years before there had been the greatest war between the English kings Edward II and his son Edward III, and Robert the Bruce, the king who led the Scots to victory over the English. Berwick had been a major point of contention during those wars, and had remained in Scottish hands since. Edward wanted it back.

"I do," Richard said, though he wasn't sure. He was sure they could hold the city on their southern side of the Tweed, but he wasn't sure he could take the northern half and hold it for any great length of time, if at all.

"I'd go with you," Anne said at last, and Richard sighed.

"Anne," he said quietly, because they'd already talked about it, several times, long into the night. She wanted to go with him, but he wanted her safe from harm. She'd been in the centre of one war, he never wanted her even near another one. He had half a mind to send her and the children to Nottingham or even to London, as far south and away from the fighting as he could.

"I know," she muttered. "I know. But I'll miss you," she said, finally looking at him, tears in her eyes, and he took a step closer, leaning down to kissing her softly.

"I'll be careful," he promised. "I'll come back to you."

Anne smiled, resting her forehead against his. "You always do," she whispered.

225

1481

Richard left Middleham in May, meeting up once again with Francis, Ratcliffe, and Henry Percy. The other three men looked exhausted, but there was relief now that Edward seemed to have finally taken the threat from Scotland seriously after the marriage negotiation had fallen through in a spectacular fashion and the raids had doubled. There was an even larger force coming from the south and one way or another they would have a real fight this year. Richard would remain Lieutenant General for another year and hold Edward's authority, so he could march into Scotland even if the king never arrived.

Lost in thought as they rode between towns, Richard didn't notice the odd silence around them until one of his own men shouted.

"Ambush!"

Horses reeled, suddenly surrounding him, and Richard snapped his attention to his surroundings as an arrow whistled through the air, striking one of the attackers. He'd come up from behind a bush and was spinning a sling around his head. It dropped from his grip when the arrow struck him in the shoulder and he fell with a curse.

The terrain was rocky, but the men were already moving forward, their horses giving them the advantage of speed and height, and within moments half the raiders were on the ground, wounded or dead, and the rest were running.

"Stay here," Francis said, blocking Richard as he moved to give chase. "You don't need to get involved in this."

"Francis, move," Richard growled, sword already drawn in his hand.

"Stay here," Francis snapped, kicking his horse into a gallop, chasing the last of the raiders as they fled. Richard scowled, reining in his horse. Three men remained beside him, eyes darting around the rough country for any more attackers.

He dismounted, going over to the men on the ground while two of the remaining soldiers moved in front of him quickly to disarm those still alive, and to give a mercy blow to one who was breathing, but doomed to a slow and painful death from his wounds. Richard crouched in front of the first man, the one with the arrow in his shoulder.

"Who told you to be here?" he asked, and the man grunted, scowling at him. "I'm not going to have you killed, but I want to know who sent you here to kill us."

The man spat at his feet, then grimaced, hand pressing against his shoulder, teeth gritted.

"Fine," Richard muttered after a moment. "Hold still."

He reached forward and gripped the arrow, ripping it out of the man's shoulder. It wasn't deep, though someone should stitch it up. He pulled a clean handkerchief out of his tunic and pressed it to the wound.

"Hold that there" he said. "I'm afraid you're our prisoner now, but we don't treat our prisoners badly. You'll be taken to Carlisle and kept in isolation until this matter is resolved. If you choose to help us, we may see fit to return you to your own."

He stood and walked away, pausing when the man grunted something. Turning back Richard raised an eyebrow and the man met his eye for a moment, then looked away.

"Albany," was all he said and Richard nodded, the name not altogether surprising.

The Duke of Albany was James' brother, and while the Scots weren't quite as prone to fighting brother against brother for the crown, it was known to happen. It was likely Albany was remaining behind the scenes for now, which gave them an advantage. He'd make sure to get the information to Edward and maybe it would sway his own brother into action.

Francis and the others rode back to where they waited a short time later, three prisoners in tow, giving them five in all. Wounds were treated and several men were sent off to Carlisle with the Scots, while the rest prepared to return to their scouting camp. Richard waited until the men and prisoners were out of sight before jerking his head at Francis, indicating he follow.

The Last Winter Rose

"What is wrong with you?" Richard shouted, turning on Francis when they were far enough away to be out of earshot of their own men. Francis stood his ground, unwilling to back down, his arms crossed

"You shouldn't be fighting," he said simply, but his face was stony.

"I am as capable as the next man-" Richard started, but Francis interrupted him.

"But you're not," he snapped. "You're not and I have respected the you never told me, for years and years, but I won't anymore. You have a wife and a son, two adopted children, and all the people of the north who rely on you. Soldiers fight battles and leaders-"

"Lead," Richard snapped back.

He always suspected Francis has known something wasn't right, but they'd never quite spoken about it, just like there were things about Francis they had never quite spoken about. None of that ever mattered to Richard and he'd thought none of it had mattered to Francis.

"I can see you thinking," Francis said, crossing his arms. "You know I'm right."

"I proved I'm capable at Barnet, and Tewkesbury, and a dozen other skirmishes," Richard pointed out, and Francis sighed.

"I never said you weren't capable, did I?" he asked, and after a moment Richard looked away.

"No," he said softly. "You're just being overprotective."

Francis chuckled, reaching out to put his hand on Richard's shoulder, though he did it with care. Richard

229

had to fight a fond smile. Francis had always been more restrained with him, just like Anne. Anne…

"Did she-" he asked, the thought striking him like lightning.

"Threaten parts of me I'd very much prefer to keep intact, if I didn't watch out for you?" Francis laughed. "Yes, yes she did."

Richard laughed now, sighing as he shook his head, gripping Francis' arm briefly before leaning against a large rock, suddenly exhausted.

"Then I thank you for being such a good friend," he said, waving a hand at the space next to him. "But the Scots don't scare me."

"They bloody well scare me," Francis said, taking the space beside Richard and staring across the hills. "You're just mad."

Richard smiled, but his gaze was far away as he crossed his arms. Francis reached for a flask at his hip and after a good drink he passed it to Richard.

"The only thing I've ever been afraid of is losing everyone I love," Richard admitted quietly.

Francis had nothing to say to that, so he simply leaned his left shoulder against Richard's right, occupying the same place he had been for years, a shield Richard had never really stopped to think about. Francis was always on his right, a shadow that trailed his footsteps. They sat in silence, gazing at the warm green hills, each lost in their own thoughts, worlds apart despite how close they were.

The Last Winter Rose

"This is intolerable," Richard muttered, kicking the shoddy pallet that was meant to be his bed before he sat down on it carefully.

They were moving fast, trying to keep up with and catch the raiders, so they had to travel light. That meant everyone was using the same small tents and the cheapest, lightest cots that could be broken down and strapped two to a pack horse, eliminating the need for wagons. Most of the men slept on the ground.

"If we could just catch the bastards, we could be home before the snows," Francis muttered, rubbing his hands over his face. His hair was too long and his beard was nearly grown in. Richard sighed, rubbing the rough three weeks of growth on his own face. He'd been too tired for much the last few weeks, let alone shaving. Since the ambush in June, they'd had little luck in catching anyone.

"Damn Edward," he muttered. "Either he wants a war or he doesn't."

"Your brother doesn't care much for politics anymore," Francis said, collapsing onto a folding stool and leaning against the tent wall and the rock behind it.

Richard frowned. He'd last seen Edward in April, when they planned the campaign. He'd seen the changes for himself in the previous months and there was no tactful way to say it. Edward had grown fat and lazy, spending more time drinking or in bed with a mistress, than he did on the realm. It worried Richard, because if something happened, if Edward drank himself into an early grave, his son had not yet reached the age of majority. The prince would need a regent and everyone in the country knew how dangerous that was, especially with Henry Tudor and his pitiful claim to the throne lurking on the continent.

Francis had been at court as recently as six weeks ago and though Richard didn't want to know if Edward was worse, he asked anyway.

Francis shrugged, exhaustion heavy on his shoulders. "He seemed much the same," he told Richard. "Busy with his own pursuits and distracted beyond help. No one in the south seems particularly concerned with the north, it's too far away. Too abstract a concept for most who have never been farther than York. They don't know what it's like and can't comprehend the danger."

"I want to catch these bastards, before they retreat for winter," Richard said, shifting uncomfortably on the cot.

Francis frowned. "I'm not sure we can."

September was coming to a close and the weather was beginning to turn. If they didn't catch up to and confront the raiders in the next three weeks, they would melt back into the Scottish hills and any chance of catching them would be gone until spring.

"I am done with living in a tent," Richard muttered, exhausted.

Time dragged on and the weather grew colder. Richard finally returned home late in November, bringing what supplies he could to supplement them through what promised to be another hard winter. The harvest had been poor and their stores were depleted, but he brought enough grain to hold them through the worst of the cold months.

There was nothing from Edward for weeks and Richard settled himself in with his family, enjoying the time they had together. There had been far too little of it in recent years, and somehow Richard suspected there would be even less in the years to come. Trouble was brewing and not just on the northern border. He only hoped whatever happened, they would make it through.

1482

In early April, Alexander, Duke of Albany, declared his intent to take the throne from his brother, and Edward finally seemed to take a serious interest. Weeks of letters and negotiations followed, until in May they all met at Fotheringhay, the first time Richard had seen his brother in over a year.

Edward looked terrible. He was pale and exhausted and even heavier than he'd been. He was in no condition to lead an army and certainly not to fight. Worry tugged at Richard's heart when they sat in the evening playing chess and he could see Edward mind wasn't on the game at all. He seemed far away, lost somewhere in his thoughts. He wasn't the same man Richard had known all his life.

Richard tried to quell is own unease over the next weeks, but it was nearly impossible. Edward was withdrawn from him, and only attended negotiations a few times, until finally he signed a treaty with Albany, giving him support to take the Scottish throne. Then, in a blow that didn't surprise Richard at all after seeing Edward for himself, the English king returned to London.

Richard was fuming, and it wasn't until later that he learned his niece Mary, Edward's second daughter, had been ill and died that May while Edward was in the north. When he found out, his anger toward his brother died, replaced by a great wave of sadness. It was another black mark of loss on his family, but he had been commanded to lead in Edward's stead, and so he took the army, Ratcliffe, Francis, and Henry Percy at his side, and he invaded Scotland.

"We've captured the king," Ratcliffe said one day in late July, pulling his horse to a stop in front of Richard after charging up the line with the news. "We can end this now."

Richard frowned, his mare shifting under him nervously. He had the men, he had the numbers. He could sack Edinburgh and Roxburgh and be done with it, but he wasn't keen on the idea. He didn't want to spread devastation and cause massive loss of life, the people who lived in the city were just people.

"What about Albany?" Percy asked, and Ratcliffe shrugged.

"No word yet."

"All right," Richard muttered. "Prepare the troops to march, we'll head for Edinburgh. We won't attack until we know what the situation is, I don't want to raze the city unless there's no other choice, but with the king it's likely they'll surrender easily enough, or at least be open to negotiation."

Percy muttered something that Richard was almost sure was rude, but he didn't care. He was in command of Edward's army, not Henry Percy, and they would do this his way.

They camped for the night, reforming into an organised march and heading for the city. When they arrived they found no resistance, and within a week they were installed in the castle high on the royal mile and Albany was refusing to act any further.

"You said you wanted the crown," Richard grumbled, annoyed and exhausted, and Albany shrugged.

"My brother is the rightful king."

Richard's scowl deepened. This man was nothing but trouble. They'd been in meetings all day, now that the fighting had paused and the leaders had gathered. Per the treaty with Edward, Albany should have taken the crown and James would have been imprisoned for the rest of his natural life. Now it appeared that was no longer the case and they planned to install some form of interim government. At this point Richard didn't care.

"Our army will retreat and leave you to your own politics, but we have conditions," he said, looking between the brothers. James didn't seem all that interested in leading his people either, from the dull expression on his face.

It didn't matter to Richard, Edward wasn't interested in conquering Scotland, but reparations for

The Last Winter Rose

the raids and devastation must be made. All Richard wanted was to go home.

"Name your terms," Albany said, his demeanour much different now that he stood on his own soil beside his own king.

"For a start, the return of the dowery money paid for my niece, Cecily, in yearly instalments over the next five years," Richard scowled. Cecily had been promised to James' eldest son when she was just five years old and Edward had been paying her dowery since, but now he had determined the marriage wouldn't be taking place, at least as recently as Richard knew. The whole mess had changed twice in the last year alone.

"Agreed," James said without resistance, though Richard saw several men behind him shift, their faces angry. Clearly, they still wanted the marriage to take place, or they just wanted to keep the money in Scottish coffers.

"You'll pay reparations for your raids across our border, surrender Berwick to us, and all raids and incursions will cease at once," Richard continued, and the king nodded to each term. No one contradicted him.

Richard stared around at them, waiting for anyone to say anything, but no one did. Finally, he nodded.

"Very well. Documents will be drawn up. Once they have been signed and sealed and approved by King Edward, we will retreat."

Ratcliffe stepped up as Richard turned away, arms full of parchment, already speaking. Francis fell into step beside Richard as they left the room, frowning.

"That was too easy," he muttered, and Richard shrugged.

"As long as they sign the documents and keep to their promise, I don't care," he said quietly, walking into the yard where the sun shone with surprising strength. "I'm tired of this, it's Edward's problem now. We'll secure Berwick and then I'm finished."

Berwick surrendered without a fight, though a garrison had dug themselves in at the castle and refused to surrender until late in August. By the time it was done, Richard was beyond exhausted.

"I'm going home," he told his friends after the last of the Scottish troops had been removed from the castle and the town. "I'll see Edward and deal with this in the spring."

Francis nodded, sighing tiredly. Percy rubbed his beard, his bald head shining in the torchlight.

"They may try and take back Berwick over winter," he said, and Richard shrugged.

"They can try. As we saw, it's not an easy task. Dig your men in and hold it. You'll have supplies and fresh water, they'll have rain and snow and no game," he said, and Percy nodded.

"We'll hold the border," he promised.

The next morning Richard disbanded his men and left for Middleham. Francis accompanied him and they rode with just a few men and wagons packed with supplies Anne had asked for.

Six days later the sun had yet to set, but the sky had grown dark and a light rain had started as they'd climbed the hill from the village to the castle. The journey had been quick, and warm, the September sun bringing a dry heat that left them all sweating. The only thing Richard wanted was a hot bath and a bed, but there was still much to do before they could be settled for the evening. He tugged his hood farther over his face as the gate swung open and the rain started to come down harder.

"Greetings, lord," one of the guards called, though Richard wasn't sure who it was. He raised a hand anyway and followed Francis' horse through the gate, pausing to wait while the rest of the riders and the three wagons rolled into the yard.

Anne was waiting for them, standing in the cover of the gatehouse with Maggie at her side and Richard sighed as he stepped into her arms, holding her tightly.

"I'm glad you're back," Anne said quietly and Richard nodded. He pulled back far enough to lift Maggie up, holding her close. She sniffed, burying her face in his shoulder and Anne smiled.

"The boys?"

"Sleeping, they both have colds," Anne said. "They'll be fine," she assured him when he frowned.

"Boys are trouble," Maggie muttered, and Richard chuckled.

"Richard," Francis said, appearing at his elbow, and Richard turned. Francis took a moment to greet Anne, kissing her on the cheek with one hand on her elbow. "All the wagons are here and the men will see to the supplies. I have to go, there was a message waiting for me, from my mother."

"Go," Richard said at once, setting Maggie down and drawing his friend into a tight embrace. "Thank you for everything."

Francis nodded, returning the embrace tightly. He released Richard and hugged Anne before stooping and kissing Maggie's forehead.

"I'll see you soon, I hope," he smiled, and they watched as he mounted a fresh horse and rode into the night, disappearing into the rain and the darkness.

They entered the castle and Richard sighed as he sank into his seat in the hall, smiling when Anne fussed at him to eat, though in truth he was too tired. He was asleep almost as soon as his head touched his pillow that night and he slept well into the next afternoon. He was woken by both boys, freed from their room, climbing onto his bed and hugging him awake with laughter and joy.

He rested for a few days, sending messages out that he wasn't to be disturbed unless it was a matter of absolute urgency, or news directly from Edward, and then he took Anne and the children on the summer trip he'd promised years before.

They went to Barnard Castle first, a place Richard hadn't often been able to spend much time, and there

The Last Winter Rose

they enjoyed the warm weather. He smiled softly, watching the children playing and laughing. Anne was tucked against his side, no doubt dozing in the warmth of the sun. He gazed at the clouds, his mind wandering.

A shriek brought he attention back to the children and he felt Anne startle at his side. He looked just in time to see Edward trip and go tumbling on the grass. He was halfway to his knees in an instant, but Maggie was already there, picking Edward up and dusting him off, talking to him softly and wiping away his tears.

"You're not hurt, cousin," she said, ruffling his hair and looking at his hand. "The skin isn't even broken. You'll just have a nice bruise in the morning."

"Are you sure?" Edward asked, and Richard settled back into the grass, his arm tightening around Anne.

"I'm sure," Maggie nodded, holding out her hand to help Edward up. He looked at her hand for a moment then let her pull him to his feet as Ned ran up to them, no doubt wondering what the delay was. Moments later they were all running away laughing and Richard sighed.

"She's so like Isabel," Anne said softly, her voice both sad and proud. "Isabel was always so kind when she was a girl."

"I'm sorry we couldn't have our own girls," Richard said quietly, pressing a kiss to Anne's hair as he held her close. She sighed against him, her arms wrapped tightly around his waist.

"I love Maggie like my own," she whispered. "She's my blood, our blood."

Caitlin Sumner

"I feel the same," Richard admitted, and together they sat quietly, watching the three children playing as the sun warmed the summer sky above them.

They drifted, sitting together on that hot afternoon, a jar of sweet wine at the corner of the blanket they lay on, a plate of meats and cheeses and bread ready and waiting when little hands came searching for sustenance. There were even small sweet tarts that Richard had secreted under his cloak and when he presented them the children all screeched in delight.

Time slowed and the clouds rolled gently overhead and Anne dozed throughout the afternoon while Richard watched her fondly, one eye kept on the children as they played themselves into exhaustion. Edward was first, crawling between them and falling asleep almost instantly with his head pillowed on Anne's chest, her arms instinctively wrapping around him. Then Maggie yawned and curled herself into a tight ball in Richard's arms, most of her slight weight resting on his chest. Then Ned, who was fighting yawns desperately, finally lay down on Anne's skirt, using Richard's leg as a pillow, and soon they were all sleeping soundly. With a quiet chuckle so as not to disturb any of his family, Richard settled himself more comfortably and drifted off to sleep in the sun.

They toured across the northeast for the rest of the warm September and October, going to York, Sheriff Hutton, and Whitby to see the sea. The children were in awe of such a massive body of water and Richard knew he'd never forget the look on their faces when they saw

242

The Last Winter Rose

it for the first time. They returned to Middleham as November turned cold and had a boisterous Christmas celebration, opening their hall to anyone and everyone who wanted to join them. The castle had been ringing with songs and laughter well into the night, the townsfolk happy and warm and well fed, children underfoot at every turn until they were shooed out of the hall by mothers, sisters, or nurses, and put to bed.

Snow fell throughout December and January, locking them in a quiet, isolated space, away from the rest of the world. The borders were safe, the Scots had kept their side of the bargain for truce, and though Edward was once more sending letters about a full-scale invasion, for the moment Richard was ignoring him, instead embracing the quiet time with his family. Little did he know, it was the last time he would ever have such peace.

Part III - Reluctant King

April 15, 1483

There was nothing particularly strange about the day, nothing to indicate that Richard's world was about to come crashing down around him once again. The sun had risen in the east, Edward, Ned, and Maggie were underfoot in the kitchens as usual, Anne was about her tasks, and Richard was in the yard speaking to the smith about re-shoeing the new horses he'd brought back from Berwick-Upon-Tweed the previous autumn. It was, all in all, a perfectly normal day until the sound of hoofbeats broke through the calm air of late morning and the rider came through the gate, leaning heavily over his horse's neck.

"Message," he gasped, unable to raise his head from the neck of his horse. Richard was already moving toward him as Henry, one of the guards, reached for the horse and held him steady. "Message for his lordship."

"I'm here," Richard said, and the man sagged with relief, holding out a letter with a shaking hand.

"From London," he managed as Richard took the letter. He'd obviously come with haste and ridden hard through the night and morning. This was probably his fourth or fifth horse.

Richard gripped his shoulder as he slid to the ground on shaking legs and gestured toward the kitchens, seeing now that the messenger was a boy, likely no more than sixteen. He leaned heavily against his horse, still trying to catch his breath.

"Take rest and refreshments, your horse will be seen to," Richard told him, and the boy nodded gratefully.

The boy leaned on Henry as the guard took him inside while a stable hand led the exhausted horse slowly toward rest and water.

Richard stared down at the message in his hands, saw his brother's seal unbroken on the ribbon. What news was this, to come with such haste? If it was another call to war, he would not obey, he would not put his family in danger. With trepidation he broke the seal as he climbed the stairs to the hall, unfolding the paper.

It is my sad duty to bring to you the knowledge that your brother, the king, has died. He passed this 9th of April, peaceably. His son and heir, Edward, henceforth to be known as Edward V, is en route to London from Ludlow castle as I write. I have risked much in secreting the royal seal to use upon this letter, but I must warn you of the plots by the mother of the new king, and her kin, to take control and power over our good realm. I pray you hasten to London and take up the position of Lord Protector for the boy until he comes of age, and guide us away from the devices of the Lady Woodville, who would take the throne for herself in name of her son.

The Last Winter Rose

Ever Faithfully,
William Hastings

Richard staggered as he read the letter, dated the 13th. It was the 15th, and his brother was dead. His brother was dead and Hastings had stolen the royal seal to send Richard the news, because no one else would.

Six days. Edward had been gone for six days and it had been four before Hastings had sent him this urgent message. It hadn't escaped Richard's shocked mind that he'd had no other missives, that there might not have been direct news of his brother's death for weeks if Hastings hadn't acted. He knew Elizabeth Woodville was a shrewd and conniving woman, but he had never expected she would make such a clutch for power so quickly. Then again, he hadn't expected his brother to die so suddenly, or so young. Edward hadn't seemed well, but nothing indicated he wouldn't live another twenty or even thirty years.

Richard's feet carried him to his rooms, where Anne was folding the winter linens to be stored now that spring was on its way. She glanced up and saw the letter in his hand, but didn't take in his face.

"What news?" she asked, not pausing as she folded another cloth and set it on the pile. She looked up when Richard didn't answer and now saw his face was white and his hands were shaking. "Richard?"

"It's... he... Edward..." he managed to say, and Anne dropped her task and crossed the room to him, taking the letter from his hand and gently pushing him toward a chair as she read. He sank down, eyes vacant as he stared blindly toward the fire.

Anne's heart sank and she could feel her own colour drain as the words on the page made sense in her mind. Edward, the king, Richard's brother, was dead. Saying the words again in her head didn't make it any more real, but she knew it must be true.

"I must send to the lords," Richard said numbly, absently rubbing his hands on his thighs. He was already trying to think what came next, just to stop the thoughts of Edward. "I must take their oaths of allegiance to my nephew and bear them to London."

"Do you intend to become Lord Protector?" Anne asked, and he shook his head.

"I don't know, Anne, if the situation is that serious… if she is making a grab for power, if she intends to make her son a puppet king, then I feel it is my duty. But to leave you and the children…"

"Duty comes before all," Anne said quietly, gripping his shoulder. "You may be all that stands between us and another civil war."

"My father tried to stand between us and civil war," Richard muttered, still staring blankly even as his mind worked. "He tried to protect the people from Henry's insanity, he tried to make the right choice, and they killed him for it. Put his head on a spike next to my brother. My brother, who was only sixteen. Edmund did nothing wrong except for the fact that he was my father's son."

The Last Winter Rose

Anger was bubbling up in his chest as the words spilled out, anger and shock and despair.

Anne tossed the letter aside and knelt in front of Richard, putting her hands on his face and forcing him to meet her eyes.

"You are not your father," she said, giving him a little shake. "But you are as good a man as he was, if not better."

"Anne," Richard gasped, reaching for her hands, eyes wide with panic as a horrible thought occurred to him. "What if..."

"What if what?" she prompted when he didn't continue. He was shaking under her hands and she wanted nothing more than to sooth him, but she didn't know how.

"What if they try and make me king?" Richard whispered.

Anne took a sharp breath, terror filling her for a moment before she pushed it far away, stamping it down almost violently and burying it behind the iron walls she had built herself when they sold her to Margaret of Anjou's rat bastard son.

"Then you will be the best king England has ever seen," she said fiercely. "You will be strong and kind and fair and I will be by your side every step of the way. But we aren't there yet and we may never be." She took a breath and pressed her forehead to Richard's. "Now you can become protector like your father and you can do better. You can guide your nephew to become a great king and he will rule with wisdom and justice."

Caitlin Sumner

"But what if I fail?" Richard whispered.

"You will not fail," Anne told him, smiling. "Do you know why?"

"Why?"

"Because I love you."

Richard's laugh was wet and together they brushed away the tears that had fallen down his cheeks. He pulled Anne into his lap, holding her tightly, her presence helping to steady him.

"I love you so much," he breathed against her hair. "I can't do this without you."

Anne nodded, carefully settling against him. Most of her weight was on him and she didn't want to hurt him, but he was holding her so tightly that she relaxed against him, giving him the comfort he needed in the embrace.

"London is no place for the children," she said softly. "But we can bring them to Nottingham. I'll make the arrangements to get things settled here and I'll join you as soon as I'm able."

Richard nodded, his heart breaking. It seemed like he'd only just returned from fighting the Scots and now he was being ripped away again. He knew he'd have to leave the next morning, at the very latest.

He'd make for York first, send messages this evening to summon the lords to a council.

"I need Francis," he realised suddenly, thankful that Francis was already in the north. He wasn't about to walk into the viper's den without Francis at his side.

249

"Sit another moment," Anne said softly, running her hand through his hair when she sensed his panic rising again. "Breathe. Then we'll begin."

Richard nodded, his arms tightening around her as he finally let himself think of Edward.

He hadn't cried for his father, or Edmund. In truth he'd barely known his father and it had been a distant kind of hurt. He hadn't shed a tear for George either, George hadn't deserved it. He'd cried for Anne, his eldest sister, but she had been married and gone before he was old enough to know her. But Edward... he was the only real brother Richard had ever felt he had.

He thought of his mother, another of her children gone. He'd never have the kind of strength that she did, he'd never have the strength that Anne did to endure all the things that had happened to her. He felt like the least of them in the moment, a feeling he rarely let himself have. He held Anne close, his rock, his lifeline, and he wept.

Between the three of them, Richard, Anne, and Geoffrey, they had two dozen letters drafted by the early evening and Richard was carefully signing and sealing each one when Anne finally left the hall to pack his things for him. He'd leave in the morning, heading directly for York. He hoped to intercept Francis on the way, and he'd sent three messengers to try and locate him and tell him where to meet, but he wouldn't know if Francis received the message until he reached Ripon.

It was madness in the town when he arrived late the next afternoon, having left Middleham when the sky had barely begun to grow light. Clearly news of Edward's death had reached the people already, because the town centre was in chaos.

"Richard!" Francis shouted as soon as he spotted him, pushing through the crowded square and Richard immediately swung down from his horse, meeting Francis in a tight embrace. "I'm so sorry."

"I'm glad you're here," Richard said, pulling back to look over his friend. Francis looked well, if tired.

"I have rooms for the night," Francis said, nodding to the other men to follow.

It had been pure luck that the first messenger that Richard had sent had found Francis the same day, and he'd come straight to Ripon and rented most of the rooms and stables at the largest inn. That evening news of Edward's death had swept through the town and there had been near pandemonium since. He'd be unable to do anything, but wait for Richard to arrive.

Closed in a quiet room with hot food and good wine, Richard showed Francis Hastings' letter and Francis scowled, pacing in front of the fire uneasily.

"There's going to be trouble," he said, and Richard sighed.

"It looks like there already is," he pointed out, and Francis nodded.

"So what are you going to do?"

The Last Winter Rose

"I don't know," Richard said quietly, gaze on the dancing flames. "I really don't know."

April, 1483

They left before dawn, bound for York, arriving in the early afternoon. Many of the lords and landed nobles had already arrived and were waiting for Richard. It seemed many of them had left for York as soon as they'd heard the news of the king's death, a full two days before the news had come to Richard.

There was little dissent between them, which surprised Richard, and he found himself fully supported when he put forth Hastings' proposal that he become protector for his nephew until the boy came of age. Messages were dispatched and the young Edward, now styled Edward V, was riding in the company of his uncle Anthony Woodville, and his half-brother Richard Grey, and agreed to meet Richard at Northampton, rather than going directly to London. The plan was they would then all continue to London together, but when Richard's party arrived on the 23rd, Edward was no longer with them.

"The king was to meet us here," Richard said, refusing to break Anthony's stare across the room after they'd been shown in. He'd known the man a long time and he could see in Anthony's eyes that he was up to something. When they'd arrived at the arranged inn in

The Last Winter Rose

Northampton to find that only Anthony, Grey, and Thomas Vaughn, Edward's household chamberlain, had arrived, Richard had been immediately suspicious.

"He felt more comfortable continuing on toward London," Anthony said, bowing his head in apparent deference. "We can catch up with him easily enough. We would be honoured, if you would join us for the evening meal."

Richard kept his face placid as he nodded, when really all he wanted to do was scowl at Anthony. He'd always had a hard time trusting Elizabeth's elder brother, and since George's demise he'd grown ever more suspicious.

Dinner was a stilted affair, full of small talk and fake pleasantries. Nothing of much import was discussed, and Richard didn't try to push the conversation, instead using the time to plan his next move. They parted ways for the night and by the time he went to sleep, a plan was fully formed in his mind.

The next morning, they gathered near the edge of town. Quiet orders passed to a few trusted men, and Richard mounted his horse, waiting. Francis was already mounted and watchful at his right side. A few minutes later, as the sun was rising fully, Anthony and Grey rode up with their small group of men, Vaughn trailing at the back.

"Shall we, my lord?" Anthony asked, with the falsest smile Richard had ever seen.

Richard nodded.

"Arrest them," he said coldly, and men immediately moved forward to seize Anthony Woodville, Thomas Vaughn, and Richard Grey. "Lord Rivers, you are charged with treason and sedition against the crown. You will be held, pending trial, and your lands and titles are hereby revoked. Sir Vaughn, you are charged with the theft of the royal treasury in the year of our lord, fourteen hundred and sixty-one and will be held pending trial. Lord Grey, you are not formally charged with any transgression at this time, however you will be held in confinement with your uncle until such time as it can be deemed there are no charges to be brought against you."

"What, exactly, are you doing?" Francis whispered quietly as the three men were led away silently. Richard had not let him in on the reasoning behind this plan and he didn't like surprises.

"Anthony killed my brother," Richard said. "George," he clarified when Francis raised an eyebrow. "I have yet to prove it, but I know he acted on the orders of his sister and had George murdered before Edward could have his sentence reduced to imprisonment."

Francis whistled lowly. "And Vaughn? That's a thin accusation, one Edward pardoned him for. After all, the money he stole belonged to Henry."

"It keeps him occupied for the moment, until I know I can trust him," Richard shrugged. "The same goes for Richard Grey. Until everything in London is settled, I need them out of the way so they can't cause trouble."

"Smart," Francis muttered. "We'd better go, we need to reach the king."

Richard only nodded, turning his horse south and digging in his heels.

"Why have you arrested my uncle and my brother and the head of my household?" Edward asked, face calm, but voice angry. Richard looked at him for a long time, silently gaging him. He hadn't seen Edward since he was a young boy, or ever really spoken to him, but now he was on the cusp of being a man, and he was a king.

"Lord Rivers committed crimes that must be punished," he said finally. "Your brother, I have suspicions, but no charges. He is safe, but he will be held until he can be cleared or charges can be brought. Your chamberlain does not have my trust."

"And what do you want with me?" Edward said quietly.

Richard tilted his head, then indicated the chairs waiting for them. Edward nodded and they both sat, watching each other across the table.

"I want you to take your rightful place, and I want to keep your mother's influence at a minimum," he said truthfully. "Her ambitions could interfere with a smooth transition of power, so for the moment…"

"I understand."

They watched each other silently until Edward spoke again.

"I've been told tales of you, uncle, that you want the throne for yourself."

Richard snorted. "It's a shame I can't have your uncle executed for egregious lies," he muttered. He caught the look on Edward's face and sighed. "I can tell you, nothing is, or ever has been, further from the truth. You are my brother's eldest son, the rightful heir to the throne, and I will see you on that throne and act as protector until you reach the age of majority. After that, my only wish is to return north, to my home."

Edward seemed to consider this for a long moment, then he nodded.

"Very well," he agreed. "My father always spoke highly of you. I will trust your judgement, and follow your advice."

"Thank you," Richard relaxed slightly in his seat. Having the young Edward's trust meant a great deal.

They entered London a week later, under the cover of darkness at Francis' suggestion, making their way to Westminster through back roads and dark alleyways. Tomorrow Edward would enter the city with his men, but tonight there would be a late council meeting.

A group of men was waiting for them at the gates of the palace as they rode in, light rain coming down and darkening the paving stones to almost black. Richard

The Last Winter Rose

dismounted and quickly scanned the men, picking out two secretaries, a personal dresser, and the lord of the bedchamber, each with the insignia of their station clearly visible.

"Have letters been sent to our allies abroad?" Richard asked without preamble, pulling off his cloak and passing it to the footman trailing him before he tugged at his gloves. "Have they been informed of Edward's death?"

"Yes, lord," one of Edward's secretaries said, the short man half trotting to keep up with Richard's stride. "His grace Edward passed from this world and into the arms of God on the 9th day of April. On the 11th letters were sent to the courts of France and Spain, to his grace's sister in Burgundy, to his holiness Pope Innocent in Rome. Further messages were sent throughout our land in the days that followed. A letter has also been dispatched by ship to Ireland, with instructions to continue on to Scotland and deliver the news."

"Very good," Richard nodded, turning a corner sharply. The secretary, Richard didn't know this one's name as he'd never met him before, skidded and nearly hit the wall before he hurried to catch up, the others trailing doggedly behind. "I have brought the signed oaths of the lords of the northern lands pledging fealty to my nephew, Edward's first born son, and I will see the council tonight."

"Tonight, lord?" the man stammered. It was already well past the midnight hour.

258

Caitlin Sumner

"Tonight," Richard nodded. "Rouse them from their beds and have my things taken to my rooms. I'll be in the king's council chamber. Where is the dowager queen?"

"She has left the palace, lord," the secretary told him nervously. "She resides in sanctuary with her daughters and her younger son, the prince Richard."

Richard nearly rolled his eyes. Of course she was. Whenever there was any turmoil, Elizabeth ran for the vault under Westminster Abbey at the first whisper. She may not even have left to attend Edward's burial at Windsor.

Richard made his way to the council chamber and took a seat in the chair Edward had so often occupied, sitting casually, but with authority. Whatever this meeting brought, he would not show them how uncomfortable he was in this new role. He'd been a member of this council, both in person and in name, since he was seventeen years old. He had every right to be here and to wield this authority.

He took just a moment to reflect the stark change in his feelings since the weeks he took Edward place while he was imprisoned by their cousin Warwick. It seemed like a lifetime ago.

The councillors trickled in one by one over the next hour, some dressed, some with a robe thrown over their night clothes. They all stopped and stared for a moment at Richard, before moving to take their seats. When the last of them had appeared, Richard stood.

259

The Last Winter Rose

"Gentlemen, I am here to inform you that I intend to take up the role of protector and nominal regent for my nephew, King Edward, until such time as he comes of age and takes full control of the kingdom and all its dealings. I have already met with the new king, and he is in complete agreement with this, and will enter the city tomorrow in royal procession and proceed here to Westminster to take up his duties."

Richard waited, and to his surprise they each nodded, until every man around the table had indicated his assent.

"What of Lord Rivers?" one man asked at the far end of the table. "You arrested him and his nephew, as well as the king's chamberlain."

"I did," Richard nodded as eyes turned to him again. He was unsurprised that news had already reached London. "Lord Rivers will be tried on charges of conspiracy and murder. Sir Vaughn is, I suspect, under the direct influence of the Woodville family and has been removed from a position of power as a precaution, the same as Richard Grey. They will not be harmed."

"You speak of murder charges, who, exactly, is the Lord Rivers accused of murdering?" another voice asked, and Richard had to suppress a smile.

"My brother, the Duke of Clarence," he said, and the group went silent. He smirked, knowing he had shocked them all beyond anything they were expecting.

If nothing else came of this whole mess, he was at least going to see one piece of justice done. He hadn't trusted George, he hadn't even particularly liked his brother at the end, but he hadn't supported his execution, had argued against it, despite everything George had done. And Anthony had murdered him, on Elizabeth Woodville's order. Richard was sure of it.

"If there's nothing else," he said, and one by one the councillors shook their heads. Either they truly had no protests, or they were too surprised at being woken in the middle of the night, and didn't have their wits about them. That was all Richard needed for now, and with a nod he left the chamber and the councillors to their own, inevitable, discussions. If he was going to do this, he would do it with strength and surety, and not make the mistakes his father did.

June 8, 1483

"Edward's children are to be declared illegitimate."

Richard froze at Stillington's words and he felt the room tilt around him.

"Lord," the Bishop began, seeing the look that fallen over Richard's face, but his words were abruptly interrupted.

"I will not hear another word," Richard snapped, turning his back on the lords and the Bishop.

"Hear it or not, my lord, it will be law. Parliament intends to pass the decree within the next fortnight. The marriage between your brother and the Lady Elizabeth-"

"The dowager queen," Richard said, interrupting Stillington again. He may dislike her, but he still afforded her the proper courtesy.

"The marriage could never be proved," Stillington said defiantly, not wavering under Richard's glare. "And I myself married your brother to the Lady Eleanor Talbot."

Convenient he never said anything before today, Richard thought. Eleanor Talbot had died years before and had never made claims while she lived, not that Richard knew about, even marrying Sir Thomas Butler.

"The boy Edward is king, as his father before him," Richard said aloud, rounding back on them and meeting the hard stares around the room, already knowing this wasn't a fight he was going to win. They were going to put him on the throne, take the crown from his nephew and put it on his head, and he couldn't stop them. He'd done everything right and still, somehow, he was going to become the last thing he ever wanted to be.

"His legitimacy cannot be proven," the Bishop said. "Yours can. You are the next in line should your brother have sired no legitimate children. The king lived in a state of bigamy and no child of Elizabeth Woodville will be king."

Richard scowled and turned away again. This was not what he wanted. This was never what he wanted. This had been his worst fear since he was nine years old. He took a breath, clenching his hands, because he knew this was a risk when he came south. He'd just never expected it to happen. He knew there were plenty out there that didn't want a boy on the throne, not after how king Henry turned out, but he'd thought they were convinced to allow Edward to rule under a protector until he came of age in four short years.

"I will not take the throne," he said tightly, but even as he said it, he knew he'd have no other choice.

"Your mother has made it clear to me that she will reveal the truth of your brother's birth, if you do not accept this charge," Stillington said and Richard felt himself go cold as he glanced at the bishop.

The Last Winter Rose

"What truth," he asked, voice barely above a whisper, words barely a question. He was pleased to see Stillington took a half step back at the venom in his words, but he suspected he already knew what his mother had threatened to say, though she'd made no mention of it when last they spoke.

"She will confirm before a tribunal that your brother Edward was not the son of your father, that he was sired by another man and was therefore, a bastard."

"Get out," Richard said without hesitation, and after a moment, Stillington left. Ratcliffe hustled several other lords out of the room, leaving just himself, Francis, and Richard, who resisted the urge to throw his wine cup across the room.

"She would put the entire weight of this country on my shoulders to keep it from the hands of a boy not yet turned thirteen, who is quick of mind and strong of arm, well educated, well trained. A boy who will make a fine warrior and a better king. She would do this to me, all because she cannot countenance the boy's mother," Richard seethed with disgust.

He was backed into a corner now, with few options. Either he took the throne willingly and displaced the boy, allowed his nieces and nephews to be declared illegitimate and potentially start a war with Elizabeth and all the Woodvilles, or allow his mother to slander herself in front of the nation, and have to take up the throne anyway when his brother was declared illegitimate himself.

264

"You could take your family and flee to France," Francis suggested, trying to lighten the room slightly. Richard snorted and shook his head.

"An option, but perhaps not a good one," Ratcliffe said quietly. He'd always been the more stoic of the two and Richard was glad for both their company.

"I don't want to think of this now," Richard said softly, rubbing his temples. It had been a long few weeks effectively ruling the country on behalf of his twelve year old nephew. He'd been waiting for Anne, but he hadn't heard if she'd even left Middleham yet. He hoped she would come soon, because he couldn't do this alone. He needed her blunt sense, especially now.

"I don't see as you have much choice," Ratcliffe said, steepling his fingers in front of his face. "It seems you will be our new king."

"Damn George," Richard cursed quietly as he stared at the rough wood of the table, the room around him dim and hazy. "Damn him to hell."

"While I'm inclined to agree with you on that sentiment," Francis said, as he took a seat at the empty council table. "Would you really rather have had George as king?"

Richard grimaced, leaning on the table and letting his head hang between his shoulders. "No," he said quietly. Not George. Never George.

"Then it seems we have only one way forward." Ratcliffe said, and Richard nodded, sinking into his own seat.

The Last Winter Rose

"Where is Catesby?" he asked, opening his eyes again in time to see Ratcliffe frown.

"France, last I heard," he said, and Francis swore under his breath as Richard pinched the bridge of his nose.

He needed Catesby right now, perhaps more than any of them, because Catesby was a spy who had a network of spies throughout England, France, Spain, even in Rome. He would be able to tell Richard what was happening anywhere in England or on the continent and Richard would be able to trust that the information was accurate.

"Francis, can you find him?"

Francis scratched his chin with a frown then nodded tentatively.

"I think so. It might take a few weeks, it would be faster if I went myself."

"Then go," Richard said, because as much as he needed Francis here, he needed Catesby just as badly and he needed him as soon as possible.

"I'll arrange it," Francis nodded. "I won't be able to leave until the end of the month, but I'll start asking around tonight."

"I need to speak to Elizabeth," Richard muttered half to himself and Ratcliffe and Francis glanced at each other.

"She'll be informed," Ratcliffe said, but Richard shook his head.

"She'll never believe me, but I need to tell her this isn't what I wanted," he sighed. "She needs to hear it from me, even if it makes no difference."

Francis shook his head with a wry smile. "You're fighting a losing battle, my friend. At least wait until it's official. Let me exhaust a few more resources."

Richard just nodded, sinking back in his chair with a heavy sigh as he gazed out the window, lost in thought. He knew Francis would try to find some recourse, but he also knew there was none. He'd see Elizabeth soon, but first he needed to see his mother.

"Mother," Richard stared as he stormed into her sitting room the next day, but she raised a hand before he could speak any further.

"I will not have my mind changed by you, or by anyone," she said, and her eyes were furious as she stared him down.

"Then tell me, at least tell *me*, that it's not true," Richard said, taking his normal seat across from her. "Tell me this is a political move, a lie to keep Elizabeth Woodville's son off the throne."

"Will it make you feel any better?" Cecily asked, and Richard returned her glare, angry with his mother for perhaps the first time in his life.

"Of course it won't, mother, but I want to know which is the truth and which is the lie. Was Edward my full brother or not?"

The Last Winter Rose

"Of course he was," Cecily spat. "I never gave myself to anyone but your father, not that it's any business of yours. But I will not see that whore's brat on the throne. I will see you, the wisest and kindest of my sons. I will see you bring this cold, broken kingdom into the light, I will see you chase away our shadows where your father and brother failed."

"I don't want to be king!" Richard shouted, standing and pacing the room. "I never wanted to be king!"

"What you want doesn't matter!" Cecily yelled in return, and Richard nearly took a step back. He'd never seen his mother so angry, it was like she was someone he didn't even know. "This is what is right for the realm, for the people! And this is what will happen."

He stared at her for a long moment and finally her face softened and she reached a hand out for him. He came to her slowly and took her hand as he sat beside her.

"I'm sorry," she said quietly, reaching up to brush his curls back from his face. "I know this isn't what you want, I know this isn't what you would choose. I know it's the last thing you want, but Richard, this has to happen. She killed your brother, she as good as killed your cousins, and if you hadn't been so well entrenched in the north and protected by its strength, I have no doubt she'd have tried to kill you too, long before now."

"All I ever wanted was quiet," Richard shook his head, looking away. "Now you'd put me in a corner I cannot escape from."

"You may not like it, my son," she said softly. "But it's where you were always meant to be."

Somehow, Richard doubted that.

June 11, 1483

"Richard," Francis said quietly, and Richard turned so Francis could lean in and speak quietly in his ear. What he heard made his face light up with joy and he barely kept himself from smiling widely.

"My lords," he said, straightening up. "I'm afraid I'm going to have to leave you, unless there is any highly pressing business?"

There was a pause, then several heads shook in the negative.

"In that case, I have other business this afternoon," Richard said, allowing a smile to touch his lips. "My wife has arrived."

The councillors bowed as he left the room and he heard Francis chuckle as he followed, though he dropped back as they walked. He hurried down the hall, spotting her just inside the doors, her cloak still on her shoulders as she directed several footmen to pile chests filled with both her things and his along the side of the entryway.

"Anne," he called as he approached, and she turned, smiling as she hurried toward him and wrapped her arms around his neck, as his circled her waist. He lifted her off her feet and she made a sound of surprise as he set her back down, ignoring how it pulled at his back. He was too glad to see her, too happy to hold her.

"Thank God you're here," he whispered against her hair, holding her tight.

"I came as quickly as I could," she smiled, overjoyed to see him again after almost two months. "I made sure the children are safe in Nottingham and then came straight here."

Richard sighed, relieved. He hadn't wanted any of them, especially Edward, so far away. He wished they could come here, but he didn't think it was safe in London. Nottingham had been Anne's idea and he'd been too distraught to do more than trust her with the choice. "Thank you," he said, sighing, already feeling some of the weight lifting from his shoulders. Anne pulled back gently and examined him, brushing his hair out of his face.

"You've let your hair go again," she said with a soft smile, and he laughed, catching her hands and pressing kisses to her palms. "The letter found me on the road," she added softly, and Richard nodded. He'd written to her as soon as he'd learned they planned to put the crown on his head.

"Come, I'll show you our rooms," he said, keeping her hand in his as he led her through the palace and to the large set of rooms that had been given to him when he arrived in the city. He supposed they'd be moved to the king's chambers if he wasn't able to stop them crowning him, but for now he bolted the door and swore the next few hours were just for them.

The Last Winter Rose

Richard sank into a chair in front of the fire, which was roaring despite it being into summer now and warm in London. He couldn't remember a time when his back didn't ache, the pain like a shadow that followed him everywhere, the only relief coming from warmth.

"I should have stayed in the north," he sighed, burying his head in his hands and staring into the fire. The joy at seeing Anne had faded quickly into the morose terror that had sat heavy on his shoulders for the last several days. "I should never have come to London."

"They would have tried to crown you regardless," Anne said gently, brushing her hand through his hair soothingly as she came to stand beside him. She'd blanched when she first read his letter, but she'd forced herself to carry on, settling the children at Nottingham with trusted servants and continuing on to London as fast as she was able.

"It would have been easier to refuse," he muttered. "What am I to do? If I don't accept the declaration that the boys are illegitimate, my own mother will come before parliament and admit that my brother was conceived adulterously. It doesn't matter that it isn't true, and she's told me herself that it isn't, but she'll do it anyway. Buckingham would like nothing more than to see Hastings executed, Ratcliffe and Francis are barely keeping the peace in the city, and after all that, there is still Margaret Beaufort and her Tudor son just waiting for their moment to strike. I'm surrounded on all sides by enemies who are desperate to take a crown I never wanted."

Anne didn't know what to say. She'd been at the edge of a fight for the crown all her life, a pawn for her father to use. It had been such a relief to them both when they were able to retire to Middleham and leave politics behind, and now here they were, back in the centre of it.

"Tell me what to do," he whispered. "Tell me the right thing to do."

Anne was silent for a long time, then she cupped his cheek, tilting his face up to meet his eyes, searching his face.

"Take the crown," she said softly. "Take it before more dishonour is heaped on your family. Be a wise, kind, just king. Be the king that we need, the king that can bring us back together and end this fighting."

"You have far more faith in me than I have in myself," he smiled sadly at her, laying his hand over hers. "And I love you for it."

"You are the best man I've ever known, Richard," she whispered to him. "And I will be by your side as long as I live."

June 13th

Things were moving fast. It had been five days since Stillington announced that Edward's children were illegitimate and Richard would be king, and every waking moment had been spent in meetings. Richard was waiting for the councillors now, a plate of food growing cold at his elbow, barely touched. He was seriously considering abandoning them to their constant squabbles and going back to bed when Francis and Ratcliffe burst into the room.

"What is this?" Richard asked, taking the paper Francis thrust at him. The words on the page made his stomach turn and he swayed where he stood. "Is this true?"

Francis stared at the message for a long time and Richard could almost see the thoughts whirling around his head.

"It may not be," he spoke at last, "but you can't afford not to act."

"This says there is about to be an assassination attempt," Richard waved the paper, Catesby's handwriting messy and hurried. "Where is his information from? Isn't he in France?"

"Rumour says he's back in England," Ratcliffe said, glancing out the door where they could all hear approaching voices.

"I haven't been able to track him down, but he's definitely here," Francis nodded. "He must trust his source to send you this."

Richard looked at the message, a few simple words scrolled across a grimy piece of paper.

There will be an assassination attempt. Among those suspected, Hastings, Stanley, Morton, Rotherham. Use caution.

"He could have been more specific," Richard muttered, gesturing two of the guards at the door forward. "Francis."

Francis nodded and took the guards aside, not needing Richard to speak to know what he wanted. The men were quickly informed of the names they were to act on and moments after he finished, the councillors filed into the room, talking amongst themselves. They fell silent as they became aware of Richard's hard stare and then began to shift nervously.

"Search them," Richard ordered into the silence and Francis moved forward with the guards at his back.

"What is the meaning of this?" Hastings demanded, as he and several others were surrounded and searched.

"Blade!" Francis shouted a moment later and Richard could just see through the mess of people that Hastings had drawn a dagger, as had Bishop John Morton. The room erupted in chaos and Richard lost sight of who was who in the mess of dark fabric.

"Take them out of here!" he called over the shouting, trying to bring back order. This was getting out of control faster than he could keep up with and he was already losing his tenuous grip on the councillors.

The next moments were chaos. When silence finally fell again it was a taught silence, no one knowing what to say or do. In the struggle, Hastings had been stabbed, and he lay on the floor, eyes staring wide at the ceiling, his blood seeping out onto the carpet. He was dead.

Thomas Stanley was staring wide eyed and didn't struggle when the guards recovered themselves and dragged him, John Morton, and Thomas Rotherham from the room. Other members of the chamber muttered among themselves, all looking toward Richard.

"Reliable information was brought to me of an attempt on my life," he said to their stares, tossing Catesby's paper on the table. "I wanted no blood shed today," he continued, watching as Hastings' body was removed and a cloth laid over the bloodstain. "We will resume."

After a few mutterings the men settled in their seats, ignoring the four very noticeable gaps spread around the table, and resumed the business of the day.

Richard hardly heard a word of it, lost in his own thoughts. Ratcliffe took up his place behind Richard's left shoulder, nearly as tall as Edward had been and built like a bear, intimidating in the extreme. Francis returned some time later and whispered to Richard that the men who had been arrested were in the Tower, awaiting interrogation. Richard nodded and steepled his hands together, trying to listen to what was being said around him.

He had to regain control, before everything unraveled under his feet and they drowned in the mire of power-hungry men.

June 22, 1483

"I'll speak to her alone," Richard said, and Francis nodded, pulling the bolt and levering the heavy door open enough to allow Richard to pass. He set himself in front of the door where he could move quickly if there was any trouble, and where he could hear the conversation. Richard knew Francis was listening, he'd asked him to, so there would be some witness to the words exchanged between himself and the former queen.

Richard took in the arched curve of the undercroft as he walked down the hall, boots clicking on the smooth stone as he approached the wooden wall that had been built to create a private area for the former queen and her children. The door swung open as he approached and he stopped as she came out alone, though he could see several faces behind her in the open doorway.

"Bess, shut the door," Elizabeth said, and after a scuffle the door swung shut and one of the younger children started crying. "Have you come to gloat at me?" she asked, eyes cold.

"Why should I do that?" he said, genuinely confused. Did she think that he wanted to become king?

The Last Winter Rose

Did she think he was that ambitious? Of course she did. Her own ambitions meant she understood nothing else.

"You make a mockery of your brother," Elizabeth hissed. "You make a mockery of me."

"Do you think I had a choice in this?" Richard asked, waving a hand around himself to indicate the events that had taken place in the last weeks that had led to today. "I never disbelieved Edward or you about your marriage, I believe your son is the rightful ruler, but what can I do? Parliament has today declared your children bastards and all but forced me onto the throne. My own mother contrived to keep your son from the throne by threatening to tell the world that my brother, your husband, was a bastard!"

"They may hate me, but my boy is still Edward's son," she said. "Even if you cannot make him king, make him your heir-"

"They won't allow it while I have a living, true born son," Richard interrupted. He'd already tried that, tried anything to return his nephew to his rightful place. "I am sorry, I truly am. This was not how I wanted it," he said ruefully, and Elizabeth fell silent. Finally, she took a shuddering breath.

"Every day, I wake alone. I'm surrounded by my girls, but I feel so alone without him. Everything is falling apart around me, and now there is no future for my children."

"I will do everything in my power to protect you and them," Richard said, taking a step closer. "Would you doubt that? You know me, Elizabeth, you have known me since I was twelve years old. All I have ever cared about was my family. I'm not like George, I won't throw it away for power."

"But you'll take that power anyway, handed to you on a gold platter," she sneered, and Richard sighed. They were silent for a long moment, then Elizabeth's eyes suddenly grew wide.

"It was true," she muttered, gaze hard.

"What was true?" Richard asked, a feeling of unease crawling up his spine as he locked his hands behind his back, one hand around the other wrist.

"The prophecy. It was never George, it was you. The Duke of Gloucester," she spat his title like venom and Richard went cold, speaking before he could think.

"You killed my brother on a bit of mad superstition?" he demanded, anger swelling fast and hot in his chest. He'd always known she was to blame for it, but...

"I killed your brother because he aided the Earl of Warwick in murdering my father, my brother. Because he threatened me, threatened my children. I should have done the same to you."

Richard gripped his wrist behind his back so hard he could feel his bones grind together as he tried to rein in his anger. That she had the temerity to admit it aloud... he was within his rights to kill her himself right this moment.

"Be assured," he finally said quietly. "You will have no such chance with me. I am not as single minded or as power hungry as either of my brothers. I am taking the

The Last Winter Rose

crown, accepting the crown, for my son, for my nieces and nephews, be they Edward's children or George's. I am accepting the crown for England, because I swear, so long as I live and breathe I will not see that Tudor bastard take this country and tear it apart. So long as I live and breathe, the House of York will rule and care for this country and all its people."

Her face pinched as she sucked a breath in through her nose, but he'd already turned and walked away. Let her rot in Westminster's catacombs. He already had guards to stop her escape and check any communication, but he was going to double it now.

The boys would have to be moved. They weren't safe someplace as obvious as the Tower, where they had been for their protection since May. They would be vulnerable if he sent them north to Middleham, and it would put his own son in danger if he sent them to Nottingham, so that was no option. No, he needed them close, in case someone tried to use them in some way. They would either be harmed, removed to strengthen his rule, or they would be put at the head of an army to undermine and dethrone him. He knew both sides would want the princes for their own purposes, and he had so few he could trust. He couldn't even trust those who supported giving him the crown, not with the safety of his nephews. He simply couldn't afford to trust them.

He could send the boys to Francis, who had no children of his own, but who was currently fostering three boys and a girl at his estate. It wouldn't raise suspicions much if Francis were to take two more orphans in, two princes with disguised identities. The boys were dangerous in the extreme, but they were his brother's children, his blood, and he would do everything he could to protect them.

And Elizabeth, he didn't know what to do about her or her five daughters, all claiming sanctuary under Westminster Abbey, along with two of her sisters and half a dozen odd servants. There was nothing he could do, except try and negotiate so they would leave of their own free will. He would protect the girls as best he could, for the same reason he would protect their brothers. Contentious as their mother was, they were his family.

"What happened?" Francis asked, as he fell in step at Richard's right shoulder, the same place he'd taken to remaining as often as he could since they'd first come to London all those years ago. He waited at Richard's side as if he expected an assassin to come after his friend. It was not an unprecedented suspicion, especially now, especially after the mess with Hastings, but sometimes Richard thought he hovered too close.

"I won't speak of it here," Richard muttered, as they left the abbey and he went to his horse. "But we must speak tonight, alone."

Francis nodded as they mounted and rode back to the palace. They could very well have walked, but apparently a king didn't walk, even if it was barely more than a few dozen yards, nor did he go anywhere without half a dozen men at arms.

The Last Winter Rose

Though it was late there were still duties for Richard when they returned to the palace. He was not even crowned, yet it seemed everything needed his approval or signature. In the morning, he swore he was delegating most of the day-to-day tasks to Ratcliffe. He could assign duties as he saw fit and run the king's household. There was no need for Richard to personally approve what meals the kitchen would serve him throughout the week, he didn't care, as long as the food was hot.

He entered his rooms to find the bedroom door securely shut and Edward's former master of the bedchamber waiting with a stack of papers at the table by the fireside. Richard suppressed a sigh and crossed the room, keeping his voice quiet so as not to disturb Anne, who was likely already asleep. She was still tired from her journey south and the weeks it took to arrange.

Francis disappeared briefly while Richard was signing the stack of papers and listening to the man drone on about the daily responsibilities of the king. He soon returned with a tray loaded with food and a jug of ale, shooing the obsequious little man out and barring the door. Blessed silence descending on the sitting room as Richard heaved a sigh. He still hadn't taken Edward's old chambers, but he suspected he'd be forced to soon.

"Eat," Francis said, as he dragged a chair over and sat across from Richard, being sure to keep his voice quiet. Richard heaved a weary sigh, but reached for the nearest bread roll without complaint, accepting a cup of wine and a slice of cold beef and some cheese when Francis shoved them toward him.

282

They ate their fill in silence as Richard thought, trying to find the best way to broach the subject of the princes with his friend.

"I must ask something of you, something that may put you and your family in grave danger," he said finally, and Francis nodded, face placid. There wasn't much he wouldn't do for his friend and king, so he simply waited, the crackling of the fire the only sound in the otherwise silent room.

Richard took a breath, then clasped his hands in front of his mouth. "My brother's sons must be hidden," he said quietly. "You know I would have had Edward take his father's place as king, but since they have been declared illegitimate and I have no power to restore them, that has become impossible. I fear there are others who will use them or harm them, and I would see them protected. I would hide them with you at Minster Lovell, if I can. I would keep their identities hidden, and spread word that they've been sent north, as well as that they're being housed in the Tower, a deception to keep them from being easily tracked."

Francis was silent for a long moment. "You think the boys will keep their silence? They're young, but they understand who they are, and they are proud," he pointed out.

Richard sighed, leaning on the table and staring at the candle. "I don't know. I haven't spoken to them yet. I hope they're smart enough to realise it's in their best interests to simply vanish, to have a normal life."

The Last Winter Rose

"I will happily take them and protect them," Francis said. "But you might speak to them first. Be sure they won't betray themselves at the first turn."

"I will," Richard muttered. "Can you see they're brought here tomorrow morning?"

"Of course," Francis said gently. "But only if you agree to sleep."

Richard chuckled, but he agreed readily, exhaustion heavy on him as he sank into bed after the door shut quietly behind Francis and he locked it securely. He was asleep in moments.

June 23rd

Richard approached his nephews, both of whom were watching him cautiously. He waved at them to sit as he sank into a chair and after a moment both of them sat on the opposite side of the table. Richard clasped his hands together and stared at them for a long moment before he sighed.

"I am sorry," he said, glancing first at Edward, then Richard. "It's likely you haven't been told much because of your age, but the truth is this was never what I wanted. Bishop Stillington has convinced parliament that your mother and father were never legally married in the eyes of the Church, making you and all of your sisters illegitimate."

"Bastards," young Richard said quietly, and Edward hushed him.

Richard nodded stiffly to his nephew. "Yes, that is a word for it. Not one I would use, but it is what most people would say."

"They made you king," Edward said, and Richard nodded again. Both recalled the conversation two months before when Richard had made his feelings on the idea that he wanted the throne quite clear.

"Against my express wishes," he said tightly. "When I was not much older than you, before you were born, I was your father's heir for a few months. It was the worst time of my life, the dread the something would happen to him and I would become king. I never wanted a crown, I never wanted power. I wanted a simple life."

"But you've always been a prince," young Richard said, obviously confused.

"Being born to something doesn't make you who you are," his uncle said. "It just takes away your choices. I would see you on the throne, Edward, but the people have been thoroughly convinced by the Bishop. They won't support you, and short of a war, there is nothing any of us can do about it."

"So you'll be king?" Edward asked, and Richard nodded, frowning.

"You know of Henry Tudor?" When both boys nodded Richard continued. "He sits in France, waiting for England to weaken, waiting for his moment to sail across the sea and take the throne. If we are fighting each other for the crown, it will give him every opportunity to plunge us into a war worse than fought when I was a boy. Thousands will die."

The Last Winter Rose

"You have a better chance of keeping him at bay," Edward nodded, wise beyond his years. He looked tired, exhausted in a way no twelve year old prince should be. "I understand," he said quietly.

"I know I'm asking much of you," Richard said to them, splitting his gaze equally between the brothers. "But you must go into hiding. You must give up your old life and your old names, for your own safety and that of your mother and sisters. There will be factions that would rather see young Edward on the throne, and they will try to rip the country apart to do it. You must vanish."

Both boys were silent for a long time and Richard let them think. He knew this was a great deal to put on two boys of twelve and nine, but they were his brother's sons and he would let them make their own choices.

"It doesn't seem fair," Edward said finally, and Richard turned his gaze to the elder boy. "You're offering us the life you never got a chance to have," he said quietly, and Richard smiled.

Edward was like his father in many ways, but he was also so like Edmund, the brother Richard hardly remembered. He was quiet and thoughtful, and had a kindness that Edmund had possessed even when Richard was a small child. Young Richard was more like George, quick to anger and impulsive, but he followed his brother's lead in everything.

"One of the harshest lessons you'll learn is best learnt early," Richard said with a sad smile. "Life isn't fair, and it never will be."

Edward nodded and took a breath, clasping his hands together to mirror Richard, determination on his face.

"Where would you have us go?"

July, 1483

"You're not going to like this," Ratcliffe said, as he handed over the parchment. "Percy has gone too far this time."

Richard sighed, the knot of dread in his stomach not even twinging at whatever this latest disaster was going to be. He'd already reached his highest level of exhaustion and worry, what could possibly make it worse? He scanned the paper and fought a shrug.

"It takes the choice out of my hands," he said, handing it back to Ratcliffe, who eyed him.

"He executed three men without authority," he said, and Richard tried to make himself care.

Anthony Woodville was dead. Nothing else really mattered. Richard Grey was an unfortunate casualty, but clearly Percy had found, or made, charges that stuck, and he'd acted.

Richard shook himself, his chin dropping to his chest as his head hung. This wasn't him, this was the crown talking. Already it was changing him, this horrible duty they were forcing on him. He wanted to go home, he wanted nothing more to do with this.

"Richard, there must be some reprisal at least," Ratcliffe pointed out gently, and Richard sighed, sinking into his seat and leaning back with his eyes closed.

"I know," he said. "Do whatever you think it fitting to Henry Percy. The little bastard was always too big for himself anyway. Verify the trial and the judgement, whatever process needs to be done. But don't think I'm upset that Anthony Woodville is dead, because I'm not."

"No," Ratcliffe said tiredly, by now fully familiar with the truth of George's death five years before. "I don't suppose you would be."

"Just deal with it," Richard said softly. "Please."

A week later the coronation was over and there was no turning back. Richard and Anne were king and queen of all England, roles neither had ever wanted. It was their siblings who had always aspired to such heights, and neither of them were comfortable sitting above everyone in the audience chamber. Still, comfort aside, it was Anne who was already shining in her new role. She had learned to put her own feelings aside a long time ago behind a mask of steel.

"Is it wise to leave so soon?" she asked, glancing around the table filled with councillors. She stood at Richard's side, one hand resting gently on his shoulder, her spine straight and her chin high, every inch a queen.

The council had suggested that the new king and queen depart from London on a progress around the country immediately, leaving the city and the government behind, and show themselves to the people as their new monarchs.

"It's a gamble," Bishop Russell, the new Lord Chancellor, admitted. "But it would be better for the people to see and meet their new king. Edward spent his last years in the south, indulging as often as ruling. With the setting aside of his descendants as the next in line, and in putting your graces on the throne, it may raise trouble. You're popular in the north, much more popular than your brother was, and if you're seen to include all the corners of your realm, it may help your standing, and dare I say it, popularity."

"May," Anne said, her voice like steel. "You offer no guarantee, Bishop."

Bishop Russell sighed, considering in silence for a long moment before he spoke again. "I can offer no guarantees," he said quietly. "I can only offer the course that may best help your graces to keep power and peace."

Anne could feel Richard sigh, his shoulder dropping under her hand, but then he spoke.

"Very well. How soon do you suggest?" he asked quietly, leaning back in his chair. It was late in the evening, the summer sun dropping below the horizon and torches and lamps were being lit around the room by two young boys whose job it was to keep the palace lit.

"We can be ready to embark on a royal progress in a fortnight," Catesby said, shuffling a pile of papers in front of him. "Most of the preparations are kept at the ready, it seems, to minimise the time it takes to begin a progress."

"I'd be happier with three weeks," Francis interjected. "I would prefer to ride the route before, create contingencies. Security is paramount."

"Ten days," Richard said with finality. "Francis, leave as soon as you're ready and plan us a route. In ten days, Anne and I will ride to Nottingham to visit our son, and our niece and nephew. Catesby, you will meet us in two weeks time and our royal progress can begin."

He stood, nodding to them as he offered Anne his arm and they left the room, leaving no space for any argument to be brokered. He didn't want to do this at all, but the Bishop had a point. He needed to be seen if he wanted to hold his crown and show the people he was a king who cared for his people more than his indulgences. He had loved Edward dearly, had always looked up to him, but Edward had enjoyed being king perhaps a little too much. It had weakened the realm, along with the plotting of the dowager queen's family. Richard needed to bring unity back to England. This may not have been a responsibility he wanted, but it was one that lay on his shoulders and he would not shirk it.

"Who will you leave to act in your stead in London?" Anne asked, as they walked toward their rooms, guards following behind at a discreet distance, the few people they encountered stopping and bowing. She still wasn't used to it. She'd always compelled a level of respect because of her family name, but as queen it was almost beyond belief. Everyone bowed to her, barely anyone looked at her, and when they did it was either with deference, or with awe.

"Perhaps Ratcliffe, I'll have to think on it," Richard said, as they entered their rooms and he closed the door behind them, bolting it and sighing deeply, resting his head against the wood and letting his shoulders sag, now they were alone.

"Are you in pain?" Anne asked, touching his shoulder softly. "This can't be good for your health."

"I'm exhausted, Anne, and I don't remember a day I wasn't in pain," Richard said quietly, and her heart broke for him.

She'd been the first, and she suspected only, one that he told when he'd found out about his back, that it had begun to twist when he was thirteen and would continue to do so, worsening as he aged. It hadn't stopped him from learning to fight, from pushing through the constant pain to become a warrior, but the weight of it must have been immense, to know he would never be free of it. He'd shown her when he was fifteen, the slight curve in his spine. They'd hidden behind the chicken coop and he'd lifted his tunic with his back to her, and she'd run her fingers along his spine. She had wanted to weep when she saw it again nearly five years later after their wedding. She suspected by now others knew, but she doubted Richard had specifically told anyone.

"What can I do?" she whispered, carefully wrapping her arms around him and holding him against her, smiling when he covered her hands with his and laced their fingers together. He turned his head and leaned his cheek against her forehead, eyes closed.

"Just stand by me," he said softy, and she smiled.

"Always, my love."

Richard stepped out of the carriage with a sigh of relief. It wasn't that he didn't appreciate the way the carriage shaded them from the sun, or the cool wine and foods, or the wonderfully padded cushions and comfortable seats, but as soon as the wheels started rolling all the cushioning in the world didn't stop the swaying and jarring.

"No more," Anne grumbled as she clambered out behind him, shoving his hand away when he went to help her. "We're riding the rest of the way."

"Take that up with Francis," Richard said, nodding his head to where Francis was organising their guards in an orderly line.

"I will," Anne said fiercely, and Richard hid a chuckle as she shook out her skirts and pushed back a few tendrils of sweat soaked hair out of her eyes.

The sound of pounding feet distracted them and a moment later they both had their arms full, Ned and Maggie throwing themselves forward with gleeful shrieks, while Edward came a little slower, trying to appear dignified. He didn't seem to mind, though, when his cousins enveloped him in the pile, and Richard held him close, worry weighing on him as he pressed a kiss to

Edward's hair. He was so young, and so often he was sick or tired. Richard wanted so much more for him than a life of perpetual struggle.

A veritable hoard of servants took their things inside to their rooms, leaving them a blessed few hours alone with the children.

"Father?" Edward said once the excitement had settled and dinner had finished. Richard drew the boy over to sit on his knee.

"What is it, son?" he asked, though by the look on Edward's face, and the worry on Anne's, he suspected he already knew the question.

"Will I be king someday?" Edward asked in a small voice, and Richard grimaced.

"You are my heir, which means it's likely," he said quietly, glancing at Maggie and Ned. Technically they were in line even before him, but having been removed from the line of succession by George's actions, they would never have that power. "But, nothing in life is sure. I was never meant to be king, and yet here we are. For now, we will act as if you will follow me on the throne, yes, but that may not be the life that you are destined for."

Edward nodded, leaning against Richard's chest. "I don't want to be king," he said, barely audible, and Richard sighed, holding him close. Ned wrinkled his nose in distaste, as if agreeing, but Maggie's face remained serious, wisdom clear in her eyes.

Richard glanced at Anne, her own eyes worried as she watched their son, her face clearly showing how helpless she felt in this moment. Edward was eight, the same age Richard had been when he had been forced to flee in exile. He'd always wanted a simpler life for his son, but now it seemed that he too would be forced into this political storm from a young age, along with all his cousins.

"It will be many years before any of that happens," Anne said softly, reaching out to stroke her boy's hair. "Your father will be a good and wise king for many years, and when your time comes, you will be an even better king."

"All right," Edward nodded sleepily, eyelids dropping. It was late, and Ned had fallen asleep tucked up against Anne, though Maggie was still awake and watchful as ever.

"Come on," Richard said after another moment. "I think it's time for sleep."

Together they got the three children ready for bed, able to forget their new life for a few moments and lose themselves in the familiar routine. When all three were sleeping soundly Anne took his hand and led him to their own bedroom, closing the door securely behind them.

"Take me to bed," she whispered against his ear, and Richard was happy to lose himself in her for a few hours.

September, 1483

Even on progress there was a rigid schedule to keep. Richard took his evening meal with Ratcliffe and Francis three nights a week, and Anne the other four if he could, though some nights he ate in the brief time the smaller council meeting paused, before returning to the business of government, often late into the night. A dozen or more messengers came and went from their party both morning and evening, conveying letters and decisions and petitions back and forth from London.

This particular evening Francis was absent, and only Ratcliffe sat across from him. They'd already discussed most of the things they needed, but Richard could sense there was something Ratcliffe wasn't saying, so he simply waited.

"Catesby brought me a report that I'm sure you will not like," Ratcliffe said finally, pushing his plate away with a frown. Through the entire dinner Richard had suspected his friend had something he hadn't wanted to say and this simple statement confirmed that suspicion.

"I never like the reports Catesby brings," Richard admitted. "I suspect that's why they're of use to me so often."

Catesby had appeared briefly in London after the whole mess with Hastings, and Francis never had to go search for him, but he'd just as quickly vanished back into the shadows. Sometimes he appeared for almost an entire week, then he'd be gone ten days or more, but his reports and his trusted messengers always found Richard, and so far they had been invaluable.

Ratcliffe chuckled. "This one is about Edward's bastards."

Richard leaned back in his seat, folding his hands over his stomach with a sigh.

"Of course it is," he muttered. "How old are they now?"

"The boy, John, is fifteen, and the girl, Margaret, is just turned thirteen. There was another boy, he'd be about eight now, but a fever took him last spring."

Richard grimaced. "Just the two? No more?"

"No more that we've found," Ratcliffe shrugged. "That doesn't mean there weren't more."

"Well, what about them?" Richard asked, the feeling of unease settling in his stomach once again.

"There may be an advantage to you claiming them as your own. Edward never acknowledged either of them, and they could be used against you," Ratcliffe said bluntly.

"I'm sure you plan to explain how, exactly," Richard said, voice icy. He did not like this idea at all, though he could see the sense in it, his mind already three steps ahead of his emotions, like it usually was.

The Last Winter Rose

Ratcliffe's explanation and idea weren't far off where Richard's mind had gone and at the end Richard just sighed, closing his eyes and wishing once again his life had been anything else.

"You'll have to tell Anne, this should be a decision you make together," Ratcliffe said gently and Richard glared at his empty plate.

"That is not a conversation I want to have," he said quietly, and Ratcliffe sighed.

"And I don't envy you for it," he said. "But you must consider it."

"I will. I just wish you were wrong."

He waited almost a week, trying to gather his courage. He couldn't, so one night when they were sharing dinner he decided just to say it anyway. He stared at his plate, trying to think of the worlds, but they were stubborn, and didn't want to come. Normally he had no qualms about talking to Anne, about anything, but this...

"Anne," he said quietly, eyes fixed on his plate and the half-eaten food there. He'd lost his appetite. "I need to talk to you about something." There was no better way to say it then just to say it.

Anne's knife clattered slightly as she set it down, worry on her face at his tone. "What's wrong?" she asked. "Why won't you look at me?"

Richard sighed, setting his goblet down and looking up at his wife.

"You know there are those who didn't want me to take the throne," he said, and she nodded. She knew all too well. "Catesby has been listening to the whispers, and Ratcliffe brought me some of his concerns last week."

"About what?" Anne questioned, knowing there must be something specific Richard wasn't saying, something Richard didn't want to say. He wasn't usually evasive like this.

"Edward's bastards, John and Margaret," Richard looked away again. "It's complicated, but he's concerned that because of their ages someone might try to use them against me, put John on the throne as a puppet king with Edward's blood, but none of the Woodville influence."

Anne was silent for a long moment, staring at the candle on the table.

"What's his suggestion for this problem?" she asked, meaning Ratcliffe.

Richard sighed deeply, running his hands through his hair. This was what he didn't want to say.

"He suggested, and he's lucky I didn't break his face for it, that I claim them as my own."

There was silence for an uncomfortably long time, then Anne sighed.

"I'm not sure he's wrong," she said, her voice so reasonable that Richard looked up in surprise. "Too many of the nobles that Henry, or my father, raised up high with their schemes are angry that you're a good man and a fair one. They don't want a fair king, they want another puppet that will give them wealth and lands to please and appease them."

"They know I won't be that puppet," Richard muttered.

Anne nodded. "And if someone put a son of Edward, especially an unacknowledged bastard son, on the throne, that bastard would owe him everything."

"And the Woodvilles would have no claim to power either," he sighed. "But if they're my bastard children, then they're of no use to anyone. That's essentially what Ratcliffe said."

"Like I said," Anne shrugged. "He's not wrong. I don't like it-"

"I don't like it," Richard interjected, and Anne smiled.

"But," she continued. "I think it's a good idea. I think you should."

Richard stared at her for a moment then frowned. "Sometimes I hate how reasonable you can be," he muttered. He'd honestly hoped for an excuse not to go through with this utter nonsense. Anne just smiled wider, shrugging her shoulders as she reached for the bread and continued her dinner as if nothing odd had been discussed.

August, 1483

"This is better," Anne sighed, tilting her face up to the light summer rain. "I wish they had left that carriage back at Nottingham."

Richard chuckled, glancing back to where their gilt carriage was following meekly behind the train of wagons. "You know Francis would never let either of us ride in the open in the cities," he said, and Anne grumbled under her breath. It was true they'd both been forced back into their carriage to approach cities and large holds, but when they were travelling between stops, they rode in the open air.

"We could just go home," Anne said wistfully and Richard raised his eyebrows at her, surprised at the faraway look on her face. "Forget all of it…"

Richard smiled, reaching out for her hand, twining their fingers together. Their legs bumped as their horses grumbled, walking along with only inches separating them, but Anne turned her face to him and smiled.

"I know, it's just a dream," she said with a smile, and Richard squeezed her hand.

"There's nothing I'd like more," he told her softly, leaning across to press a kiss to her forehead. "I'm just surprised to hear you say it, not me."

The Last Winter Rose

Anne was quiet for a moment, gathering her thoughts, and Richard just watched her. Her hair was so long now, loose and brushing along the back of the saddle, the red in it even brighter in the sunlight that shone down on them, the day surprisingly pleasant and warm. Her face had aged in the last few months, as Richard knew his must have as well, and there was a hint of grey hair just brushing her temples. He didn't often look at himself in a mirror, but he suspected his own hair was already changing colour as well.

He sighed, turning to stare ahead of them again, eyes following the gentle winding path that took them through the hills to the next town on their progress, their procession strung out in front and behind them, protecting them from all directions, always alert. He'd been many different men in his life. Son, brother, prince, heir, duke, uncle, husband, father. And now king.

"I've always understood when you said you didn't want any of this," Anne said quietly, and Richard's eyes snapped back to her. "I never wanted any of it either, I didn't want to be my father's pawn, married off to a spoiled, cruel brat. I didn't want to be someone's bargaining chip for my family's lands and wealth. I didn't covet a crown or power or jewels. The only thing that truly matters to me, that is more important than wealth or status, is that you must be true to your own duty, and act with honour. And I think that is the most important thing to me because my family failed to uphold that at every turn."

She sighed in frustration, rubbing her face tiredly, wiping away a stray tear before Richard could see. His hand squeezed hers and she smiled at him softly.

"Sometimes, most times, duty clashes with what we want as people," she continued. "And the hardest thing we do is to honour our duty over what we want."

Richard's smile was sad as he nodded. Given a hundred years, he could never have said it better than she did in a few simple worlds. She had taken everything that had been going through his head for years and condensed it into a single thought.

"I don't want the crown to change me," Richard admitted with a heavy sigh. "I feel like it already has."

Anne shook her head, frowning at him. "Richard, no one can change who you are, you are a good man who will do everything he can to uphold justice and honour. You're not a cruel man and you never will be, even if sometimes you have to make the hard decisions."

"Henry Percy killed Anthony Woodville and I'm not sorry about it. I'm not even sorry he executed Richard Grey without authority, because it means he's out of the way and Elizabeth has lost another pawn. Does that make me a horrible person?"

"It makes you a practical person," Anne said, her shoulders straightening, ready to defend him even to himself. "It makes you human."

"I feel like the world is closing in around me, like I'm suffocating," he said.

He'd always been able to talk to Anne about anything and it had been so hard the first two months after his brother died, when they had been apart. Since they'd been crowned, they hardly had the time to see each other, much less speak of the harder things. If Richard wasn't in meetings he was sleeping, something he had far too little time for, and Anne was always busy making sure the whole palace ran smoothly. It wasn't usually the job of the queen, but it was something she had always loved. He hadn't bothered to try and tell her that overseeing the washing was no longer something she had to do.

They were so busy, they barely had time for each other. A wistfully thought came to him and Richard chuckled.

"What?" Anne prodded him when he didn't say anything and he shook his head, chuckling.

"Francis suggested I should take all of you and flee to France, when they first told me I'd be king instead of Edward. Maybe I should have listened," he mused, staring up at the clouds, missing the look of disgust on Anne's face.

"Maybe not France," she said with distaste. "I've always wanted to visit Italy though, or maybe an island where the sea is clear down to the bottom and it's always warm."

"Dreams hurt," Richard said after a moment, and this time it was Anne who squeezed their joined hands.

"They do," she whispered, and something in her voice made him turn to look at her. His breath caught at the look of love on her face as she smiled at him and he wished they weren't on horses right now, because all he wanted to do was hold her.

"Anne," he said, but she shook her head.

"They hurt, but sometimes they come true," she said and Richard pressed her hand to his mouth, not even caring that he was crying now.

He loved this woman so much, with his whole life and soul, and he didn't know if he would ever be able to live without her. He prayed every day that he would never have to live life without her at his side again. It had been bad enough when he was younger, before they were even married, but he thought now that if he lost her, it might just kill him. He would have nothing left to live for if Anne was gone. She had been his only dream for so long, he wasn't sure he'd ever had another.

They fell into silence as they rode, each weighed down with their own thoughts, hands held tightly together in an unspoken promise never to let go or turn away from each other. They were each other's forever.

"Richard, could we speak to you?" Francis said quietly, Catesby a shadow by his side, and Richard nodded, glancing around the room. There was nothing that needed his immediate attention, most of the people mingling together and talking after the meeting had broken into something more casual. He caught Anne's eye and nodded to her. A few moments later she joined

The Last Winter Rose

them and Francis led them out into the hall, to a room that was empty except for Ratcliffe.

"We bring news," Ratcliffe said, closing the door behind the four of them, sliding the bar across.

"Not good news," Richard said bluntly. It wasn't a question, there was no other news that put a look like that on both his trusted friend's faces.

"There's rebellion in the south," Francis said grimly, and Richard glanced at Anne.

"Henry Tudor?" she asked, and Francis nodded.

"It's worse," he told them both, and Catesby shifted his feet restlessly. "Most of the nobles involved are known supporters of the old regime, political dissenters or supporters of Henry or Warwick, the ones who slipped through the cracks and were pardoned or never implicated, but known to us. There are also several former members of Edward's household, men with grievances for their dismissals, even though it's to be expected on the death of a king. The blow is Buckingham."

Richard clenched his teeth to keep his jaw from falling. "Buckingham?"

Catesby spoke at last. "There is no doubt this latest is the doing of Margaret Beaufort, another new bid to put her son on the throne. It's possibly she had the collusion of the dowager queen, but there is no proof of that. All of the dowager's correspondence and servants are thoroughly searched each time anyone leaves or enters Westminster. However, her elder son Thomas Grey roams free, and you can be sure anything he does

306

is on his mother's orders, it does not matter if those orders were given long ago. There is also Lionel Woodville, one of the dowager queen's brothers, who may be causing trouble. There is no doubt the family is involved in this, but whether she herself is pulling any strings, it's impossible to know."

"And never forget that Buckingham's wife is a Woodville," Ratcliffe muttered, arms crossed where he leaned against the wall.

"There are movements here, and here," Francis said, spreading a map of the southern half of England out on the table. He set flags on Kent and on the Welsh boarder. "Tudor sailed a small invasion force from Brittany, but half his ships were forced to turn back." Francis placed a trio of markers along the coast where ships had managed to get through.

"Are we facing an armed uprising?" Richard asked, already thinking of raising the northern lords.

"Thomas Grey is organising men and according our sources, he's headed Exeter," Francis nodded. "It's too early to tell if there will be a serious support behind them, but there are enough pockets that if they organise and come together, we'll have trouble."

"How likely is that?" Anne asked, coming to stand beside Richard. "In my experience, lords don't often work together easily."

Ratcliffe and Francis chuckled. "You're not wrong," Ratcliffe nodded to her. "For now, we should raise a force, but wait and see what happens. The ships being forced to return to Brittany already helps us, and our information says the Duke of Norfolk is holding the Thames crossing at Gravesend. His messages are on their way to us now, with Catesby's spies."

Anne raised an eyebrow, impressed with the speed and spread of Catesby's network. She had no idea news could travel so fast, but if Catesby was involved it seemed almost instant.

"Damn," Richard suddenly swore, staring hard at the map.

"Richard?" Anne asked, laying a hand on his shoulder, feeing him shaking.

"Hastings was never involved in anything," Richard growled, striking his fist against the table. "Buckingham was behind it. He made sure Catesby was fed false information to implicate Hastings. He planted Morton in the room to make sure Hastings died when we moved to arrest him, and accused Morton to throw suspicion off him, make it look like Hastings' death was an accident."

Francis frowned hard, putting the pieces together in his mind. It was possible. The more he thought about it, the more likely it became and he was suddenly furious with himself.

"Damn," he echoed. "I should have seen it... I'm sorry, I didn't-"

"It's not your fault," Richard interrupted. "It's no one's fault, we were played and Hastings paid for it."

They all fell silent for a long moment, the implications sinking in.

Caitlin Sumner

"What are you going to do about Buckingham?" Anne asked finally, staring down at the map of the south coast. Three ships had landed and another four had been turned back by a storm, but if Henry Tudor was on one of those ships, it was an opportunity. She just wasn't sure they'd be able to act on it.

"Kill him," Richard snapped, and Anne glared at him.

"Yes," she said patiently. "But how? If he's marshalled his men in Wales and there are pockets of rebellion across the south, what are you going to do?"

Richard scowled, but there was only one thing he could do. Decision made, Richard looked to Francis and nodded. Francis knew Richard well enough to know exactly what he was thinking and returned the nod, taking the flags and rolling up the map.

"I'll have messages sent out immediately," he said as he worked. "We can leave here in two days."

"Muster the men at Leicester. We leave in the morning," Richard said, before sweeping out of the room, a deep scowl on his face. Francis sighed, but nodded, even though he was already gone.

Anne gave them both a soft smile, gripping Francis' arm. "I know how much you do for him, Francis," she said quietly. "Thank you. And please, remember to eat?"

Ratcliffe's booming laugh made them both jump and they chuckled with the large man as he shook his head.

309

"Girl, you might as well tell a man not to piss in the wind, for all the good it does," he said, and Anne laughed loudly.

"That's your queen you're speaking to," Francis managed around his laughter, and Anne just shook her head.

"I miss being just a woman," she said. "Thank you, Ratcliffe, I needed that."

"Anything for you, great lady," he swept an exaggerated bow, which caused more laughs, and offered her his arm. "Might I escort you to the hall for dinner?"

Still chuckling, Anne took his arm and they left Francis to his work. Catesby had vanished after Richard and she hadn't even noticed him slip away, though for Catesby that was just how he was.

By the time they reached Leicester the rebellion was practically over. Storms had gorged the rivers, preventing any crossing from Wales, and Buckingham's support had evaporated into the mist in the face of several lords on the border who were loyal to the crown and blocking any movement across the river bridges. Buckingham fled, putting his trust in the wrong person, and by the 1st of November he had been brought before Richard and his execution was ordered after he gave a full confession.

Richard swept south and along the coast and encountered no resistance, only tentative welcome. By the time he reached the place where Henry Tudor's ships were meant to be anchored, they were gone, fled back to France. By the end of November, they returned to London and Richard had no plans to leave again until well into the new year. He was king. It was time to be king.

December, 1483

Francis Lovell was not a man who was shaken easily. He was always calm, always had a smile on his face, always had a joke at hand to make a tense situation light. That was why Richard immediately knew there was something wrong when Francis pushed open the door, an exhausted messenger close on his heels, and a look on his face that Richard had never seen before.

"The boys are gone," Francis said without pausing for breath, the door swinging shut behind them with a loud thump. Beside Richard, Ratcliffe swore quietly.

"What?" Richard said, his blood turning to ice.

"Edward's boys, they're gone," Francis said again, and Richard went still.

"I am going to imagine, Francis," Richard said after a long moment, voice deadly quiet, "That you did not just come into my council chamber and tell me that my nephews have disappeared."

Francis and Ratcliffe glanced at one another at the anger in his voice, and Francis' man swallowed before he spoke. "Your majesty, I wish I brought you other news, but it is so. The boys are gone, we found no trace of them." He twisted his hat nervously in his hands and glanced at Francis.

Richard closed his eyes and turned away. "You found no blood? No bodies?"

"Nothing," the rider shook his head. "It's as if they were spirited away by a ghost. The locks on the gate had not been tampered with, nor the doors. The servants saw nothing, they were not drugged, the night watchman swears all was quiet. It was the tutor who discovered it, when the boys failed to appear for their noontime lessons. There were no tracks out of the ordinary, no sign of struggle or break in."

"When was this?" the king asked, putting his hands behind his back with a wince and gripping one wrist tightly with his fingers, trying to remain calm.

"Three days ago," the rider said quietly. "We searched high and low, every inch, before I rode here immediately on ascertaining that the boys were not somewhere in the manor, or on the lands of Lord Lovell, or those that surround the Minster. We searched the village and all the way to Witney and Burford. Young boys will sometimes wander."

"And you checked the river?" Richard asked, turning back to them. He knew Lovell's hall was just alongside the River Windrush, but the water there was calm, narrow, and shallow. It should have been no danger to two boys their age who both knew how to swim, but anything was possible.

"Among the first things, sire," the man said, and Richard turned away again, to the window.

"So they were taken," he said, a statement not a question. Francis and Ratcliffe glanced at one another

313

again, but they had nothing to refute that claim. Francis handed his man a purse with a quiet word and the man bowed deeply before near scuttling from the room.

"It... would appear so," Ratcliffe said in response to Richard, his voice tired. He had been up before the dawn and it was only midmorning now, but it felt like he had been awake for days. "There are those who would seek to harm them, and also..."

"They're going to blame you," Francis said without preamble, not bothering to hide the truth behind lacquered words. "This is as much an attack on you as it is on the boys. With them gone, it will look like you removed them to consolidate your own power. Maybe it won't be said right away, but Henry Tudor could use this as a way of discrediting your rule."

Richard glanced over his shoulder at his friend, who was staring him down almost defiantly. "And you believe I had nothing to do with this?" he asked, ignoring Ratcliffe shifting nervously. Francis quirked a sardonic smile.

"I know you better than that," he said, and it was true. He was one of Richard's closest friends, they had known each other since they were children. Richard was glad to know his friend didn't think so little of him. He stared at Francis for a long moment, the ghost of a thought shifting through the back of his mind, then he shook it away.

"Has the former dowager queen been informed?" he asked, and Francis shook his head.

"I am unaware of such, however someone may have dispatched a message to her in the chaos of the search. My man came straight to me, and I came straight to you."

Richard grimaced. He supposed he'd find out soon enough.

"Where are they?" she screeched as she crossed the vaulted chamber, the girls huddled together in the doorway of the sanctuary. "Where are my sons?"

Grace and dignity were forgotten in her rage. This was not Elizabeth the queen, this was Elizabeth the mother, the mother who had already lost four children that he knew of, among them her youngest, George, who had only been a babe in arms. Grief twisted her beautiful face and brought tears to her eyes at the thought that two more of her children were gone.

She lunged for him and he caught her wrists as gently as he could, but still with enough strength to stop her fierce attack.

"I don't know," he said, trying to calm her. "Elizabeth, I swear, on the life of my own son, I don't know where they are."

"Liar!" she screamed at him, but he shook his head, remaining stoic.

"Why would I lie?" he asked carefully. "They are my family. You are my family, my brother's beloved wife. Why would I harm them, why would I take them?

The Last Winter Rose

You know," he said, voice dropping as curious ears inched closer. "You know family is the most important thing to me."

Her eyes blazed for a moment longer, then she sagged against him, her tears wet against the velvet of his shoulder, and he cautiously wrapped his arms around his sister by law. As tenuous as the years might have been, no matter the break caused between them after Edward's death, or her admission of guilt in George's death, she was a grieving mother and he would not belittle her pain.

"Where are they?" she sobbed quietly. "Where are my boys?"

Richard only wished he had an answer for her.

"We think they've been taken. We're searching, but whoever took them was smart. They were able to learn their real identities and their location at the home of Francis Lovell, and they were able to enter and spirit them away and leave no trace. They were discreetly guarded day and night, none of the servants are missing or suspicious, none of the guards have been bribed. We don't know how they did it, or who."

"But why?" Elizabeth asked, pulling herself away and reaching for a handkerchief to wipe away her tears.

Richard sighed, taking a step back. "I wish I had an answer to even one of your questions, but I don't have any answers, only suspicions."

Elizabeth turned away for a moment to compose herself before turning back to him.

"What suspicions?"

Richard glanced pointedly over her shoulder and Elizabeth turned, waving the children back from where they'd been watching and listening. When the door shut behind them Richard took a breath.

"Catesby thinks they've been taken by one of two factions, either those who would see me off the throne, or those who would keep me on it. I can only hope it's the former, because that means it's unlikely they've been harmed."

Elizabeth nodded, her mouth pinched.

"I also hope," Richard said softly, "and perhaps it is a foolish hope, that there is a chance they were spirited away for their protection, for them, not for any motive."

"If they were, I have no knowledge or part in it," Elizabeth said, and Richard felt his shoulders dropped. He had hoped perhaps...

"Neither have I," he said. "Perhaps one of your brothers?"

Elizabeth shook her head. "They wouldn't do something like this without my knowledge."

"Then I have no further recourse. I will keep looking for them, but with no trail to follow..."

"I understand," Elizabeth nodded.

"Will you reconsider moving from this place? I can see to your protection better at one of the royal residences, you and the girls."

Elizabeth frowned, then nodded, her poise returned. "I will consider it."

April, 1484

"Richard," a soft voice called him, breaking through his restless dreams. "Richard."

Richard blinked awake, confused when he found Francis kneeling by his bedside in the darkness, his face stricken.

"What's happened?" he asked. Anne was still asleep beside him and he carefully pushed the covers back, grimacing and grabbing Francis' hand when he offered it, pulling himself up and out of the bed without waking her.

He followed Francis into the sitting room, wrapping a long robe around himself against the cold as Francis shut the bedroom door quietly. There was one candle lit on the desk and a letter sat beside it. Richard froze when he saw the parchment, a sudden cold washing over him. He didn't want to take another step, his arms tightening where they were crossed across his chest.

"Tell me," he said, as Francis came to stand before him, tears now visible on his face and Richard's knees threatened to buckle. "Edward," he whispered, because what else could it be?

"They found him this morning," Francis whispered. "He never woke after going to bed last night. The message just came."

Now Richard's knees did buckle, his ears roaring. He was only vaguely aware of Francis catching him, both of them clinging to each other as Richard sobbed against his best friend's shoulder.

His son was dead. His son was dead and he'd never have another. They had tried and tried for years and never had more children. He couldn't understand how his mother had been so strong in the face of losing so many of her own, it felt like someone was carving his heart into pieces with a hot knife.

He lost track of time, barely aware as he clung to Francis. It was a dim haze when he felt his friend pull away, then there was warmth somewhere next to him and then Francis' arms wrapped around him again, this time with a heavy blanket.

The fire was roaring in the hearth when his ears finally stopped ringing and Richard drew a shuddering breath, leaning against Francis, who just held him silently.

"How do I tell her?" he said finally, voice raw and shaking. Francis' arms tightened for a moment and Richard felt him sigh.

"I can-"

"No," Richard said, knowing his friend would offer. "I... thank you for coming to me as soon as you knew, but I have to tell her."

The Last Winter Rose

He pulled himself back finally, wiping away the tears on his face, grateful for Francis' steady hand on his shoulder, keeping him upright. They'd somehow crumpled to the carpet in front of the hearth and he had no memory of sitting, or of Francis kindling the fire, but he must have.

"I am so sorry," Francis told Richard softly. "I can't even begin to imagine."

Francis had no children of his own, his brief political marriage never more than words on paper, but the children he fostered were like his own. It had torn him up enough when the two princes vanished the year before, but he had no comparison for the loss of a child of his own.

"I don't know how much more I can take," Richard admitted softly. "I'll... I need to tell her. Just give me another moment."

They sat quietly until the sun began to rise, then Richard hauled himself to his feet, waving away Francis' help. He ached all over and he felt like a man of sixty, not thirty-one, and he slowly made his way back to his bedroom, easing the door open softly.

He walked to the windows and opened the curtains, turning to watch Anne sleep in the soft morning light. He heard the outer door closing as Francis left and he wanted to stay here in this moment forever. He didn't want to be the one to tell her that her only child was dead. He wanted to rush north to Nottingham and find Edward, berate him for joking with them all, but it was a fool's want.

"Richard?" Anne whispered sleepily, one eye half open, her voice shaking him out of his thoughts. "What's wrong?"

Richard opened his mouth, but no sounds came out. He tried again, his voice grating like he'd been screaming.

"A message," he said. "Francis, he came... Anne..."

"It's bad," she said, sitting up slowly. He could see her shaking and he crossed the room, falling to his knees beside the bed and taking her hands in his, pressing them to his lips.

"I'm so sorry," he said, fresh tears streaming down his face. "I'm so, so sorry, Anne."

"Edward," she whispered, and Richard sobbed, nodding. He thought he'd cried all his tears, but the pain rose up in his chest, threatening to rip him apart.

"He went to his bed and never woke in the morning," he said softly, and he could feel the way she rocked back and forth as her hands tightened on his before she sobbed quietly and leaned down, pressing her head against his.

Richard pushed himself up awkwardly, wrapping his arms around her as he sat on the edge of the bed and she cried almost silently against him until the sun was well up outside the window, their room flooded with morning light. Finally, she went still and silent, then pulled herself away, wiping her face with the corner of the blanket.

"I need to see to the kitchens," she said quietly. "There's washing to be done."

Richard didn't protest, letting her slip out of bed and dress, helping her with the ties when she turned to him. She left without another word and Richard stared out the window for a long time before he turned and buried himself back under the covers and fell into an exhausted sleep.

They left for Nottingham that evening. Francis arranged everything and a plain carriage was waiting for them in the yard as the sun began to sink below the horizon. Neither of them protested, both too exhausted to think of riding. They travelled through the night, stopping only for the small party to change horses, and they arrived late the next afternoon. They were all exhausted now, but the men had been willing to forego sleep to get them there as fast as possible.

Francis, looking as exhausted as Richard felt, held the door and helped them both climb from the carriage. It was Maggie, to Richard's surprise, who came running to him almost as soon as they'd stepped down, falling into his arms as he leaned down to catch her. He lifted her with a soft grunt and settled her on his hip, stroking her hair as Anne accepted an embrace from Ned. Maggie was almost eleven now, far too old to lifted up, but she was slight like her mother had been and Richard had little trouble carrying her inside.

He found out later from their nurse, Jane, that Maggie was the one who had gone to wake Edward and found him, so Richard made sure to make time for her later, asking her if she was all right. She insisted that she was, but she was sad, because it had reminded her of when her mother went away. That night when Richard went to sleep it was with Maggie tucked under one arm and Ned under the other. Anne refused to sleep, instead sitting in the private chapel with Edward, eyes locked on his still form beneath his shroud.

They buried him three days later, all of them crying as the blessings were said over his little coffin and Richard held Anne as she finally broke down, screaming her sorrow to the darkening sky. The rain started as Edward was lowered into the ground, as if the very heavens were weeping, and Richard could do nothing, utterly helpless and feeling so alone, despite being surrounded by Anne, Francis, Maggie, Ned, and more than two dozen other people who had come to pay their respects to Edward, people who had loved and cared for him, people who had been their friends for long years. Geoffrey Frank had come from Middleham with shocking speed and stood solemnly in the rain, his hat in his hands, and Richard knew he too was weeping.

Days passed in a quiet haze of grief until they were forced to return to London and Richard had to return to the awful business of being king. Never in his life had he wanted to run away more, to just leave it all behind and start again somewhere new, somewhere nobody knew him. He spoke passable French, they could disappear into the countryside and never return, but like before, it was nothing more than a dream. Only this time it was a dream that just brought more pain. It no longer held even the smallest glimmer of hope or joy.

He sighed heavily, standing in the hall and staring at the throne that had been his nephew's, however briefly, had been his brother's, could have been his father's. He'd never wanted any part of it, and now whatever legacy his family might have would die with him. He supposed it was a fitting end to the tragic comedy of errors that had been the succession to the English crown for the last hundred years, that he was the last, a youngest son with no son to carry on their name. In a way, he almost felt relief.

September, 1484

Summer passed in a haze. It became hard to tell time, one day much like the next. There were days Richard couldn't get out of bed, days when his pain was so bad he could barely move. Anne was silent, rarely speaking, and when she did it was only ever a few words. She ate less, and grew thin and pale, moving through the halls like a spectre. Most days Richard felt like one himself.

"Richard?"

"Mm," he mumbled, staring at the fire that was always burning in their rooms. He hardly noticed Anne had come in.

"What are you thinking?" she asked him, setting down the basket she'd been carrying.

"Dark thoughts," Richard mumbled behind his steepled hands.

"About what?" Anne questioned with a sigh, settling on the arm of his chair and carding her fingers through his hair, heart aching.

It still hurt every day, twice as badly when Edward crossed her mind, but Richard was a broken man, unable to move forward from the death of their son.

The Last Winter Rose

"About who I will name as my heir," he said softly, and Anne bit her lip, tears welling. The grief was still fresh and felt like a knife to her heart every time she thought of Edward.

"I suppose it must be Ned, then," she said.

There was no one else, now. The search for Edward and Elizabeth's boys continued, though Richard strongly suspected they were too well hidden to be found, though he wouldn't come right out and ask Francis if he'd had a hand in their disappearance. He knew either Francis had, and he had neglected to tell Richard precisely to protect the boys even further, or he hadn't and they were gone forever. Either way, their Edward had been gone almost half a year and the lords were clamouring that Richard appoint a new heir.

"He's barred from holding the crown, because his father committed treason," Richard said tiredly. "I don't think I could restore him, and I doubt Ned has any wish to become next in line for a throne with so much blood on it. He's a quiet child, he would find this life torment."

"Who would you choose, then?" Anne asked, because someone had to, and the council was getting nowhere with their badgering.

Richard glanced up at her, weighing his words. "Honestly?"

Anne nodded, wondering why he was being so reticent. She'd never found any of his thoughts particularly troublesome, so she didn't know what he could be thinking that he was worried he'd upset her.

"Princess Elizabeth."

There was silence for a long moment, then Anne frowned.

"She's the same as her brothers, though, declared illegitimate, and has no right to the crown," she muttered, not particularly bothered by the idea, though she expected most of the councillors would have fits, and perhaps one or two might have his heart give out. But trying to give the crown to any of Edward's children faced the same problem that had put the crown on her own husband's head.

"And yet, Henry Tudor would marry her and use her to claim the throne for himself," Richard sighed, pinching the bridge of his nose. His back ached and he was exhausted. He'd been king for barely a year and a quarter and already he'd been fraught at every turn. "She is my niece, whether legitimate or not, and the granddaughter of a man who would have been king if he hadn't been killed. On those grounds alone I can declare her legitimate and make her my heir, and it will still be a better claim than Henry Tudor."

"They'll never accept it," Anne said and Richard slumped further into his seat.

"I know," he mumbled. "But you asked for honesty."

Anne sighed, her fingers still running through his hair in what she hoped was a comforting gesture. "You need to appoint someone," she said softly.

The Last Winter Rose

"Why," Richard said petulantly, though he knew the answer. Anne pursed her lips around half a smile and sighed.

"Because if you do not, there will be another war," she said firmly, pressing a kiss to his head as she stood. "I'll see you at supper," she whispered as she left him alone to his thoughts.

Richard sighed. The last few months had been... worse than hell. Worse than any damnation the bible said was waiting for them. For the first time he realised just how different he and Anne were.

She wore her grief like a cloak and held her head high, back straight and eyes blazing with defiance. She was quieter, but still the strongest person he'd ever met.

Richard... Richard carried his pain like the Promethean boulder and every day it was a little heavier than the last. His heart was broken beyond healing, and he didn't know where he'd even begin. Maggie helped a little, sticking closer to him than she ever had before, both of the children now living with them at Westminster. Neither he or Anne could bear to be away from the two who had become like their own, but even they couldn't fill the void left by their son.

Most days Richard was late to rise, often finding the bed empty when he opened his eyes. Anne was awake with the sun and she made herself busy throughout the day, while Richard wondered why he bothered to get up at all. His councillors ran the country, not him, every decision he tried to make was a fight, and he had no strength left for fighting. Instead, he sat vacantly in

328

meetings while Francis, Catesby, and Ratcliffe did what he should be doing. He should be ruling, but he couldn't shake the haze from his mind, couldn't stop thinking about how much he had lost over the years.

With a groan, Richard scrubbed his face with his hands and pushed himself out of his chair. It was late morning, and the day was clear. There were other things he knew he should be doing, but he was going to go see his mother, because for one afternoon he needed to not be a king, not be a leader. He needed to be a son and be comforted by the woman who raised him.

December, 1484

"You're drunk," Anne said quietly, and Richard shrugged. All around them the Christmas feast roared with noise and laughter, no sense of decorum left after how heavily the wine had flowed all night.

Why shouldn't he be drunk? His kingdom was threatening to fall apart around his ears, his son was dead, his brothers were dead, he had a barely held together truce with the former queen and her still powerful family, and on the other side of the channel, Henry Tudor was baying for his throne like a bloodthirsty hound.

"It's not seemly," she said softly, and Richard scoffed.

"I don't care," he said harshly. "All my life I've been the quiet one, the moderate one, the brother that didn't cause trouble. All I wanted was a simple life with my family, and instead…"

Anne gripped his wrist, tears threatening to fall, and she looked away from his vacant gaze, her own heart still so tender. She understood his anger, she felt it herself every single day, but she hated to see him like this. Turning away further she coughed into a cloth she carried with her, as gently as she could, but it still made her lungs ache.

Richard looked over at her as her hand tightened on his arm and he winced as her fingers dug in. There was blood spotting the white cloth in her other hand and he looked away again, unable think about it tonight.

Anne sighed as the coughing subsided and she reached for a goblet of water that had been boiled with herbs and slowly sipped it, slumping back into her seat in a show of exhaustion she rarely allowed in public. It didn't matter now, everyone else was already so drunk they weren't watching how their queen sat, they barely acknowledged that she or Richard were even there. The din of noise was overwhelming and with a last glance at Richard she squeezed his arm and stood, excusing herself from the feast. She doubted anyone even noticed that she left.

Richard reached for the wine and poured himself another goblet, intent on forgetting his own name, even if just for a few short hours. It was well past midnight already and the people in the hall were likely to carry on until morning or until they passed out, whichever came first.

When he woke sometime the next afternoon, everything was a blur. He'd drunk far too much once when he was younger, egged on by Edward while they were across the channel in Burgundy, and he'd woken feeling much the same. A decade and a half later he felt significantly worse and it took several minutes before he could sit up enough to take in his surroundings.

The Last Winter Rose

He wasn't in his own room, he was sprawled rather uncomfortably across Francis' much smaller bed, and Francis himself was asleep in the chair in front of the fire, head tilted back at an angle that made Richard wince, snoring loudly.

Richard groaned, pressing a hand to his head. He reached for the pewter cup by the bed and drank the contents, making a face at the mix of herbs that would help clear his head, then he lobbed the cup at Francis, who startled awake with a shout.

"For all the love of God," Richard moaned. "Stop making so much noise."

"Alive, are you?" Francis asked, stretching and picking lint from his doublet. "That was quite impressive last night."

"Go away," Richard said, pressing his hands into his eyes. "Before I have you executed."

Francis snorted as he stood on mostly steady legs. "You should be thanking me for not taking you back to your own room and your wife. I doubt Anne would be very happy with this," he said, waving vaguely at Richard.

With a string of colourful curses he hadn't realised he'd committed to memory, despite hearing them from George often enough when they were younger, Richard hauled himself up to a sitting position with gritted teeth, breathing hard as every muscle in his body screamed at him. He stank like ale and wine and mud, and several pieces of his clothing were missing. Squinting near the door he saw them piled up in a filthy heap and he wondered what exactly he'd done the night before.

"You fell in the pig pen," Francis said, catching the direction of his gaze. "Very undignified for a king, I must say."

"If you weren't the only friend I have, I would kill you with my own hands," Richard threatened as he finally managed to regain his feet. The table in front of the fire had a second chair and a plate of plain food and Richard sat down heavily, reaching for a chunk of bread to soak up the wine he could still feel in his stomach.

"Catesby and Ratcliffe would be hurt to hear you say so," Francis yawned, reaching for a piece of cheese. He was significantly less damaged by the night before and seemed to be waking up with ease. Richard just grumbled into his bread and ignored his friend.

The night was a blur, but Richard remembered some of it. He remembered sitting in the hall, surrounded by people, and feeling so alone he thought he would shatter. He remembered Anne at his side, but the feeling that she was slipping through his grasp like water, like she was already so far away and untouchable, just as when they'd been younger.

Her illness had started in the summer, just a gentle cough. Over the months it grew harsher and took more and more of her strength, what little she had after they'd lost their son. He'd held her tight in his arms as she sobbed for him night after night for weeks, he'd held her when she coughed and coughed, so long and hard she brought up blood for the first time. Now that happened

The Last Winter Rose

nearly every time a fit took her, and they both knew she didn't have much time left. Anne, ever practical, had already told him he should remarry when she was gone, but he'd refused to even consider it.

No one else knew, except a single healer who was sworn to secrecy. Richard had wanted to consult the royal physicians, but Anne had refused, instead quietly bringing the woman who had tended their bumps and scrapes as children in Middleham, who had been there when both she and Isabel were born. She was a kind woman, now aged and stooping when she walked, but she was honest and didn't mince her words. That, at least, Richard appreciated.

"Richard?" Francis asked, and Richard shook his head, breaking out of his morbid thoughts.

"What?" he muttered, frowning at the food he'd stopped even trying to eat, the bread dry and tasteless.

"What's wrong?"

Richard was silent for a long moment before he looked away, into the fire. "Nothing."

It was obvious Francis didn't believe him, but he didn't press Richard, he never had. Anyone who looked at Anne knew she was dying, but Richard couldn't bring himself to say the words aloud. They ate in silence and Richard's headache slowly receded. His clothes were a lost cause, but Francis had a pair of trousers that just fit him and a fresh shirt, so he was able to make it to his own rooms with some dignity left.

Anne wrinkled her nose when he entered, but there were already two men carrying buckets of hot water in and filling the tub in the bathing room off the main chamber, thanks to Francis doing what he did best.

"Did you sleep with the pigs, or just roll about in the mud?" she asked, and Richard scowled.

"How do you know?" he asked, stripping his shirt as the door shut behind the two who had brought the water and kicking off his mucky shoes. They were probably lost too, but he didn't really care. He had a dozen pair of shoes, since people seemed to think a king needed more clothes than a family of twelve.

"Gossip like that travels fast," Anne smiled, returning to the letter she was writing as Richard sank into the bath with an uncharitable grumble under his breath.

Silence except for the scrape of a quill descended and Richard stared blankly at the window.

"How do I go on?" he asked finally, and the quill paused. His words were barely loud enough to carry across the room, but Anne heard him nonetheless. "I don't know if I can…" he trailed off, unable to say the words, unable to even think of a world without her at his side.

Edward's death had broken something between them, something that would take too long to heal, she would be gone before it could, and Anne's death was going to destroy the little that was left of his heart.

"You will put one foot in front of the other and be who your people need," Anne said quietly, eyes fixed on her letter. "You will be the man I fell in love with when I was a girl, the strongest, wisest, kindest man I've ever known, you will be a good and fair king and you will leave this realm better than it came to you."

"You really believe that?" Richard asked, rolling his head to the side, watching her profile, seeing her fingers grip the quill tightly, almost to breaking. After a moment she relaxed her hand and set the quill down, turning and meeting his eyes, her gaze strong and clear and focused fully on him for the first time in months.

"With all my heart," she said softly and, for the first time in months, Richard's smile, though weak, was genuine. He would never stop loving her, it was part of who he was, but maybe, if he remembered her unwavering belief in him, he could cling to that like a lifeline and get through each day.

February, 1485

Anne's health deteriorated at an alarming speed, and by the middle of January she had handed most of her duties off to her ladies and was no longer actively running the household. Richard shirked his own duties three days of four and sat with her, talking quietly, reading, trying to persuade her to eat something, but she didn't have much time left.

They'd moved to Windsor for the winter, but the castle was cold and draughty and needed hundreds of pounds of upkeep work, hundreds of pounds the they didn't have. Edward had run the kingdom to near bankruptcy before he died and two years had done little to recover it. They were lucky that the harvests had been abundant and they hadn't had to try and buy grain from the continent, but war was looming ever closer and all rumour and report said Henry Tudor would make an attempt to land on English soil before summer was out.

The talked long and often about Henry Tudor, much to Richard's distaste. They circled the topic again and again, never seeming to reach a satisfactory conclusion.

"You can't trust Thomas Stanley to control his wife," Anne said, coughing roughly into a handkerchief.

The Last Winter Rose

"Margaret Beaufort has wanted to put her son on the throne since he was a boy."

Richard rubbed his face tiredly, having heard this a dozen times before. "I know," he muttered. "Even Edward told me not to trust either of the Stanleys, but what choice do I have? They haven't actually done anything. There was never any proof that Thomas was involved in Buckingham's plot and the death of Hastings. William stays on his lands and rarely ventures out. I can't even arrest Margaret Beaufort on suspicion of sedition, because if I did I would guarantee Henry's invasion. For the moment he still hasn't gained much support from across Europe."

"But he's gained support here," Anne reminded him, much to his chagrin. "That is more dangerous than an entire French fleet."

"Not if that French fleet makes it across the channel this time."

Anne sighed, glancing toward her window. She was so tired. She imagined this must be what Richard had felt for so many years, the constant pain, the exhaustion. She slept more hours of the day than she was awake, she could barely eat, and every breath was like a dagger in her chest. She had nothing left and she knew it.

"I want to go back to Westminster," she said one afternoon, shifting the topic away from impending war. Richard looked up at her, surprise and hesitance crossing his face.

"Anne," Richard started and she shook her head.

338

"I know you have to stay here for now," she said softly. "But I want to go."

Richard was silent, his lips a tight line. He could hear what she wasn't saying, that she didn't want him to see her die. His heart rebelled at the notion of being parted, but he had vowed early to always respect her and her choices, so he kept his thoughts to himself and nodded tersely. He watched the tension drain from her shoulders as she sank back onto her pillows, a soft smile curving her dry lips.

"You'll have to remarry," she said softly. "Promise me, you can make a good political marriage and get the support you need."

Richard looked away. He was tired of arguing this with her, so he chose to say nothing instead. Anne sighed, letting it drop. She'd said it a hundred times if she'd said it once and he would either listen or he wouldn't. She would be gone soon and he would do what he wanted.

They lapsed into silence, both lost in their own morbid thoughts.

The carriage was waiting and Richard walked with Anne from her bedchamber, supporting her weight and pausing often when she needed to rest. He offered to carry her, but she wanted to make this last trip herself, even though she was weak.

The Last Winter Rose

The sun was breaking through the clouds when they emerged into the yard. She closed her eyes and tilted her head up, sighing as the weak warmth of winter touched her pale skin. In the daylight she looked like a ghost, gaunt and pale and so, so small. Richard drew her into his arms and pressed his face to her hair.

"I love you," he whispered, holding her close, his voice tight with unshed tears. She was so small in his arms, so frail. "I wish I could be with you."

"You have a kingdom to run, and enemies on every side," Anne said softly, her voice weak, almost snatched away by the breeze. She pulled back and caught his hands in hers, looking up at him with a soft, sad smile. "You're needed here now, and I'll fare better at Westminster, where the fires are warm and the soup hot."

"Anne-" he started, unable to hear her joke.

"Shh," she hushed him. They both knew she wasn't coming back to Windsor, where he was effectively trapped by the court and business of law until spring, but she wanted them to have one more moment of illusion, one more moment of happiness.

"I swore I would always come for you," Richard said, cupping her cheek, trying to memorise her face, the feel of her skin. She was cold, pale, but still as beautiful as the day of his sixteenth birthday when he realised he loved her.

"And you always did," she whispered, laying her hand over his. "I will not be a burden."

Richard swallowed, nodding. He'd always respected her wishes, her choices, and this was no different, as much as he hated it.

"You were never a burden," he whispered, taking her into his arms. "And if you were then I have carried you gladly."

She held him tightly, but didn't say anything. After a long moment Richard pulled away and kissed her forehead before he helped her into the carriage and pressed a lingering kiss to the back of her hand, eyes damp as he looked up at her, undone by the soft love on her face.

"Come back to me," he said softly. "I need you with me."

Anne smiled, but said nothing else as she settled back into the cushions and Richard slowly closed and latched the door. He rested his forehead against the wood for a moment before he stepped away, locking his hands together behind his back as he nodded to the driver and the guards. They each saluted him as they sent their horses forward and the carriage slowly pulled away. He watched long after it had disappeared into the distance, before he turned and went back inside, pulling his cloak a little tighter against the chill February air.

He had work to do.

March, 1485

For three short weeks Richard was able to pull himself together and act like a king again. He appeared at meetings and listened to the problems throughout the country. He ordered a second parliament for as soon as could be organised, and he looked to raising men to guard against the promised invasion. He came back to himself, in appearance if not in spirit. Inside he still ached every day, waiting for the inevitable.

"We must prepare for Henry Tudor," Richard was saying when a man came into the room in the middle of March, wearing messengers livery. Richard waved him over, already knowing today was the day. The council session had ended and Francis had remained next to Richard at the massive table to talk just between the two of them.

"I come from Westminster, my lord," the man bowed, his face far from neutral.

"She's gone?" Richard asked quietly. He'd known in his heart that the time had come, he just hadn't wanted to admit it.

"Aye," he said softly. "Just an hour ago, when the sun became darkened."

Richard nodded, shoulders drooping a little more as he glanced out the window. The sun was shining again, but the world was a little duller now. "Well," he said, reaching for a sealed envelope of papers. "These must be delivered to Bishop Kempe. Everything is prepared for her burial at Westminster Abbey within the week. We'll be ready to ride there by this evening."

The messenger stared for a moment before he took the letters and bowed deeply. "At once, your grace. The country will mourn the loss of its queen, may she rest in peace."

Richard gave a sharp nod as he left and Francis shifted next to him.

"You knew?" he asked quietly, and Richard quirked a half smile that didn't reach his eyes.

"We both did," he told his friend tiredly. "The winter was hard. She was ill in the late summer, and I think we both knew she didn't have the strength to carry on any longer, not without Edward. When she left last month, I knew I wouldn't see her again. I'd have liked to have been with her, I'd have liked to have been there. You may think me callous, but she forced me to prepare, to acknowledge her illness, made me promise to carry on without her. She's at peace now, and I'm glad her suffering can end. I have been morose these last months, mired in pain and grief, but I will try to do better."

Francis pursed his lips, nodding. He didn't know how long the set to Richard's shoulders would last, but he knew it wouldn't. Instead of calling his friend on his unrealistic promise, he diverted. "We outnumber the

The Last Winter Rose

Tudor brat five to one," he said, returning to the topic, and Richard gave half a shrug, wincing as it tugged his back and sent a shooting pain into his right leg.

"You've seen how quickly the tides can turn," he said, and Francis sighed.

"Richard, you're the best king we've had in a century," he said fiercely. "Please don't give up on us. Please don't... please," he trailed off, unsure what he was asking. He thought perhaps he was asking Richard to live, especially now.

Richard chuckled darkly, because Francis knew him as well as Anne did, as Anne had. He clenched a fist as he thought how he'd never see her smile again, hear her laugh. He had so little left to live for, but he'd made a promise, a promise that one way or another, he was going to keep.

"If Henry Tudor wants my throne," Richard said, fists curled as he leaned against the table. "He'll have to take the crown from my cold, dead body. He'll have to kill me and that is not something I plan to make easy for him. I promise you that."

Francis blew out a breath, something almost like relief settling over him, but he had known Richard a long time, and he was always going to worry about his friend, especially in the face to yet another loss. Richard continued to talk about the preparations they would make for war and Francis listened, doing what he had been doing for years, standing at Richard's side and holding him up when he was ready to crumble.

344

It wasn't until late that night, alone in what had been their bedroom in the palace of Westminster, that Richard wept. With only one candle burning and all the servants dismissed, he wept for his son and for his wife, his rock, his guiding star. She had been everything to him, every moment of true happiness in his life had come with her smile or the brush of her fingers. He longed for the days in Middleham, when Edward was just a small boy, when they would sit together at the long table and Anne would leave her hair unbound, the sunlight bouncing off it from the high windows as she laughed. He had loved making her laugh, there was no better sound in the world than her laugh.

He had ridden back into the city as dusk fell, unwilling to be away from her, even if she was gone. He hadn't been able to bring himself to go to the chapel to see her yet, but in the morning, he promised himself.

He would have to marry again, he knew it, but the thought was abhorrent. He wanted no one else, even less a match that was politically motivated. He would be expected to produce another heir, but he didn't know if he could face the prospect, much less press that on a woman who likely didn't want to marry him anyway. Perhaps he could delay it a year or two, at the very least. He was still young, and maybe they would find his nephews and he could finally make young Edward his heir. Now that he didn't have a son of his own, there were few choices remaining and the council was running out of arguments.

The Last Winter Rose

Sadly, the chances of Edward reappearing were growing slimmer by the day. It had already been over a year since the boys disappeared from Francis' home without a trace and they had found no clue, no tracks, no hints. No one knew anything, and if the boys were alive, they hadn't found any way of making contact. As much as he hated to believe it, there was every chance now that they had been killed and they'd never be seen again.

There was only one other possibility, one he had chosen never to investigate, one question he'd never asked. There was a chance, a small chance, that Francis had spirited the boys away for their protection, someplace even Richard didn't know about. He'd wondered, in the weeks after, watched Francis more carefully, but if that was what happened, his friend never gave away even a hint that he had gone behind Richard's back.

Richard couldn't blame him, not really. He was doing all he could to protect the realm and making the princes harder to find, keeping them out of the hands of their enemies... it was a smart move, if they were alive and in hiding, if it had been Francis all along.

Richard didn't dwell on the thoughts, though he let them gain more clarity in his head than he ever had before. Perhaps someday he would ask, perhaps someday he'd be ready to know if the blood of his nephews was on his hands or not. It didn't matter now though, even if Edward were alive and in London the very next day, they still wouldn't accept him as the next king. They would force Richard to marry again before they let the son of Elizabeth Woodville sit the throne.

The funeral was peaceful, though the chapel was filled with mourners, including, to everyone's surprise, the dowager queen and her daughters. Richard stood silently, dressed all in black, Francis and Ratcliffe standing behind him, and even Catesby made a rare appearance. Duchess Cecily stood next to him, her face hidden behind a black veil and her hand in his. Maggie and Ned huddled together, silent tears on their faces as they held each other's hands.

Anne had been their last direct relative, aside from their grandmother, Anne's mother, who they rarely saw and barely knew, and Cecily, who saw them occasionally, but they had never been close since she didn't often leave her own home and never travelled, and they had grown up far to the north.

When he and Anne had taken the children in after George was arrested, their own Edward had still been young enough to take most of Anne's time the first year or two, but she'd had enough love for all of them. They had treated Ned and Maggie as their own, loved them as their own, though now Richard knew he must find someone else to look after them, someone he could trust. He would look in on them as often as he could, but he couldn't be a father to them now, he wasn't what they needed. He was a broken wreck and he wouldn't burden

The Last Winter Rose

any child with that. He was able to maintain his public face most days, though some were harder than others. As soon as he stepped out of his rooms the mask slid into place, he became the hard king everyone thought him to be, and at night, alone in his empty bed, he wept.

After the service and burial were over, Richard found himself in the audience chamber. He sank down on the king's chair, head in his hand as he slumped in the only way that didn't cause his spine to burn with agony. He glanced through his fingers, not raising his head when the door was pushed open and he was surprised to see Maggie slip in and shut the door behind her before walking over to him, stopping just short of the raised platform where the chair sat.

"Are you sending us away?" she asked without preamble, and Richard dropped his hand, staring openly at her.

"You want to stay here?" he asked, incredulous. Would the eleven year old girl in front of him never stop shocking him?

Maggie frowned, her hands bunching in her skirts. "You're the only family we have left. The only one who's been there for us, who's taken care of us. And now that Anne is gone, you're going to send us away."

"Maggie," Richard said tiredly, his heart clenching at the unshed tears sparking in her eyes. "I'm king. I don't have time to be what you need me to be, and I'm-" his voice broke and he looked away.

"I miss her too," Maggie said softly, and Richard stopped fighting the tears. He leaned forward and opened his arms and a second later Maggie was in them, holding on to him tightly as they both cried.

"I don't know how to live without her," he admitted, cradling his niece close.

"You just do," Maggie sniffed. "One day at a time."

"You're too young to be so wise," Richard said quietly, but he was so proud of her, as proud as if she was his own daughter. She had always been so smart, so much older than her years.

"You're the only father I've ever had," Maggie said softly. "Ned too. Please don't send us away."

"Oh, my sweet girl," Richard sighed, holding her close. "I won't. I promise I won't unless I have no other choice."

May, 1485

"Did you kill my brothers?"

Richard stilled. Slowly he straightened and set down the papers he'd been shuffling through and looked up.

Bess was fierce, just like her father, face defiant, hands clenched at her sides, and she had her mother's fire to fuel her determination.

"Do you believe I did?" he asked in turn, and for a long moment she just looked at him, before her shoulders sagged and her hands loosened.

"No," she said quietly, looking away. "I don't. I never did."

"Despite what your mother might have said," Richard muttered and Bess huffed.

"My mother isn't right about everything," she said quietly. "You don't have the character of a murderer."

Richard smiled sardonically. She didn't need to know about how badly he'd wanted to murder Warwick all those years ago, how he'd done nothing to stop her uncle Anthony's execution, but he appreciated her faith in him. In that, at least, she was more like her father than her mother. He bent over his papers once again, searching.

"Why did you want to see me?" Bess asked, curious now why she'd been called to an audience with him, alone.

"I've drawn up the necessary documents with the intent of making you my heir-" he started.

"No," her voice cut through his with a single word.

Richard froze, then looked up at her, eyes narrowed. He knew he'd be fought at every turn to make her his heir, but he was determined to try.

"What do you mean, no," he said, annoyed at her interruption and blatant denial.

"Henry Tudor already wants to use me to take your throne," she spat angrily. "If you make me your heir it will be all the easier for him to do it."

"It will come with the caveat that whomever you marry will not become king," Richard told her, because he was already drafting the documents to say just that. "And thank you for your faith that I'll keep my throne."

"I don't want to be queen," Bess said, her voice petulant now and her young age showing. She was wise beyond her years, just like Maggie, but she was only nineteen and had lived a sheltered life, more so than most princesses. She ignored his sarcastic comment entirely.

"I never wanted to be king," Richard told her patiently. "For a while I was your father's heir, after George was taken out of the line for trying to commit treason, more than once, and before your brother was born. It was the worst few months of my life. I never

The Last Winter Rose

wanted any of this, and it has cost me everything. Do you want to protect your family?"

"Of course I do," she snapped. "But how will this protect them? I'll never be allowed to stand alone as queen."

"Who would you suggest then?" he asked, going back to his papers and sitting carefully. He didn't have to listen to her, and she couldn't refuse him if he made her his heir, but he respected his niece enough to tell her his intentions before he called parliament to make his case.

"Anyone else," she said, striding to the window and staring out silently. "This isn't for me."

Richard tilted his head, watching her, before he spoke softly. "I've found that it's the ones who don't want power who are usually best suited to wield it."

Bess huffed a half laugh, turning back to him, her arms wrapped around herself.

"My answer is still no," she said, and Richard sighed heavily.

"Will no one in this wretched land simply do as they're told?" he said, Bess smiled.

"You're a king, uncle," she laughed. "Not God."

Richard waved his hand at her. "Go away," he muttered, and she laughed again, curtsying as she left him to his thoughts. He'd hoped she would accept and fight beside him to become his heir. Her mother certainly would have supported it, for once, but now he would have to find someone else. He would never make the people accept her if she herself wouldn't stand up and accept the challenge. It seemed the only one in their family who had ever truly wanted the throne had been George, the only one of them not to wear the crown.

He cast his mind about for anyone he might make an heir, but came up with few possibilities. The last thirty years had decimated their family, leaving them weak and scattered. He could repeal the writ barring Ned from taking the throne, but the people would be hesitant to accept the son of a traitor, just as they would outright refuse to accept a woman. He could name someone not his own family, but again...

The closest option still of royal descent then, was his nephew John, the son of his elder sister Elizabeth and John de la Pole. It wasn't ideal, but he was within the line of succession, though it was a complicated claim. It would have to do.

And if Henry Tudor invaded and won the throne, none of it would matter anyway.

August, 1485

On the 11th the news they'd all been waiting for came.

"He's landed," Catesby told the silent room. "Four days ago, at Milford Haven. His uncle, Jasper Tudor is with him and they have already captured Dale castle. They have two thousand French troops, at least, making his numbers close to four thousand as it stands now."

There was silence all around the table and Richard's fists tightened.

"So be it," he said finally. "He wants a fight, we'll give him a fight. Send the orders."

For two months a set of envelopes had gone everywhere Richard had, written, signed, and sealed, orders for lords to muster their men and gather at Leicester. They had known all along that Henry Tudor would land in Wales, his father's homeland, and had chosen a point from which they could cut him off if he went north, east, or south toward London.

Since June they had been at Nottingham, just to the north, a strategic point in the centre of the country, waiting, and now the time had come. Unlike the last attempt, Tudor had landed his troops and was making his way across the country. There would be no storm intervening this time.

"Tudor has crossed the border," Catesby reported five days later, hurrying to Richard's side with the most recent missives. "His army is in England, and from what we can tell they're heading for Shrewsbury. They have the Earl of Oxford with them, and their numbers are close to seven thousand."

Francis swore loudly and Richard grimaced. Their own forces were close to a similar number, closer to eleven thousand if they could muster everyone together in time. This wasn't going to be a war or a drawn out campaign. This was going to be a single battle to decide who would hold the crown.

The next two days passed in preparation, the yard around the castle alive with the sound of blacksmiths changing horseshoes, repairing armour, making new weapons. Raw recruits were trained quickly, men who had never held more than a shovel before being taught to wield a pike and short sword.

When Catesby brought a further update the night of the 18th, with a list of the men who had joined Henry Tudor, Richard cursed. They were going to be outnumbered if Northumberland didn't move.

"Get Henry Percy and his men here now," he ordered Catesby. "Go yourself if you have to. We'll move as soon as we can and meet you in Leicester."

Catesby nodded, checking his weapons before he took the sealed letter and left, half jogging down the hall and out to the stables.

The Last Winter Rose

"We have to send the princesses and children north," Richard said, turning to Ratcliffe, who nodded. He had kept all six of his nieces and his nephew close, unwilling to let them too far from his protection, but now they would be safer further away, in case they were unlucky and the battle happened close by.

"I'll arrange it," Ratcliffe nodded. "I've already sent messages to London to try and persuade your mother to retreat somewhere safer."

"It's unlikely she'll listen," Richard shook his head. "But thank you."

He said goodbye to Maggie and Ned the next afternoon, the other girls hanging back with their servants, all eyes on them. Maggie stared at him for a long time, but she refused to cry. She hugged him tightly before she stepped back, taking Ned's hand and pulling him along with her as the door opened and Ratcliffe appeared.

"We need to go," he said, ushering the other girls to the door and out. Maggie glanced back, staring at Richard for a long moment before one of the women tugged her arm and she was pulled out into the hall.

"Elizabeth," Richard said quietly, catching her elbow as she made to leave the room last. She paused and the door swung shut behind the last of the servants, leaving the two of them alone.

"What is it?" she asked, turning fully back to him. No one in her family called her Elizabeth unless the situation was dire.

"If this goes wrong," he started, and she scowled. He held up a hand. "If this goes wrong, if something happens to me, make me a promise. Take care of your cousins, as best you can."

"If something happens to you, I'll be forced to marry Henry Tudor," she muttered. "What do you think I can do for them then?"

Richard shook his head, dropping his grip from her elbow and turning away. He walked to the window and leaned on the frame, staring out at the rain.

"You'll be Queen of England," he said. "I'm not saying the outcome of this fight is already decided, but if, God forbid if, that bastard kills me and takes you, he'll be digging his own grave. He might think he's won a beautiful prize that puts him on the throne, but he'll never control you. You have your father's strength and your mother's cunning. You can keep our family alive."

"It's bad luck to talk like you're already dead," Bess finally said after a long silence. "I promise, I'll do all I can for Ned and Maggie, but I don't know if it will be enough."

"All I ask is that you try," he said, and he could hear her sigh.

"I will," she promised, and he could hear her skirts rustle as she walked over to him and lay a hand on his shoulder. "I'll see you after the battle," she said, and Richard nodded, glancing up at her.

"I'll see you after," he whispered. She held his gaze for a moment before she nodded and turned to leave. In

The Last Winter Rose

the doorway she paused, one hand on the door, one on the archway.

"My father always said you were the best man he ever knew, and that you would have made a much better king than he did," she told him softly. "Prove him right."

The door shut before Richard could summon up an answer and he let his forehead drop to the glass as his eyes drifted shut. He was so tired, and everyone expected so much of him. Even only taking it a day at a time, he didn't know how he was going to get through another invasion, another war. He just wanted to rest. He felt so much older than thirty-two.

Bess and her sisters, Cecily, Anne, Catherine, and Bridget, along with Maggie, Ned, two dozen guards, a dozen servants, and four nurses left for Sheriff Hutton as the sun began to sink below the horizon and he watched from the window. They were all that was left of his family, his blood. And he would never see them again.

August 22, 1485

Richard pulled on his gauntlets, staring across the field, exhaustion evident on his face. Francis stood at his shoulder like a spectre, armed for battle and bristling with weapons.

"Not going to tell me I have no business fighting?" Richard spoke quietly, and Francis glanced at him.

"I'm not going to stop you," he said softly after a long moment.

"I expected you to," Richard said. "Maybe I wanted you to."

The fog was thick, the air heavy. A breeze was blowing gently from the north, pushing the bank of white around them faster than clouds crossing a summer sky.

"We can't win this, not here, not now, not when it's likely that one or both of the Stanleys have betrayed us."

A long pause. "But?" Richard prompted, and Francis sighed, turning to fully face him. Richard met his gaze steadily.

"You want this battle?" Francis asked softly, watching the emotions play across Richard's face.

"I do," he said after a moment, and Francis took a breath, nodding.

The Last Winter Rose

"Then I will follow you."

"As your king?" Richard asked, his voice barely audible. All around them the sounds of thousands preparing for battle grew louder.

"As my friend," Francis smiled. "And as my king."

Richard held his gaze for another moment then looked away. He was exhausted, he couldn't remember the last time he slept without nightmares, and his back hurt so badly that some days he could barely stand without help. The circle of people that knew about Richard's painful spine had grown to a few servants, another physician, and two tailors, though he long suspected everyone knew, they just refused to say a word.

After... Richard could hardly bear to think about Anne. After she had died, Francis had quietly slipped in next to the hole her presence left. Francis had come to wake him one morning, not long after she had passed, and he'd been unable to force himself from bed, mentally or physically. Francis had helped him up and helped him wash and dress in the complicated doublet designed to hide how his shoulders were slumping unevenly, and then forced him to eat. It was a routine after that, and some dark part of Richard's mind knew if not for Francis he would have likely starved months ago.

"Thank you," Richard said, and Francis looked at him, face puzzled. "I don't think I ever did. Thank you."

"For what?" Francis asked, though his face softened into a smile.

"For everything," Richard said simply. There weren't words for everything Francis had done for him over the years. Thank you would never be enough.

They stood silently for another moment, then Richard asked the final question that had been weighing on his mind.

"Are they safe?"

It was barely a whisper, barely audible over the growing noise, but Francis heard, and Francis didn't have to ask what he was talking about.

"They are," he said simply, gripping Richard's shoulder. "Both of them."

Richard nodded, jaw clenched as he gripped his sword and turned away from the line of enemy soldiers and called for his horse.

The mist swirled low, dimming the already weak morning light, and every face along the line was grim. They were ready to fight, to die, for their country, for their king, but there was no air of glory here, no joy of battle, no great hope of victory. The odds were in their favour, yet still a pallor was cast across the prevailing mood even as the sun rose, bringing only enough light to see by to the day. Richard glanced to the east, toward York, toward his one true home, the place he had always felt safe, secure, the place that had nurtured him and protected him from all the evils of the world. He knew in his heart, he would never see her again.

The Last Winter Rose

Turning back to the field he gazed over what he could see of the enemy troops, the Tudor banners, the banners of Oxford, Pembroke, William Stanley, all those who stood against him, against his England. He could win this battle, despite what Francis said, but at what cost? At what purpose? His son was dead, his wife, his beautiful Anne, gone. His brothers, his father, all gone, his sisters scattered to the wind. His nephews had still not been found, despite over a year of searching, and he knew they never would be, not when Francis had done his job so well. His nieces... he hated to think what would happen to them if he lost here today, especially Elizabeth, so strong like her mother, but still so young. He hated to think of Bridget, only four years old. And Maggie, Maggie who was like his own daughter. Family was everything to Richard, the most important thing, and yet his family had been torn apart and he found little reason left to carry on.

He looked around, the faces of the men staring back at him, meeting him openly as comrades, not as subjects, and he realised this was what he had. He had his people, he had England. They were his family, and he would fight for them until his last breath.

He turned his horse and drew his sword, wincing as the movement sent pain roaring down his spine, but he couldn't think of that now, it didn't matter. He'd trained his whole life to ignore the pain, ignore the odd set of his spine, he'd learned to fight around it, use it to his advantage. Today would be no different. He stood tall in his stirrups and held his sword aloft.

"To me, men of England!" he cried. "To me!"

The roar of sound drowned everything out. The pounding of a thousand hooves cut the morning, followed by the cry and boots of infantry as they charged toward the Tudor lines, such as they were. They were England, and this was their day of victory.

June, 1515

Thirty years had passed since that fateful day at the battle now known as Bosworth Field, and few knew the true story of what had really taken place. A second Tudor king stands before the throne, hands behind his back, crown heavy on his head. He remembers the stories his mother told him, about his great uncle, about how brave a man he was, how brave a king. He remembers huddling up against his big brother, now gone, on cold winter nights as she whispered words their father had forbidden.

Richard was a traitor, a monster, he had killed his own nephews, perhaps even his own brother before them, all for the crown, a crown he couldn't even hold. He was weak, he was nothing.

Those were the words his father wanted known. Those were the words the world knew. But Henry knew something else.

He knew the soft words of his mother, spoken in the shadows and the deep silences of the night, words of valour, gallantry, bravery. How Richard never stopped looking for the two boys who simply vanished, how he had protected them all as long as he could, her mother, her sisters. How he had promised they would be safe, how he had fought to protect them, how he had died to protect them.

His mother was gone now, along with his youngest sister. His brothers, his father. Only Margaret and Mary remained, though they were far from him. All of his children had died in the cradle. Only one elderly aunt remained. His family was broken, scattered. He was alone.

Family cost you everything, he thought bitterly as he turned away from the throne. It was a chain around his neck that weighed on him day and night. Even if they were gone, their ghosts still haunted him, the ghost of his father most of all. His father who had no honour, who had no valour, who sold Henry's sister away to France for peace, peace that was barely holding.

Not for the first time Henry wished he had been born into any other family. If Henry knew anything at all, it was this; his family was cursed, and just like Richard, he would leave no legacy, no heirs, no future. He may accomplish something, it may even resonate through history, but even if one day he had a living child, he knew there would be no more beyond, that his line would end soon, end forever.

There would be no Tudor dynasty stretching through the ages. They would wither and die, just like their rose did every autumn, just as the white rose had done. His father had joined the roses, but that didn't make them stronger, it only made them more fragile. It made them weak. He made them weak.

The Last Winter Rose

History had been written so effectively that now Henry had no hope of changing it, no one left to contest the things his father had told the world. No hope of telling the truth about his family, about what really happened to his uncles Edward and Richard, how Edward had nearly taken the throne back and sent Henry Tudor to his grave. Henry Tudor, who was never meant to be king, just the same as he was never meant to be king. It should have been Arthur, the brother he'd barely known, raised away from court as the Prince of Wales.

But now here he was. King of all England, Henry of the houses Tudor and York, and he would write his own history.

Acknowledgements from the Author:

A very heartfelt thank you to my mother, who puts up with everything on a daily basis, from the crisis of 'What do I put in this chapter?' to 'What did I have for breakfast and where did I put my other shoe?', and who acts as my editor for free and tells me that my writing is amazing and I can capture character's voices with so much skill. This book would not have been possible without you, because if you hadn't taken me to Middleham castle when I was barely 6 years old, I would probably not even have known who Richard III was and I would probably think he was evil, like so very many people still sadly do. I love you so much mama, thank you for always being there for me.

To my Dad, who has supported me in every way possible, even if it's a quiet hug rather than a 6 hour brain storming session, thank you so much for everything you do for me.

I would also like to thank my best friend. She has *also* put up with all my nonsense, *but* she also helped me format and final proof this book in four days so I could rush it to print, and she formatted, printed, and hand bound me a copy because she is amazing!

To my sister, who sometimes doesn't know what on earth I'm talking about, but listened and encourages anyway. ♥

And last but not least, thank you to the Richard III Society, and Philippa Langley, not only for finding Richard in 2012, but for coming to Penrith in Cumbria in 2023 and planting a white rose bush, because less than two weeks after that event I started writing this book, and I would never have started it without the wonderful and welcoming people of the society.

Also from Caitlin Sumner

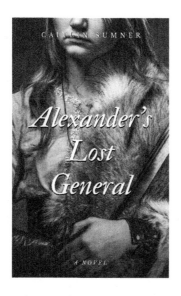

Alexander's Lost General

A female warrior in a time dominated by men, a general in a time ruled by kings. Alexis was born with a fire in her spirit that could never be quelled. She grew up at the side of giants, Alexander, Hephaistion, Ptolemy, Cassander. Two would be her brothers, one her lover, and one her greatest enemy. For twenty-two years they stood together, winning wars, conquering the known world, bringing in a new age. For ten more Alexis fought to hold Alexander's empire, side by side with Ptolemy. She became known as 'The Warrior Queen' or 'Queen of Asia', ruler of the known world after Alexander.

Love. Death. Betrayal. War. This is the story of Alexis of Macedon.

Also from Caitlin Sumner

The Lost General Saga: Hephaistion

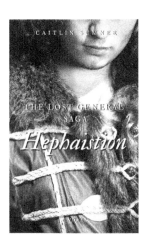

You know her story, but you don't know his. See the world of Alexander, Alexis, Ptolemy and Solon through the eyes of Hephaistion, his life spread before you in a sweeping tale of a soul caught between times, in a place that will never be right for him. He dreams of the past and the future. From the beginning, he knew how it would end. Follow in his footsteps as he tries to navigate a life where he has never felt quite right in his own skin, hear his words, and see the world as he saw it.

The Lost General Saga: Alexander

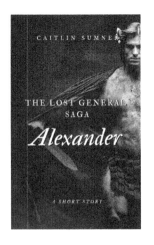

What drove Alexander? What did he think and feel when he set out to conquer the world? In this short companion story to Alexander's Lost General, see through the eyes of Alexander, the great feats he accomplished and the demons he fought as he sought to be king of the known world.

Caitlin Sumner was born in California and began writing almost before she could read. She has attended University in Scotland, studying Classics and Ancient history.

Currently she enjoys spending her time writing, and continuing her historical studies, two ongoing passions of hers. She enjoys horseback riding, fibre arts, gardening, rock climbing, and going to the beach.

Visit her website at **caitlinsumnerauthor.home.blog** for updates on upcoming projects and current publications.

She can also be found posting the very large and varied number of books she reads on Instagram:

@caitlinsumnerauthor

Printed in Great Britain
by Amazon